For Sean

Also available:

A Blanket of Blues

Everybody gets the blues sometimes. Fingers Flaherty had them all the time. He lived the blues and sang about his every ache.

Flaherty's blues gave him nothing but hardship, sore feet, and a shattered heart. Every one of his songs told a fraught story. His characters walked many a dark path and twisted lane on their troubled journeys.

And now they get to share their tales, wrapped in dark humour and a blanket of blues.

A collection of short stories inspired by Flaherty's songs, A BLANKET OF BLUES presents its varied cast at turning points in their lives. Some yearn for change, whereas others seek self-improvement. And others want nothing more than a little peace of mind, even for just a few hours. Each character struggles through the daily conflicts and irritations of his or her life, fighting back with proud confidence, caustic wit, mule-headed defiance, and a dash of reckless optimism.

Dimestore Avenue Blues

Jesse believes that the future will be better. One day, he'll make up for all his mistakes and achieve perfection.

He still has some bad days as he lives out his autumn years in Dublin. But his worst days were in New York in 1976. After that city had nearly crushed him, he'd fled to Dublin, a broken man. But he was determined to rebuild himself, brick by brick, improving day by day.

Back in the 1970s, Jesse was a successful young ad man on Madison Avenue. He'd succeeded because he was willing, indeed eager, to do anything to advance his career. It all seemed like a good plan, right up until the day he brought a pistol to work. For years in those offices and meeting rooms, they all thought they were kings, living it up in their high palaces of power. As it all fell apart for Jesse in 1976, he realised they were all just fumbling in the dimestore.

Jesse knows he isn't perfect. He's made many mistakes and will probably make more in the future. Now, with the possibility of contentment finally within his grasp, will he be allowed one final chance to be happy? Or will the ghosts from his past once again refuse to lie down in their graves?

Talkin' Squirrel Blues

Who speaks the most sense, a dead blues singer or a live squirrel? Moses McNamara isn't sure.

After his girlfriend suddenly leaves him, Moses must rebuild his shattered life. His companions in this quest include a trendy squirrel, an elderly neighbour, and a blues singer with six strings and a grudge.

Moses was never the world's most motivated marketing copywriter. After a disastrous performance review, he feels lost in a career he hates, glaring at a cruel world through defeated eyes.

When his self-esteem is on the floor, Moses meets Floyd, a talkative squirrel who helps restore his confidence. He also consults his neighbour, Jesse, an old man with little patience for the young man's martyr complex. And through it all, Moses listens to Fingers Flaherty's songs. The melodic ranting of the belligerent bluesman helps Moses to keep his own problems in perspective.

Can Moses find a new love to help him forget the girlfriend who walked away? Or will the past always rattle in his brain like a half-remembered song? As his romantic quest becomes more complicated, Moses doesn't always know whose advice to follow: the well-dressed squirrel or the dead blues singer.

Which one would you listen to?

1

Broken Engine Blues

Our Father, who art in heaven, won't ya come down here for a while,
Show her how to love me, show her how to make me smile.
She drives me crazy in the mornin' and sets fire to my fuse,
My little bitter angel got them broken engine blues.

As her car careened through another red light, Tiffany finally accepted the hard truth. Her driving skills had indeed deteriorated since she'd left Bill.

Never the most considerate of road users anyway, she'd recently developed an alarming disregard for the rules of the road, the safety of other drivers, and the health of her ailing car. For her, a car was simply a means for getting from one place to the other with the minimum of fuss. And every obstacle along the way had to be mercilessly overcome.

Bill had constantly complained about her driving. He'd tried to patiently explain to her the reasons why there were rules of behaviour on the road. He'd gingerly suggested that this was one place where she should perhaps consider taking the feelings of other humans into account.

What would that tosser know about human feelings? The little shit

1

weasel never cared about mine!

When Tiffany ignored Bill's reasonable approach, he'd tried screaming, hectoring, bullying, begging, and weeping. None of these approaches worked either. Improving her driving skills moved further and further down her list of priorities. It was currently relegated to a footnote on page 257 of her mental to-do list.

And now that she had no Bill to worry about, she'd almost entirely forgotten about the rules of the road. Especially this morning.

I can't believe I'm going to be late for work. Again! That stupid bastard of an alarm clock. It's all Bill's fault, of course.

Looking at the situation objectively, Tiffany could accept that forgetting to set her alarm clock could arguably be seen as maybe being *her* fault perhaps. However, for the time being, every problem in her life that wasn't verifiably an act of God would be blamed on Bill, her ex-boyfriend.

Tiffany's speeding was having limited success in the traffic jam. The cars on Dawe Street inched agonisingly forward for a few seconds before groaning to a halt once again. Some car horns bellowed in fury. A lorry growled menacingly. A bony-arsed courier tried to slither into the bus lane.

Tiffany thumped her steering wheel when she saw that it

was already 10:15.

The insistent throb of her headache reminded her why she was late.

If Bill had been a proper boyfriend, I wouldn't be wasting my time going on blind dates set up by Martha.

Martha was Tiffany's sister and had almost danced for joy in the streets when Tiffany finally left Bill last year. She then wasted no time trying to set Tiffany up with *any* single males who didn't scurry out of the way quickly enough. Martha didn't have a strict vetting process. As far as she was concerned, *anyone* (or indeed *anything*) was better than Bill. It was the only thing Tiffany wholeheartedly agreed with her sister about.

Too many vodka bombers last night. Too drunk to set the alarm clock before going to bed. Too tired to wake up on time. And, when she finally awoke, too tired to move.

Tiffany glared at the traffic. An elderly woman sat in a yellow wreckage in front of her. While the traffic was stalled, the woman delicately applied some lipstick, adjusting her rear-view mirror to better inspect the result. She frowned at her reflection, unaware that the traffic had begun to move again.

"Move it, you old bat!" Tiffany blared her car horn, accidentally setting off the wipers in the process. "You can daub your face on when you get to the graveyard."

The woman glanced around and drove on for a few feet, before the traffic settled back into inertia.

Pedestrians ambled along Dawe Street, soaking up the morning sunshine. Cyclists whizzed through whatever cracks they could find in the smouldering traffic. Some drivers had fallen asleep. Others whiled away the time by arguing on their phones. Some fraught souls, like Tiffany, counted the minutes by thumping their steering wheels.

"It's a warm, sunny morning across Dublin," the DJ on the car radio enthused as Ron Carter's "Satellite Sunday" faded away. "Certainly a morning to leave the car at home and walk to work. Get some fresh air into those carbon-monoxide lungs, folks!"

The lights at the top of Dawe Street turned green and the traffic growled into life. In front of Tiffany, the yellow wreckage stuttered along reluctantly.

"The traffic's completely jammed across the city, as usual." The DJ laughed. "There are reports of a car moving in Inchicore, but these haven't been confirmed yet. Estimated time of arrival to anywhere is–"

"Wanker!" Tiffany switched stations. "Hopefully, someone will run him down when he's walking home."

Tiffany closed her eyes, wondering if she could meditate herself to another planet.

Focus on breathing. I breathe out all the tension. I breathe in all the energy. I breathe out. I breathe in. I breathe…

All this did was remind Tiffany of the disastrous blind date last night.

His name was Decker, apparently. He'd told Tiffany what his real name was, but she'd stopped listening by that point. Anyway, it seemed that everyone called him Decker so why bother trying to remember two names?

He was out of breath because his bus was late, and he'd run all the way from the bus stop. When he finally arrived at the bar, he was breathing hard and his face was drenched in an ample layer of sour sweat.

The first thing Tiffany thought was that he looked like a turtle. A turtle in a cheap suit with a completely ridiculous pseudo-punk haircut, but a turtle nonetheless. His skin, while not exactly wrinkled, had the texture of an abandoned banana.

However, convincing herself that beauty rarely resides on the surface, Tiffany decided to give the Turtle a chance. For now.

Unfortunately, Decker failed to hide his disappointment when he finally focused his eyes on Tiffany. He obviously wasn't too concerned about inner beauty.

Tiffany fought the urge to run out of the bar and murder her sister. She knew the blind date was going to be a disaster. The unsavoury cocktail of sweat, heavy breathing, and disappointment in front of her made that obvious.

But she was academically curious to find out how this encounter would end. And she'd nothing else planned for the evening. She decided to begin proceedings by making Decker even more uncomfortable.

"So, what's the problem?" she asked him. "Were you expecting Scarlett Johansson?"

"It's not that." The Turtle shook his moistened head. "It's just that—"

"Yes?"

"Well, you're older than I thought you'd be. An *awful lot* older."

"Did Martha tell you that I was a teenager?"

"Well, no…" the Turtle conceded with a frown. "But she did say that you were… *still* young."

"I'm only thirty-four, for Christ's sake!"

"Thirty-four?" The Turtle blessed himself, shuddering. "God, I didn't think you were *that* old!"

The evening never really regained its footing after that.

Tiffany had to admit that he was vaguely interesting, once she started actually listening to him. He worked for a security firm that specialised in protecting very minor forgettable celebrities. He was gloriously indiscreet about his clients' foibles. Once his breathing stabilised and his sweat evaporated, he got into his stride with a litany of libellous anecdotes.

As the night wore on, in spite of her misgivings, Tiffany found herself getting more and more interested in the tales. The steady stream of vodka bombers helped her to engage in the conversation.

The Turtle, perhaps inevitably, misread the signs and assumed that Tiffany was growing more and more interested in *him*.

As they prepared to part ways outside the pub later, Tiffany was already erasing her memory of him.

"Well, thanks for an… unusual evening," she mumbled. "It was–"

"My pleasure." The Turtle leaned towards her face. "It doesn't have to end–"

"Oh dear God, don't kiss me!" She gasped, recoiling. "I don't know where you've been."

Tiffany gave up on her breathing exercise. Nothing was

going to calm her down today.

Shit! I haven't phoned the Seagull yet.

Tiffany accelerated through a break in the traffic as she tried to fumble her phone out of her pocket.

"We play that for Lillian and Gerald," the Radio Red DJ said as Justin Waiver's "Frozen Lover" melted away. "Lillian wants all Dublin to know that she loves you, Gerald. What a great way to start the morning!"

Tiffany sighed as she flicked to her boss's phone number. She opened the car window, hoping some fresh air would make the impending conversation bearable.

Her boss was Gordon Byrne but was known to everyone (except himself) as the Seagull because of his tendency to squawk around in a flapping panic and basically shit on everything.

Tiffany braced herself as the phone was answered.

"Yes?"

"Gordon, it's Tiffany."

"Tiffany! Good to hear that you're not dead."

"Yeah. Look, I'm afraid I'm running a bit late this morning because—"

"I had already noticed that! We were beginning to wonder if you had been kidnapped by angels. Or perhaps had another improbable accident–"

"Okay." *Shut up, you sarcastic dildo!* "I'll be in as soon as I can. The traffic's completely messed up beyond all repair this morning."

"So is the presentation we were supposed to give to the client this morning. You knew I was relying on you to fix that up before the meeting."

"As I said, I'm on my way in now." Tiffany had completely forgotten about the presentation. But, having worked in Sunrise Event Management for eight years and been ignored for promotion twice, she didn't feel that she had to apologise to her boss for *anything*. Most days, she barely managed to be civil to him. "I'll be in soon."

"Soon is still late–"

"It's not my fault I'm late!" Tiffany had to slam her brakes to avoid crashing into the back of the yellow wreckage. "You stupid cobwebby bitch!"

"What on earth did you just call me?"

"Not *you*! There's an escaped mummy driving a pile of rust in front of me. She's more interested in her lipstick than the road. Look, I'll be in the office as soon as I can get there. However, given the state of this traffic, I can't promise miracles."

"I know not to expect miracles from you, Tiffany, because—"

Tiffany put the phone back in her pocket before the Seagull could elaborate.

The traffic moved off Dawe Street and was now merging with the gridlock on Monaghan Way. It was 10:30 now. Judging by the speed of the traffic, Tiffany reckoned she'd make it to the office by nightfall.

Sod this for a game of poker! If I can sneak on to Remington Lane, I might then be able to wriggle on to North Road.

Tiffany glanced behind her to make sure there were no buses coming. Then, remembering that the planned manoeuvre was probably illegal, she checked to make sure that there were no police either.

The DJ announced that he would now play George Lemon's "Crease" for Sam and Betty, celebrating thirteen years of wedded bliss.

Carefully inching her way into the bus lane, Tiffany wondered what thirteen years of wedded bliss with the Turtle would be like.

Please don't kiss me. I don't know where you've been.

She allowed herself the first smile of the day.

Well now, baby, I woke up this mornin', and I was already dead.
I just dunno how the hell these ideas get inside my head.
I'm a little bit crazy, all right, but that's yesterday's news.
My little bitter angel got them broken engine blues.

The smile faded as her phone started ringing again.

And it turned to a glare when she saw Bill's number on the display.

"What the hell do *you* want?"

"Hiya, Tiffs! How are you keeping? Hope all is—"

"What the hell do you *want?*" Tiffany balanced the phone against her ear as she sped down the bus lane. "Make it quick or I'll hang up now."

"Well, as you probably know, it's my birthday next week and—"

"You didn't seriously think that I'd remember your birthday, did you?" Tiffany was surprised to discover that her brain had actually retained the date. She tried to make a conscious effort to wipe it out of her system. However, the effort of getting off the bus lane and on to North Road was taking up most of her attention. "I can barely remember what you look like at this stage."

"I know when you're lying, Tiffs!" Bill laughed. "Your

voice takes on that shrill harpy edge. I bet your left eyebrow is twitching too."

"Again, what the hell do you want?" Tiffany tried to steady her eyebrow. And her hold on the steering wheel. "I'm about to hang up before I'm involved in a pile-up. I don't want my last conversation on this planet to be with *you*."

"At least try to stay alive until after my birthday. It's a big birthday too. Thirty-five. Can you believe I'll be thirty-five?"

"I don't care what age you are! Life's too short to be worrying about trivial—"

"I still look twenty-five, of course. Must be those energy tablets I've been taking. Pity about the strange side effects…" Bill got lost in a private reverie for some seconds. "I'm full of energy these days. Out nearly every night of the week and—"

"I'm going to hang up now, Bill, and then murder—"

"Just listen, okay. I know you find it difficult to talk and drive at the same time, so, for the sake of the other road users, just listen for now. I'm going to be going out for a few drinks with the old gang next week to celebrate the big three-five. They'll all be there, hopefully. Suzie and Jeff. Wigwam. Pac-man. Joey. Silvio. Lucinda. Crusher."

"I could barely stand those tossers and tossettes when I was going out with you." Tiffany settled herself into the traffic jam on North Road. She actually did miss some of Bill's friends. They made being with him bearable. "Why would I want to see them now that I've freed myself from that toxic circle? I'm trying to build new contacts. Meet normal people."

"Percy. Giggles. Jugsy. Bob and–"

"Oh, will Giggles be there?" Tiffany realised immediately that she'd blurted that out too quickly. She'd always had a soft spot for Giggles. Although he was an assistant for the local undertaker, he had a face and attitude that belonged on the vaudeville stage.

And a body that belonged in surfer movies!

Rarely was a man more unsuited to his chosen profession. Giggles had once been beaten up after a funeral because he'd started laughing during a particularly pious eulogy for one of his drug-dealing neighbours. But he always made Tiffany laugh with his inability to take anything seriously. Oh yes, she was still *rather* fond of him.

Yummy!

"Maybe I will pop along–"

"You don't have to bring a big present." Bill, of course, was completely oblivious to Tiffany's feelings for Giggles. "You can save the big present for my fortieth."

"Okay, let me make things clear." Tiffany took a deep

breath. What was that sudden smell? "I'm not going for your birthday. I'm just going because it might be nice to see that old gang for a few—"

"You just called them all tossers and tossettes!"

"Everybody becomes a bit tossy when you get to know them well enough." *Hold on, I remember that smell. Jesus, that brings me back!* "Anyway, sometimes it's good to take a step back and have a giggle… have a laugh with the old gang, just to remind yourself of what you've escaped from."

"There's a really cool new box-set of early blues out, by the way." Bill's neighbour Jesse had been educating him on the joys of blues music over the last year. Bill had loved discovering that there were some people in the world who were even more miserable than he was. "That'd make a good present if you were having difficulty deciding—"

"Goodbye, Bill!"

Tiffany switched off the phone and flung it to the car floor. She took another deep breath and listened to the radio. The Sinister Sisters' latest hit, "Chain Gang", rattled around the car. Tiffany began to slightly relax.

*

They tell me sisters are now doin' it for themselves,
And leaving losers like me on the old dusty shelves.
My dignity's down the drain, I've got nothin' left to lose,
My little bitter angel got them broken engine blues.

The wistful smell caressed Tiffany out of her reverie.

My God, that smell again. I'm right back there. His mangy bedsit. The Che Guevara posters on the cracked wall. The tins of beans and pots of noodles. Those dreary socialist magazines. That ginger goatee. And the warm haze of smoke.

Before she'd met Bill, Tiffany had gone out with what she'd affectionately called a "politically active pain in the arse". Oscar. Complete with defiant goatee and strident opinions. For a whole summer, she'd been madly in love with Oscar, despite his indie music and rudimentary hygiene. They spent entire weekends lost in fluttering blankets and clouds of hash.

Ah yes, those were the days, my friend!

Shaking herself out of her hazy memories, Tiffany looked out the window to see where the hash smoke was coming from. She didn't see any students or buskers. Perhaps it was coming from one of the cars.

She looked over to her right. A car full of grim-faced banker types, all delicate spectacles and nailed-down shirts.

The smoke was unlikely to be coming from there. Powdered noses were more their style!

She looked over to her left. Two nuns were smiling beatifically at the traffic, lost in reverential prayers.

Tiffany had had a hatred of nuns ever since Sister Agatha called her a "wanton little slut" during the school quiz back in primary school. She'd decided way back then that she'd never let anyone judge her again, not even God. Or the devil.

But it was hard to hate those two smiling angels in their sensible blue convertible. They looked so happy and peaceful, completely unperturbed by the carloads of tension all around them. And from their window wafted a seductive smoke that sent another nostalgic shiver through Tiffany.

Surely that's incense... It must be... They couldn't be...

Just as Tiffany was contemplating the possibility that there were stoned nuns loose on North Road at this hour of the morning, one of the nuns turned to face her.

"Good morning, my dear," the nun said, with a beaming smile that would make Satan himself simper with coy embarrassment. "Isn't it wonderful how technology sometimes forces us to slow down and contemplate the beauty of God's creation around us?"

"It's a pain in the hole," countered Tiffany, wondering

how anyone could smile so freely before lunchtime. "I'm late for work and my dickhead boss is already having kittens."

"We're always late for something," the nun replied, nodding. "But the really important things in life will always wait for us. I'm sure your boss will wait for you. And I'm sure your friend will wait for you. Even though it's his birthday."

"Were you listening to my phone call?" Tiffany felt all her nun-related hatred rush to the surface. "Who the hell are you to eavesdrop on private–?"

"We couldn't help it, my dear. I'm sure everyone on this road heard you. Your anger is there for all the world to see. And hear."

"I'm not angry," Tiffany snapped. "You holy molies always think you know everything, but let me–"

"Oh, we don't know everything." Another dazzling, compassionate smile. "But we know a cry for help when we hear it. We'll pray for you. We'll pray that a guardian angel will guide you through your–"

"I don't need any angels!"

Why the hell won't this traffic start moving?

"We're just here to help–"

"I've got enough sanctimonious, interfering bitches in my life already."

"Learn to relax, my dear. Accept your angel. We all need help on our journey." And with a parting smile, the nun rolled up the window and disappeared back into her veil of mysterious smoke.

Tiffany closed her eyes, visions of Sister Agatha and Giggles and Bill and the Seagull and Martha and Oscar the Goatee all jiggling around her head.

Jesus, I must have inhaled some of that smoke. This day just gets worse by the minute.

"Well, looks like the traffic has frozen all over the city for today," the DJ declared. "So here's a song to take your minds off your troubles."

Fingers Flaherty's "Bitter Angel Blues" started thrashing its way from the speakers.

Tiffany got lost in the demented chords. It wasn't until the cars behind her started honking that she realised that the traffic had finally started moving again.

She rammed the car into first gear and got ready to face the workday.

*

Make me some coffee, baby, pour it on down my mouth,
Let's try to have a laugh before the whole day goes south.
You can stop that stupid lecture, there's no room in the pews,
My little bitter angel got them broken engine blues.

The Seagull was in a good mood this afternoon. Indeed, from a certain angle he looked happy, jovial even.

This should have been good news for Tiffany.

It wasn't.

The client meeting had gone surprisingly well, despite the alarming typos in the presentation, the lack of drinkable water or comfortable chairs in the conference room, and the wholly inadequate (and fictitious) progress report. Sunrise was blessed with clients who were willing to overlook obvious shortcomings in its project management because it could usually cobble together reasonable corporate events on budgets that ranged from miserly to embarrassing.

So the Seagull was full of the joys, bubbling with irrelevant anecdotes and unprofessional curiosity about inane aspects of his team members' personal lives.

He chose to share his sunshine with Tiffany in the canteen during coffee break. Tiffany noted approvingly that the Seagull did not comment on the fact that she was on a coffee break three minutes after turning on her computer.

"Jesus wept!" The Seagull collapsed into another paroxysm of laughter, biscuit crumbs flying across the table in Tiffany's general direction. "The look on his face was only priceless. There must have been a dispute on in the factory when they built him."

He took off his glasses and wiped his eyes, still giggling.

Tiffany stared at him, wondering whether to join in the laughter or drown him in her coffee. She contemplated her options and waited for her wretched hangover to finally recede for the day.

This sorry tale has been going on forever and he still isn't approaching the point. If he doesn't shut up soon, I think I'll hang myself. Or him. One of us definitely has to step up to the noose.

Tiffany had retreated to the canteen to get away from the nagging of her co-worker Paul, known to all as Jehovah. A born-again Christian with a neat line in judgemental put-downs, Jehovah had started lecturing Tiffany about her "road to ruination" as soon as her shadow darkened her desk. The canteen had seemed like an oasis of tranquillity.

Until now.

"Anyway, where was I?" The Seagull smiled as he put his glasses back on and adjusted his rampant hair. "Oh yeah.

Pedro and the nurse. He didn't know where to look. This was, needless to say, the first time he had ever thrown up on a nurse."

"Get away." Tiffany sighed. Pedro was the accounts manager and the Seagull's drinking buddy. Indeed, he was probably the Seagull's only functioning friend. The only times Tiffany had to interact with Pedro was when she needed to go war with him over mistakes in her payslip. She enjoyed seeing the blood drain from his face every time she stormed into his office. "Anyhoo, I suppose it's time I got back to—"

"Well, Pedro isn't the most eloquent fish in the net at the best of times, but his shock had now rendered him completely incoherent." The Seagull was too caught up in the flow of his narrative to be distracted by the fact that Tiffany was no longer even pretending to listen to him. "And his babbling just made Delia angrier. You know how it is when someone just doesn't know how to shut up. All you want to do is kill them."

"Yes." Tiffany glanced at the teaspoon on the table, assessing possibilities. "Indeed."

"Well, Christ on a broomstick, I thought her face was going to explode at any minute."

Tiffany knew it was time to kill this anecdote. Talking to her boss always made her a bit uncomfortable. It wasn't just because he elevated breezy incompetence into an art form. He also carried a slightly sinister torch for her. He'd made this obvious too many times for her liking.

"Anything interesting happening in the world today?" Tiffany asked, hoping to steer the Seagull away from his own feathery little world.

"Not much. I was reading a snotty-nosed blog about college life in Dublin these days. It was letting all the spoilt, grubby little teenagers know what joys lie ahead of them when they finish school."

"Don't get me started about college life!" A smile flickered across Tiffany's lips. "All that free time and never entirely sure what you're supposed to be doing with it."

"I was a complete disaster at college." The Seagull unleashed his dreaded squawking laugh. Tiffany realised too late that she'd just handed him another conversational bone to gnaw on. "If I wasn't drunk, I was hungover. If I wasn't hungover, I was asleep. I kind of miss all that hazy chaos."

"I don't," Tiffany lied. "Chaos becomes too much after a while. You get fed up wondering what the hell is going on!"

"Don't you miss those free-for-all days?" The Seagull leaned in closer to Tiffany. A bit *too* close, the HR manual would have said. "I'm sure you'd some wild times at college."

22

"Perhaps…" *And what exactly is he getting at now?* "But nothing that threatened the international balance of power."

Tiffany glanced out the window, hoping that he would drop the bone and go back to whatever it was he did in his office all day.

"Tell me, Tiffany, what was the wildest thing you ever did at college?"

"Oh, I was very tame," Tiffany lied.

She could have told him about at least twenty different incidents. Her twenty-first birthday party, which lasted four days and three nights. Her graduation celebration. The night she threw paint at a lecturer during a debate about abortion. Her attempt to seduce the gay male stripper at Alison's hen night.

"One night," the Seagull announced, "my flatmates got me drunk on tequila horseshoes and tied me to the railings outside the house."

"Lovely." *I'm still not going to tell you anything.* "Sound like nice people to know."

"And not only that!" He laughed. "They ripped the clothes off me and left me tied there, stark naked. Jesus wept! They could be a shower of shites, those lads. There I am tied to a railing, shivering to death because it's five below zero. Of course, there had to be a full moon out, so everyone could see the show. Can you imagine that?"

"That's a... compelling picture." She tried to erase the image, but it was too late. She knew it would stay etched in her memory. "I hope the experience did no lasting damage."

"You'll never guess who rescued me." The Seagull squawked again, eyes alight, gripped by his own anecdote. "These two old dears on their way home from bingo. I'm telling you, Jesus wept!"

"I'm sure He was bawling by this stage."

"One of them had a pair of scissors in her handbag, so she was able to set me free. They got a good long look at the crown jewels before they let me go, though."

"There probably wasn't much to see," Tiffany said before she could stop herself.

"I had a rotten cold for a week after that..." The insult had apparently soared over his head. "So, Tiffany, have you ever been tied naked to a railing?"

"That'd be telling." *I hope you're not forming an image in your head.* "It's certainly not something I've done recently."

They sat in awkward silence for some minutes. Tiffany glanced into her coffee, thinking about Alison's hen night. The stripper had been called the Masked Miguel. A shock of wild bleached hair and a pale, tall body. Turned out to be a twenty-five-year-old farmer from Mayo. Oh well…

As that night had worn on, Tiffany had felt the tequila galloping through her head. The room spun faster as she stumbled through the crowd. She flung her arms around Miguel when he tried to leave. He smiled a nervous rural smile and made his farmer excuses. She thought she could wear him down, but he wriggled free and scampered out of the room. Alison didn't talk to her for weeks after that.

"I'd better get back to the desk, Gordon." Miguel faded into Tiffany's memory. "I need to catch up on some… things."

"What are you doing after work?"

Tiffany pretended she didn't hear him as she walked out of the canteen. She was already trying to invent excuses for leaving work early today.

You can tie me to the railings, baby, you can tie me to the bed.
You can even tie me up on the cross when I'm all good and dead.
Just don't let me go hungry, feed me plenty of warm booze,
My little bitter angel got them broken engine blues.

2

Cross Jesus Blues

Hail Mary, full of grace, full of guile and wit,
The bottle's empty, send your son out for another hit.
Put away your rusty nails, put away them stupid views,
Give me a break from these cross Jesus blues.

"How lovely to see you again, Sparrow!" Tiffany plucked her reluctant teenage nephew from the café chair and violently embraced him. "How are you keeping?"

"It's Robin." Her nephew tried to wriggle out of his aunt's vice grip. "And everything is going–"

"My God, you're awfully thin, Sparrow. Martha, why have you stopped feeding your child?"

"I haven't stopped feeding him!" Martha glared at her son. "It's not my fault that he never puts on weight. He never finishes anything I put in front of him."

"Well, you'd better do something about him, or the ducks will start throwing bread to him when he walks in the park!"

As she sat down at the café table, Tiffany scrutinised her sister.

Oh dear...

Martha's marriage had obviously entered another dark intersection. Her clothes were just a little bit *too* revealing. She had just a little bit too much make-up on. And her voice was just a decibel too shrill.

"You need to keep a close eye on your son, Martha," Tiffany said, settling into her lecture. "The males in our family haven't been blessed with brains."

"I'm still here," Robin protested.

"There's nothing wrong with Robin!" Martha instinctively saw any comment about her family as an unwarranted assault on her parenting skills. "He takes after his father a bit, that's all. A touch vague and–"

"I'm *still–*"

"Not much happening north of the neck," Tiffany persisted, ignoring the protests of the indignant teenager beside her. "He certainly got that from George's side of the family. We always knew there were a few bats missing in your husband's attic."

"And you were dating Stephen Hawking, Tiffany?"

"How's school these days, Sparrow?" These lunches with Martha usually descended into a battle, and Tiffany knew when she was defeated. So she retreated down a safer conversational alley. "All good?"

"Yes, it's good." Robin's shrug was as bored as his voice. "I just need to finish this geography project and try to–"

"Have you not finished that *yet*?" Martha found a new focus for her rage. "What the hell are you doing sitting here gabbing with your bitter aunt? Get back to the library and try to get to your desk without collapsing in a starving heap in the middle of the road!"

Tiffany watched her nephew scurry out of the café.

"I still think he's a bit delicate in the head," she said, seeing no need to wait for Robin to be out of earshot. "You should take him to the doctor."

"I did," Martha replied. "Dr Lambchop couldn't find anything wrong with him, apart from the usual pointless male teenage drama. But let's be honest, the cat is more qualified than that chancer of a doctor. About as much use as a chocolate kettle. He never knows which end of you to look into when you go to him with any ache or pain."

Tiffany had to concede that point. Dr Lambchop lived in a haze of vague generalities. He could never concretely diagnose a problem. When she went to him with a persistent stomach cramp, he informed her that her ache was most likely a belated manifestation of fin de siècle existential ennui.

There was no shortage of ennui in the office this week, so

Tiffany was in no hurry back to work. Her volatile sister provided a welcome distraction from the unwanted attention of her boss and the meaningless deadlines.

"I was talking to Bill earlier this week," Tiffany said. "He's invited me to some bullshit party in–"

"God almighty, some women deserve their chains," Martha said, shaking her head. "The problem with some people – people like you, for example – is they don't know that they've escaped. Instead of kicking back and living a little, they end up wishing they were back in their padded cells."

"All I said was that Bill phoned me." Tiffany recoiled at the sudden switch in the conversation. "This doesn't have to turn into another pointless therapy session. Not every little incident is a life-defining moment!"

"You've been cut adrift ever since you left that disastrous excuse of a boyfriend." Martha stirred her tea with a vengeance. "You're only pining for old milk."

"Pining for old milk?" Tiffany couldn't help smiling. "Jesus Christ, he's been called everything now! He went past his sell-by date a long time ago."

"Your own sell-by date is approaching too, Tiffany. Don't let life roll on over you."

Sometimes Martha's savage realism was too severe to take.

Other times, she provided exactly the right shot of reality to clear Tiffany's head.

Martha was approaching forty and getting into her middle-aged stride. A teenage son and distracted husband ensured she was never short of things to complain about. As they got older, she and Tiffany came to rely on each other more and more, despite their well-honed ability to scrape each other's nerves.

They enjoyed a relatively amiable lunch break, complaining about the food and plotting revenge on every person who had wronged them over the last week. As usual, Martha's list of targets was longer than Tiffany's.

But Tiffany didn't want to spend the day dwelling on the past. The encounter with the nuns earlier in the week had shaken her. She needed to strike out for the future.

"Anyway," Tiffany said, "I've decided to pop along to the farce of a party. Giggles will be there. He's always good for a laugh."

"I'm sure he's good for other stuff too." Martha laughed. "Which of course is why you're going to the party."

"That is absolutely not–"

"You might have more luck with him than you had with poor Franklin."

"Who's Franklin?"

"Decker. Have you forgotten him already?"

"Oh yeah. The Turtle!"

"Look, no one cares what his name is. Anyway, he phoned me in an awful state the other night after your knicker fit. Could you not have given the poor turtle a chance?"

"I spent years giving Bill chances. I've lost the enthusiasm for it now. If the fire doesn't light after the first match, it's time to go home."

"No, Tiffany, it's time to go back to work."

Tiffany ordered another cup of coffee. The future couldn't wait.

But work could.

I know you think that I'm the devil, and I swear that I ain't,
But I gotta let you know that I sure ain't no saint.
So start to say your prayers, start to pay your dues,
And brace yourself, baby, for the cross Jesus blues.

Most of the rest of Tiffany's afternoon was taken up with catching up on her social media updates. She was responsible for monitoring the company's online presence and enhancing its digital footprint. It was a gift to her as it gave her the perfect cover for whiling away hours on the internet.

Jehovah was wrapped up in his own work, efficient and productive as ever. But not too busy to get in random digs at Tiffany about her increasingly frequent hangovers.

"So, Tiffany, how's the head now?" There wasn't the slightest trace of concern in his tone. "It'll soon be five. You'll be able to get the hair of the dog then."

Tiffany tried ignoring him. This was difficult for two reasons.

First, Tiffany could never resist rising to the bait. Of all the men she'd known, only Bill could annoy her more than Jehovah could. And part of her enjoyed the spats with Jehovah. They helped to kill the hours between projects.

Second, Jehovah had all the missionary zeal of a true convert. In his early thirties now, he used to fancy himself as a man about town, lighting up all the parties and making off with the prettiest pair of legs in the room. His thirst for flirtatious skirts was matched only by his thirst for tiger cocktails and expensive sins.

After one room-spinning party a year ago, he'd tried to convince a shy young receptionist to come back to his snake pit. He unleashed all his charm and money on her, but she resisted with a decisiveness that intrigued Jehovah. Turned out that she was a born-again Christian, belonging to some vague sect out in some vague suburb.

Jehovah saw her as a challenge. She saw him as a project. Three months later, she'd baptised Jehovah into her pious circle and he'd forgotten why he'd been chasing her.

Now his reformed heart flamed with the passion of a judgemental prophet in the wilderness. As far as he was now concerned, Tiffany was the scarlet whore of Babylon.

Tiffany wished her life were that interesting.

"The only hair I'll be taking this evening, Jehovah," she replied, "is the scant hair right off your head if you don't shut up. Save your sermons for the grannies on Sunday morning."

Tiffany considered getting caught up on some work admin bits and pieces that she hadn't got round to this month. That might take her mind off the buzzing anxieties inside her skull.

Nah, too late. It's nearly five. Far too gone in the day to start bothering with work. What to do?

She took out her phone and searched through the names. She'd deleted a lot of contacts after leaving Bill. Making a new start meant cutting off the ties that might bind her to the past. But some names she'd held on too. Just in case.

She found the name and took a chance.

He picked up after a few seconds.

"Tiffany!" Giggles started laughing, as a matter of course.

"How are you, babes? Haven't seen much of you since you escaped from that lunatic. How's freedom treating you? Ha ha ha ha."

"I'm good, Giggles," Tiffany replied, already infected with his enthusiasm. "I just took a wild notion and thought I'd give you a quick call. See how you're keeping."

Across the cubicle, Jehovah starting humming George Langton's "High-End Harlot".

"I'm just great!" Things were always great with Giggles. His blind optimism was almost admirable. "Work is wonderful. No shortage of corpses to doll up. Even though the competition is stiff these days, ha ha ha. Speaking of corpses, I was talking to Bill last night. He's looking very scrawny these days. His harmonica has more meat on it. He must miss your cooking."

"I doubt it." Tiffany had never cooked a single meal for Bill during their entire time together. She had never even made him a cold sandwich. Some precedents were best not set. "He's probably just forgotten how to eat."

"Maybe he's on a diet or something," Giggles conceded. "He was talking a lot about getting fit and losing some flab. I think he's even joined a gym or something ridiculous like that. The mid-life crisis has kicked in already!"

"Getting fit?" *Why's the bastard only now deciding to get fit? I'd begged him to take some exercise. If only to get him out of the flat.* "Anyway, I didn't call to talk about that gobshite. We should catch up sometime. Have a few drinks and… whatever. Bit of a laugh, you know."

Loud tut-tutting drifted over from Jehovah's desk.

"Well, I have a work night out tomorrow night," Giggles said. "We'll all be out drinking and talking the same body language, ha ha ha. That'd bore you into a coffin. And then I'm off to see the brother for the weekend. His wife has given birth to their first baby and I have to… Well, I'm not sure what he wants me to do. Check it out for alien DNA or something, maybe. I've already told him I'm not available for babysitting. The last baby I looked after still hasn't been found, ha ha!"

"Will you be at Bill's birthday farce next week?" Tiffany wasn't going to let Giggles get away that easily. "I might drop in there."

"Good God, don't tell me you remembered his birthday?" Another explosion of laughter. "I thought some memories are best repressed."

"Well, some dates live on in infamy, Giggles," Tiffany replied. "Anyway, what harm could it do? Indeed, it might be a good idea to show him how well I'm getting on without him."

"Well, I'll definitely be there. Someone will have to pour him into the taxi at the end of the evening."

"He's lucky to have friends like you. You're the only one who's managed to stick with him all these years. You must have been a limpet in a previous existence."

"I need someone to laugh at my jokes. Look forward to seeing you next week then. Anyway, I'd better get back to work. Another deadline to meet in the mortuary, you know!"

"See you then."

Jehovah was still tut-tutting at the other desk.

And Tiffany was still smiling as she put the phone back in her bag.

Take a walk with me, baby, I'll sweep ya offa your feet,
You can chew my ear off, you can chew my meat.
If you wanna know my pain, take a walk in my shoes,
But be ready to carry the cross Jesus blues.

A shower, a quick snack, and some trashy TV helped Tiffany to relax when she got back to her tiny studio apartment. She needed a quiet evening and some time alone with her thoughts.

Of course, half an hour of silence in the apartment was enough to drive her over the edge, so she decided to go for a walk.

Since leaving Bill, Tiffany had found solitary walks to be an effective and cheaper alternative to counselling. Some evenings, she would go to Fitzroy Park, wandering aimlessly among the trees, ducks, squirrels, and skateboarding teenagers. Other evenings, she strolled around the suburban residential areas, wondering what secret scenes were being acted out behind the locked doors. Often, she went further, strolling up into the hills, trying to be at one with nature and also scouting out possible sites for burying bodies, if it ever came to that. Ten thousand steps a day closer to her future.

Bartley Road, another suburban ghost-estate hell, was eerily quiet this evening. Tiffany enjoyed the peace, listening to rhythm of her footsteps on the pavement. She tried to shut out every other sound.

In these rare moments of silence, Tiffany could almost convince herself that the world was made for love, tranquillity, and happiness.

She suddenly heard a woman screaming.

It wasn't a scream of terror. It was a scream of blind fury. Tiffany knew that sound. She had used it often with Bill, when words alone failed to convince him.

That woman's right in the centre of the fury. I wonder if she's Bill's new girlfriend.

Her ears tuned into the sporadic noises that now crackled the silence. A car engine roaring to life. Passing birds twittering and squalling. A washing machine spinning its last cycle. A frustrated child crying. Dogs suddenly erupting into barking fury.

Another scream.

A front door swung open at the end of Bartley Road and a young woman stormed out.

"You degenerate scumbag!" The woman trembled, white with rage. "You lousy, two-faced, backstabbing, good-for-nothing, treacherous bastard!"

Inside the house, a man's voice shouted, indistinct.

The woman was about twenty-five, her black curly hair fluttering in the breeze. She wore a grey tracksuit that looked like it had been flung on.

"Get that cheap whore to do it for you. I've had enough of you and your pathetic excuses. I'm out of here!"

Tiffany slowed her walk, watching the unfolding scene.

The woman was taking a silver bracelet off her wrist. In her rage, she was having difficulty unclasping it. Having eventually freed it, she held it in her hand for some seconds, staring at it. Frowning. Then, with a shudder, she flung it back into the house.

"You can give this to your mangy little minger slut!"

She fumbled with the gate handle, cursing.

The man's voice started shouting again.

Kicking the gate open, the woman turned and ran down Bartley Road. She didn't even glance at Tiffany as she dashed past.

Tiffany stood still, watching the house.

Any second now.

A young man appeared in the doorway.

"Geraldine! What in the name of Christ are you playing at?"

Small and chubby, he was older than the woman, closer to thirty. His blond hair was a dishevelled thatch. He stood shivering in his T-shirt and Batman shorts, darting glances up and down the road, clenching the bracelet in his right hand.

"Get back here, you stupid wagon!"

He noticed Tiffany staring at him.

He glared at her for some seconds, then shook his head and stormed back into the house.

And now, the closing chord.

He slammed the door shut.

Tiffany recognised the look of baffled fury on the young man's face. She had seen it on Bill's face many times over the years. As she walked down Bartley Road, she wondered how long it would take Geraldine to forgive the young man.

The wind was beginning to chill, so she increased her pace, burying her hands in her jacket pockets. Just as she was beginning to warm up and enjoy her walk, unpredicted rain began spitting down.

Useless bastard of a weather forecaster!

Tiffany had no umbrella, and her jacket was too light to give much protection. She looked around for shelter as the spits of rain became a steady, unforgiving drizzle.

It was time for Tiffany to go to church.

Curl up into my arms, let me be your shelter,
Enjoy the steady calm before the helter-skelter,
If you wanna read my mind, take your time and peruse,
But you won't see nothin' but the cross Jesus blues.

St Anne's church, a small grey-brick building, stood at the end of Bartley Road. The car park was deserted, but the church door was open.

As the rain began to soak through her jacket, Tiffany ran

towards the church.

I hope I don't run into Jehovah in here. I'll never hear the end of it.

All was quiet inside. Tiffany shook the rain from her hair and took off her jacket. She glanced around the church, feeling a strange tingle that someone was watching her.

The rain rat-a-tatted against the stained-glass windows. The church had a minimalist 1960s design with sparse decoration. Wood carvings of the Stations of the Cross dotted the light-blue walls. Two aisles of wooden seats led to a white marble altar.

Tiffany slowly walked around the church, the heavy green carpet muffling her footsteps. She looked at the wood carvings. Jesus and the women. Jesus falling. Simon helping to carry the cross. Looking at the faces of the stern soldiers and the weeping women, Tiffany found herself getting lost in each scene.

She turned her attention to the paintings of the saints. One particularly deranged one caught her attention. It showed an overweight middle-aged man balancing precariously on a rock, preaching, a city blazing to the sky behind him. Beneath him, a woman knelt in prayer, looking up at him in awe.

He's one savage-looking bastard!

The saint was engulfed in some passionate sermon, his

eyes aflame, his mouth open in a furious roar. The face contorted with emotion as his hair blew in a storm of grey around his head. Down his chest, a long beard flowed in torrents and a grey cloak swirled around him, caught up in the fit of his sermon.

In his left hand, he clutched a lily. His right arm stretched out before him, pointing into a shameful darkness that extended beyond the frame of the picture.

Tiffany gazed into his eyes. The painter successfully hinted at the fires that blazed inside them. The eyes stared into the distance, cursing the evil that they saw.

"Those eyes just burn right into you, don't they?" a gentle voice suddenly said.

Tiffany jolted and only just managed to suppress a curse. She turned around.

There behind her stood the two nuns she'd seen on North Road last week. They stared up at the painting, rapt.

Tiffany could hear her own breath in the silence of the church as she looked back up at the picture.

The painting seemed to have changed. She gazed into his eyes. There was no fire in them any more. They seemed to twinkle with mischievous merriment, the saint's cloak rippling at some private joke. The roar on his face had melted into the tiniest hint of a smile.

Those twinkling eyes seemed to be looking at her.

I must have had too much coffee today. My nerves are wired.

"Don't be afraid of him," one of the nuns said.

"Who the hell's afraid?" Tiffany's voice ricocheted around the church. "And why the hell are you two following me?"

"We're not following you," the smaller of the nuns replied. "We often come in here. Why would you be surprised to find nuns in a church? If this were a rave club, then you could be surprised to see us. But the real surprise is that *you* are here. What called you inside, my dear?"

"The bloody rain!"

"We told you we'd pray for you," the taller nun said. "And it looks like your prayers have been answered."

"Are you two still stoned?" This was all too much for Tiffany. Outside, the rain continued to pelt down. "The only reason I came in here is because–"

"Is because you're unhappy," the taller nun persisted, sweet and patient and relentless as a swan. "We all could hear your pain and anger that morning. But you don't have to go through your journey alone. We all need angels to guide us."

"Well, I don't need an angel to guide me out of here." Tiffany certainly wasn't going to let herself be hypnotised by a doped-up nun. "Goodbye!"

"We'll continue to pray for you," the nun replied as Tiffany stormed past her.

"Save your prayers for someone who actually needs them." Tiffany didn't bother looking back as she walked towards the church door. The rain had calmed itself down into a silent drizzle.

Watching the puddles seep across the car park, Tiffany again felt that tingle of being watched.

The back of her neck continued to tingle as she ran out into the rain.

You don't have to say you love me, I don't need to hear your lies,
I can see the sad, sad truth when I look into your eyes.
Don't keep me hangin' on, find someone else to accuse,
And release me from these cross Jesus blues.

3

Hallelujah Blues

Come, Holy Spirit, can you see everything I touch just fails?
Come help me, Holy Spirit, because everything I do just fails.
But it's hard staying sharp, when your toolbox is full of rusty nails.

Tiffany stumbled over to the kitchen and made her first coffee of the day.

She'd had a restless night. The recent encounter in the chapel had shaken something in her soul and left her feeling vaguely unsettled ever since. Whenever she finally got to sleep, her dreams were usually haunted by visions of fire and brimstone, saints and nuns.

All I need is a good shot of coffee to blast away the cobwebs.

Tiffany had been reading up on mindfulness recently. Something about living in the moment appealed to her, especially when she was trying to forget the past.

She took a moment to savour the aroma of the coffee. She felt the warmth of the cup in her hand. After taking a deep relaxed breath, she sipped the precious liquid and let the taste engulf her tongue.

Why the hell did I agree to go to Bill's birthday party?

Mindfulness was difficult for Tiffany because her mind was always too full of toxic thoughts that kept bubbling to the surface. Even in the morning silence of the studio apartment, she found it hard to shut off the racket in her head.

Still, the coffee was doing its job. She began to feel more alert. She'd give herself some more time alone in the studio to settle her thoughts before venturing into the chaos outside.

Tiffany didn't particularly like her tiny apartment. Martha referred to it as a brick cage, which was closer to the mark than Tiffany would care to admit. Sometimes she felt like the walls were crawling inexorably closer to her. There was always some weird smell or noise that couldn't be logically accounted for. There was the constant vague threat of imminent rodent infestation. The human neighbours could be noisy, nosy, and nasty. And the landlord had the personality of a vindictive scorpion.

So, obviously, the apartment wasn't perfect. But it was Tiffany's refuge *for now*. Until she found somewhere better. And when the thunderous silence of loneliness got too oppressive, she could always stay in the spare room in Martha's house.

The coffee tasted good. The silence sounded good. The peaceful apartment looked good.

Tiffany smiled to herself, drinking in the silence, enjoying the uninterrupted solitude, living in the still, quiet moment.

Someone rapped loudly on the apartment door.

"Shit!" Tiffany jumped, startled. Coffee splashed on to her blouse. "God almighty!"

Tiffany slammed the cup down on the kitchen counter and stormed towards the door.

Another sharp rap. Louder. More insistent.

"I'm coming!"

More persistent rapping.

"What?" She flung her door open. "Are you on fire?"

A stout middle-aged man stood in the hallway. He was about six feet tall with a wild beard and a shock of grey bushy hair tied into a scruffy ponytail. His shiny silver tracksuit barely covered his ample frame and was fraying noticeably at the zip.

Ignoring Tiffany for now, he continued to shout into his cracked smartphone.

"Yes, I'm here… I already told you that… Of course… I know it's the right one… Don't you trust me? You must think I came down with the stork in the last shower… That's what I'm trying to tell you… I know… Just leave it with me and stop bothering me… How the hell can I if you keep phoning me?"

Tiffany stared at him in disbelief.

"Look, I'm here now, so that's all that matters," the scruffy man continued. "Yes, I can handle it from here... Yes, I know... No, I haven't forgotten... Leave it with me... I know... I know... *I know!*"

He shut off the smartphone with a snarl and stuffed it into his tracksuit pocket.

"Unbelievable!" He bundled past Tiffany into her studio. "There's just no arguing with someone like that. Give anyone a bit of power, and he becomes a dickhead. Give him infinite power, and he becomes an infinite dickhead. Such a bloody ego!"

Tiffany stood frozen in the doorway for some seconds, and then stormed in after him.

"Hey! Come back here! Who the hell are you?"

"Me?" The scruffy man turned around, beard and ponytail swishing. "I'm Bruno, of course. We met last week."

"Where?"

"In the church. When you were sheltering from the rain. Is there any food in this dump?"

"What?" Tiffany followed him over to the tiny kitchen counter. A niggling sensation told her that there was indeed something familiar about this unexpected visitor. "I didn't meet anyone in the church. Except those two stoned sisters."

"Can I have a glass of wine, please?"

"No, you bloody can't! Now, you'd better start explaining yourself quick or I'm going to start screaming the building down."

"Oh, spare me the amateur theatrics!" He rummaged in Tiffany's press and took out a small chipped glass. After rubbing the glass on his tracksuit, he poured himself a glass of water from the tap. "I'm enjoying this encounter even less than you are."

"Who are you?"

"I've already told you, haven't I?" He sipped some water, then grimaced. "This water tastes putrid."

"I don't care about the water!"

"I'm St Bartholomew Balbanna of Pantica. My friends and lovers call me Bruno. When you were in the church last week, you prayed to me."

"No, I did not." Tiffany now remembered the face in the painting. The austere, vehement eyes. The ferocious face. The man in front of her looked a little less ferocious, a bit more *alive*, but the resemblance was still there. "I was just trying to get out of the rain."

"Maybe you weren't praying consciously." Bruno

shrugged. "However, your subconscious mind was screaming out for help."

"And how exactly do you know what my subconscious mind is saying?"

"Because I'm a saint." Bruno poured the water down the sink and began cleaning the glass. "As soon as we saw you, we knew you were in trouble."

"We?"

"Me and the two doobie sisters."

Tiffany tried to look away, but the man's dark blue, bloodshot eyes were hypnotic.

"I really should get to work now," Tiffany said, looking for a reason to run out of the studio. She made a mental note to throw out the coffee jar when she got home. "I have a lot of urgent—"

"Urgent?" A hearty laugh sent the saintly ponytail jiggling. "Since when have you cared about work, Tiffany? The cockroaches in the office kitchen are more productive than you."

"I have better things to do than stand here talking to some figment of my over-caffeinated imagination." Tiffany threw on her coat, wishing she had a bucket of raw sewage that she could throw over her unwelcome intruder. "The fresh air will help to clear my mind."

"I'll walk to work with you then," Bruno declared, "just in case–"

"I'm perfectly capable of–"

"Look, you've got your job to do, and I've got mine. So let's just–"

"What job?" Tiffany started walking towards the door.

"I'm sorta like your guardian angel. The two doobie sisters interceded on your behalf. It took them a while. They're not very focused, as you can imagine! And now the boss man – that was Him on the phone – has sent me down to look after you."

"You were sent by God?" Tiffany allowed herself a laugh. She couldn't remember the last time she'd laughed this early in the day. "Why is God interested in me?"

"He's got to get involved in everything." Bruno sighed. "A total control freak, to be honest."

"So what, are you like my patron saint?"

"Not exactly. More like a guardian angel, as I said. You see, I'm here as a punishment." The ponytail had got entangled with the tracksuit zip. Bruno took a few seconds to rearrange himself before continuing. "I was having another argument with the boss. That's always the problem with omnipotent beings. They hate arguing. Anyway, the long and the short of it is that He threw me out of heaven. Yet again. He set me this task. I have to look after you for the next few months. Make sure you don't fall into bad company or do anything stupid."

"And what makes you think I'm going to do something stupid?" Tiffany stood in the hall, looking for her door keys. "I've haven't done–"

"Well, you already agreed to go to Bill's birthday party, didn't you?"

This was too much for Tiffany. She turned around, ready to unleash a torrent of abuse on the dishevelled guardian angel.

But the studio was now empty.

I work all day, and I play by the rules.
You know, I work all day, and I make sure to play by all of them rules.
I follow the leaders, but Lord have mercy, them leaders are all fools.

Tiffany found it even more difficult than usual to concentrate on work, following her encounter with Bruno.

My guardian angels are just like my boyfriends: useless in every way.

It was a rough morning at Sunrise.

Problems kicked off early when half the office rang in sick.

Then a group of customers was protesting online, wanting to know why the Bluetooth speakers had started emitting smoke during yesterday's dancing convention. There were nearly twenty Twitter rants to respond to.

The Seagull arrived in hungover just before lunch, looking like he'd slept in a septic tank. He spent the next hour rasping orders at Tiffany, snapping at her most timid queries. Everyone in the office realised that he was best avoided, so they placed all their problems on Tiffany's desk instead.

Unable to bury her head in a pillow, Tiffany buried her head in some mundane work instead. Soon, she'd almost forgotten about Bruno and was busy composing responses to the burning speakers, using the hashtag #HotMusic.

"Hi @YoyoGirl. Sorry to hear your interpretive dance presentation was thwarted by the smoke coming from the speaker. Please confirm that you didn't have any aromatherapy candles burning near the speaker. Think fire safety at all times. #HotMusic"

Tiffany suddenly became aware of a whiskey-soaked feathery presence behind her. She turned around and, sure enough, the Seagull was standing – no, staggering – there. She wasn't sure how long he'd been looking at her.

"So, Tiffany," the Seagull said, when he realised that she

had seen him, "how are we handling this debacle with the spontaneously combusting speakers during the serenity ballet?"

"Quite well," Tiffany lied. "I also spent some time this morning reading up about our sexual harassment guidelines again."

"What the hell does that have to do with–?"

"You know how it is these days. We must be much stricter in our definition of sexual harassment." Tiffany noticed with satisfaction a nervous sweat break out on the Seagull's forehead. "Sexual harassment takes many forms, including staring–"

"I still don't see what–"

"It's important to know boundaries." Tiffany saw Jehovah's head jerk up at this. "I'm just saying."

"Anyway, back to the speakers–"

"Actually," Jehovah interjected, eager to jump on a chance to knock Tiffany off her stride. "Tiffany does make a good point. Although the exploding speakers are turning into a PR disaster for us on social media, we should listen to what she has to say about boundaries. From what I've heard around town, Tiffany has some very interesting definitions of boundaries. And the lack thereof."

"Shut up, both of you!" The Seagull massaged his fragile temples. "I'm not in the mood to listen to you two alley cats scratching each other. Tiffany, you need to keep on top of this situation."

"I've heard that she likes staying on top of things," Jehovah said, before pretending to return his attention to the complicated spreadsheet on this computer screen. "A woman who likes to take control, if you know what I mean..."

Tiffany decided that she'd maul Jehovah later. For now, she had to get the Seagull away from her desk. She couldn't handle both of them at once.

"Look," Tiffany said, pointing to her screen and trying to muster up some fake urgency, "I've been responding to the tweets and I'll reassure everyone that we're on top... that we've got this situation under control. Anyway, I'd better get myself back to–"

The Seagull was now rummaging in his jacket pocket.

"Do you still like blues, Tiffany?" he asked.

"Not really," Tiffany replied. "That was Bill's pointless obsession. Some of it just rubbed off on me, like a fungus."

"I got you a present." The Seagull seemed to be having difficulty extracting the package from his jacket pocket. "I know how much you love blues music."

55

"I literally just told you that I don't–"

"It's just a CD I found in that smelly market on Hawthorne Lane. Fingers Flaherty, I believe. Perhaps you've heard of him."

Jehovah had completely forgotten about his spreadsheet and was watching the unfolding scene with eyebrow-twitching curiosity.

Tiffany looked at the CD as if it were a disembowelled fish. Fingers Flaherty always reminded her of Bill. The same constant whining and self-pitying martyr complex. No wonder Bill adored him!

But even more disturbing was the fact that it was a gift from the Seagull. She knew that, beneath his breezy façade, her boss was an unrepentant sleazeball. She could handle that. She was used to putting misguided males in their place.

But the realisation that the Seagull was still carrying a drunken torch for her was too much. No hashtag could encapsulate her growing revulsion.

She could feel the burn of Jehovah's stare. It was time to crush this scene.

"I don't know what to say." For once, Tiffany wasn't lying to her boss. "But I really need to get back to the social media. It requires my attention *right now.*"

The Seagull had already turned an unsettling shade of grey and seemed glad of the excuse to retreat to the nearest bathroom. Two things he couldn't handle: hangovers and assertive women.

As soon as he was out of earshot, Tiffany put on her jacket and slipped out for a break.

The social media shitstorm could wait until she'd cleared her head.

I walk for hours every day, but I can't shake you out of my head.
Walking, walking, walking, and you're still rattling around in my head.
Can't shake you offa my fingers. Can't shake you out of my bed.

The mountain air felt blissfully fresh after the suffocating atmosphere in the office.

Tiffany relished each slow breath.

I breathe in. I kill the Seagull. I breathe out. I kill Jehovah.

Since taking up mindfulness, Tiffany had developed her own brand of breathing exercises. They helped her exorcise her desire to commit murder without the inconvenience of having to go to jail.

However, the incidents with Bruno, the Seagull, and Jehovah had left her more rattled than usual. It was time to call in extreme therapy.

It was time to phone Giggles.

He picked up almost immediately.

"Tiffany," he gushed. "How are you today?"

Giggles's laugh was like a pure adrenaline shot through Tiffany. She felt the tension of the last twenty-four hours immediately dissolve.

"I'm great!" *I am now!* "How's work going with you?"

"As grave as ever," Giggles replied, not missing a beat.

"Just checking in to see about this party of Bill's. What's the plan?"

"Well, Bill has organised it, so, of course, there's no real plan." Another guffaw from Giggles. "That guy couldn't organise a sick day during a plague. I think we're all going to just meet at the Yellow Carrot and see where it goes from there."

"Probably to hell in a handbasket, like everything else Bill touches," Tiffany replied. She was waiting for a suitable opening to ask Giggles about what was bothering her.

"Well, you didn't go to hell, did you, Tiffany? And presumably he touched you once or twice."

Bingo!

"Oh, I wouldn't know what hell looks like. I'm not a very

religious person, as you know."

The cool mountain air was blowing away the last of Tiffany's tensions. She was beginning to feel relaxed enough to confide in the notoriously indiscreet Giggles. Not even the faint shadows that flitted around her distracted her as she walked a steady gait, mindful of each step.

I step on Bill. I step on the Turtle. I step on Jehovah. I step on the Seagull.

"I don't think you're too religious either, Giggles. I remember you playing Pokémon during Ronnie's funeral last year."

"Actually, I do believe in God. I just don't think that He believes in me."

It was a typical Giggles answer: amusing but meaningless.

"Sometimes, I think I could use a good guardian angel," Tiffany replied, tentatively. "We all need a helping hand now and then, don't we?"

"I once had a guardian angel," Giggles said, sounding almost serious. "But we didn't click. He said I was a hopeless case. Like one of our clients, he was probably dead right. So I have been alone ever since… Anyway, you've got to laugh, haven't you?"

Something in Giggles's tone threw Tiffany off. And the

shadows were beginning to distract her.

I Bill on step. I Jehovah the Seagull. Oh bollocks!

"Yes, we all feel alone sometimes." Tiffany wondered how far she could explore this side of Giggles. "There's no shame in—"

"Well, you know all about loneliness, Tiffany. You were dating Bill!" Giggles's laugh sounded more forced than usual. "Anyway, we'll see you at the Yellow Carrot, right?"

"Yes." Tiffany knew the moment had passed. But at least she now felt more motivated to go to Bill's party. "Anyway, I've got to go. I can't hide from the office forever."

The shadow engulfed Tiffany as she slipped the phone back in her pocket.

"Why *exactly* do you want to go to Bill's party?" an already familiar voice asked.

Tiffany looked up, startled.

Bruno was now striding beside her, puffing and sweating as he tried to keep up with her.

"Were you listening in on my phone call?" Tiffany glared at Bruno. But she didn't feel anger. There was something oddly reassuring and comforting about the tracksuited maniac walking beside her. "You're supposed to be my guardian angel, not my stalker!"

"Can you not slow down a bit, please?" Bruno struggled to get the words together. "You need to remember that I'm nearly seven hundred years older than you."

"And nearly seven hundred pounds heavier! For someone so fond of wearing tracksuits, you've really let yourself go!" Tiffany slowed her pace slightly. The last thing she wanted was the death of a guardian angel on her hands. "Don't they have a gym in heaven?"

"I'm banned from that too." The scarlet colour began to recede beneath the moist beard. "Mr Control Freak likes to have rules and regulations for everything. I don't really do rules and regulations. What's the bloody point of being in heaven if you have to follow an endless list of commandments?"

Tiffany began to suspect that she might have found a kindred spirit after all. Bruno would be a good addition to the Sunrise team.

Thinking about Sunrise reminded Tiffany that she should probably start thinking about maybe beginning to start going in the direction of the office soon. Perhaps.

No hurry!

"Why are you so concerned about Bill's party anyway?" she asked. "It's hardly the social event of the season."

"Of course it isn't!" Bruno shook the sweat and crumbs from his beard, prompting a disgusted yelp from Tiffany. "There'd be more excitement at a biscuit-sucking convention. I don't care about Bill. I care about you. Well, no. It is *my job* to care about you. Best to clarify that."

"I'm going to Bill's party because–"

"You're still in love with him!"

"What?" Tiffany stopped walking, causing the sweaty tracksuit to crash into her. "Are you completely insane? Is that all you've got to show for seven hundred years of wisdom?"

"Okay, let's hear your version of the story. We'll probably end up with four versions of the story, just like Himself did!"

"There'll be other people there too." Tiffany put more distance between herself and Bruno and picked up her pace again. "Martha will be there. And Wigwam. Joey too, of course. And Silvio. Perhaps Giggles."

"Ah, Giggles." Bruno gave a hearty laugh. "We all love Giggles!"

"How the hell would you know Giggles?" Tiffany felt that adrenaline rush again. She tried to convince herself that it was from the bracing walk.

"Giggles is a hero upstairs," Bruno said, his twinkling eyes shooting up to the clouds. "St Neville O'Kane was the most pious, sanctimonious, self-righteous shite ever to get into heaven. And believe me, the competition for that title is fierce up there! He said he could save *anyone*. He thought he was the hottest guardian on the cloud. So we set him a challenge. We looked for the most hopeless case we could find. And we found your Giggles."

"Why was Giggles hopeless?" *Okay, that sounded too shrill. Get a grip, girl!* "He's a nice guy."

"Six months trying to fix Giggles drove poor old Neville over the cliff. That silly bastard undertaker couldn't take anything seriously. And Neville wouldn't know a good joke if it sat on his knee and started nibbling his ear! It was a match made in the other place. So don't get too close to Giggles, Tiffany."

"Who said anything about—"

"I don't want you to make too many mistakes. I'll never hear the end of it from the boss if I do. The Seagull is a pussycat compared to the omnipotent psycho boss I have to answer to. Your problem is that you're a hopeless judge of character. You've dated thousands of men and—"

"Thousands?"

"I'm taking the long view here. Looking at your accumulated lives over eternity."

"Aren't you getting your religions mixed up?" Even Tiffany suspected that reincarnation wasn't part of the Catholic belief package. "Since when has–?"

"I'm not going to listen to a theology lesson from someone who thinks that counting her steps while walking will open up the gates of eternal wisdom. There's more to religion than finding the easiest way to make yourself feel good. All I'm saying is that you've never, in all your lives, been good at understanding other people. Even when you were a rabbit, you made bad choices. And those guys set the bar very low!"

"Enough about me." Tiffany didn't like where the conversation was lurching. Time to switch focus away from her previous life as a rabbit. "How did a smelly, hairy slob like you get to be a guardian angel?"

"That's a long, complicated story…"

"You don't have to go into detail. I've probably got to get back to work soon."

"Neither of us care about your work, Tiffany!" Bruno took a deep, gurgling breath before launching into his history. "It all started back in 1347, when I was martyred by that bastard of a duke for preaching the sacred word. Of course, I was told that an army of angels would come and rescue me before a hair on my head was disturbed."

"And did they?" Tiffany had never paid much attention during religion class. She wasn't too sure about the correct procedure for martyrdom. "Your hair looks very disturbed today."

"Of course not!" Bruno snatched a bottle of water from his pocket and took a deep gulp. "The head was sliced off my shoulders and stirred in a vat of boiling oil before I could even begin to argue my case. Never rely on an army of angels, Tiffany. What good is a heavenly trumpet blast when you're turning into someone's deep-fried lunch? Apparently, someone coughed up one of my teeth and it became a sacred relic somewhere. They actually built a cathedral in honour of it. Nobody could come and rescue me from the axe, but they had no problems building a cathedral for one of my bloody teeth!"

"Well, I'm sure looking after me will be a walk in the park compared to that." *Step one. Step two.* "A nice mindful walk in the park."

"Oh, please! Don't turn a simple everyday activity into a philosophy. Next you'll be telling me that drinking water is the path to enlightenment. It's actually just the path to constant visits to the bathroom. Anyway, I have my own sacred relic to bring me luck."

"Your tooth?"

"No. This." He handed what looked like a grilled raisin to Tiffany.

"What's that?"

"It's the earlobe of Judas Iscariot's first cousin. I never leave home without it. Neither did he until someone cut it off him."

Tiffany handed the relic back with a shudder.

"I don't need any relics." Tiffany was surprised at her defensive tone. She tried to assert more authority in her voice. "I'm perfectly fine living my life–"

"You're far from fine. You don't even know what 'fine' is anymore." Bruno finished his bottle of water and threw the empty bottle in the nearest bush. "There's an ache inside you that you can't cure, so you're trying to ignore it."

"Bugger off! Who the hell are you to pontificate to me? I've never been happier in my life," Tiffany lied. "Why, only yesterday, I was thinking–"

"Only yesterday, you were beginning to realise that you'll never be happy on your own." Bruno took a half-eaten chocolate bar from one of his deepest pockets. "You're just not like that. You need someone to spar with and scratch at. Someone to replace Bill."

"I just want–"

"It really is time that you went back to work," declared Bruno, throwing the chocolate wrapper on the path. "I'll be in touch soon and we'll sort out a plan of campaign."

"You're very untidy for a saint," Tiffany noted. "Not much perfection about you."

Silence answered Tiffany.

All she could hear was her own breathing on the empty hillside.

I breathe in. I kill the Seagull. I breathe out. I kill Jehovah.

A bottle of wine for the good times, a bottle of whiskey for the pain.
Give me a bottle of wine for the good times. Give me a bottle of whiskey for the pain.
My brain is soaked right through. Don't think I'll ever be sober again.

The Yellow Carrot was noisy and overcrowded and stuffy and smelly. Tiffany could hardly hear herself think. And that was good. She didn't really want to listen her thoughts.

Tiffany hoped the wine would dissolve the uneasy tingle that shot across her stomach. She looked at Bill awkwardly trying to negotiate a tray of drinks across the room. She expected to see the tray go flying at any minute, but he managed to unsteadily make his way back to his friends at the far table.

Not as many friends as I was expecting. Just Joey and Silvio getting steadily shitfaced as they balance wobbly on their barstools. And there's Giggles over at the table. Giggles looks hot tonight! And then Wigwam trying to chat up that unfortunate woman over there. No wonder Bill looks sad.

"Quit gawking at him," Martha snapped. "You'll only destroy your eyes."

"I wasn't gawking. I just wanted to make sure it was him."

"Of course it was him! He's like a busted sewage pipe; you can sense him as soon as you walk into the room. Though at least you can fix a sewage pipe."

Tiffany watched the young couples laughing with each other as they enjoyed their easy intimacy. Single girls danced to the guitar and organ riff. Single guys prowled through the crowd, casting grins, quips, and compliments. Their efforts were sometimes met with flirting smiles and flickering lashes, sometimes with turned heads and threatening glowers.

The whole scene made Tiffany glad that she had said goodbye to all that for now. The desperation in one guy's eyes, the uncertain twitching on one girl's lips, it all seemed too fraught for her. Her scars would take longer to heal.

A pale, skinny red-haired guy was dancing wildly with a

group of girls. He kicked his legs with abandon, his arms flailing all around him. The girls laughed, enjoying the joke. One of the girls, a slim brunette with dark eyes and a light-blue dress, moved closer to him, trying to time her sway with his.

"What the hell are you staring at now? That ginger farce throwing fits in the corner?"

"Look at those girls," Tiffany said. "They're really enjoying themselves. They look like they don't have a care in the world."

"That's because they're half-cut on gin and vodka. They'll devour that fool any moment now."

The red-haired guy had just crashed to the floor with a yelp. The girls crowded around him, trying to help him back to his feet. He seemed to having difficulty moving his left leg.

"I was talking to someone today." The image of St Bruno with his bottle of water flashed before her. "He told me that I was haunted by the possibility that I might never find real happiness."

"Who said that to you? I hoped you gouged out his eyes. The cheek of some people!"

"He was…" *No, I don't want her to think I've gone completely for the birds.* "Just one of those religious nuts. He called into the office. I tried to ignore him, but I can't stop thinking about what he said. I feel like something has laid an egg in my brain."

"It'll get well fried in there!"

"Don't pay any attention to me." Tiffany drank some wine. The tingle inside her refused to dissolve. "I've been all over the shop the last few days."

The girls were leading the red-haired guy to the door. He limped severely, his arm around the brunette's shoulder. The hunger had gone from her eyes and she tried to brush his hand away.

His fall reminded Tiffany of Alison's hen night. And the Masked Miguel. She had been thinking about him a lot today. Remembering the day she tried to book him for an office party. She had found his number online. When she called it, a woman answered the phone. Irene. His manager. And wife. Tiffany decided to hire a cheap jazz band for the event instead.

She noticed that Bill and Giggles seemed to have fallen into an argument. Voices were being raised and tables thumped.

"Maybe it's time to jump back on the merry-go-round," Tiffany said. "I've got to see what's lying around."

"Don't go rushing into something stupid." The sharp edge had left Martha's voice. She now sounded concerned. "That's how you got tangled up with that Bill calamity."

As the red-haired guy limped out the door on his own, Tiffany couldn't help smiling to herself. The chase hadn't got any easier. Yet part of her was looking forward to stepping back into the arena. She was going to prove St Bruno wrong. She would find happiness on her own terms.

As she walked over to Bill's table, she could hear that the conversation had already descended into the bullshit zone.

"Where the hell did Wigwam disappear to?" Bill asked.

"He's trying to chat up that bird in the gold top," Giggles replied. He suddenly noticed Tiffany at the table. "I mean, he's trying to engage in conversation with that woman over there. Oh, hi, Tiffany!"

"Hello, Giggles," Tiffany replied with an instinctive smile. "I see Wigwam hasn't changed. He still never knows when he's defeated."

The one thing I always did like about Bill was his friends. Well, some of them! If he had been more like them, things might have been better. Instead of being bitter.

The bar was beginning to fill up with the Friday-night crowd. A guitar instrumental gently played beneath the conversations and the tinkle of glasses.

In a dark corner, Wigwam was frantically talking to a tipsy

middle-aged woman. He was wearing a bright white shirt which seemed to dazzle the woman. His scraggly black hair was gelled back and his short beard twitched as his anecdote relentlessly rattled on.

"What about your antics last night?" Giggles asked Bill. "You said you got some rabbit action."

"I don't think I should talk about this in front of Tiffs," Bill replied, glancing over at Tiffany. "It might be too upsetting–"

"Bill," Tiffany assured him, "your sad exploits could never upset me. At worst, they just intrigue me in an academic sort of way!"

"Well then, as I said earlier," Bill continued, "she took me back to her place and we–"

"Where did she live?"

"Tyrone Terrace, I think… One of those manky ghost estates near the Rodexin factory."

"Did she have a big place?" Giggles leaned in towards Bill. "How many rooms were there? How big was–?"

"What's with the Spanish Inquisition? She had a nice hallway and a nicer bedroom and–"

"What colour were her sheets?"

"Red. Green. Magenta. Cyan with hints of azure. Any

damn colour you'd like." Bill's face was a collage of colours now too. "You don't have to believe me."

"We believe you." Giggles laughed. "Your story is just as believable as any of the other fake news that you read online these days."

"Just because *you're* not getting any action," Bill snarled at Giggles, "doesn't give you the right to take the piss out of *my* successes. You miss the thrill of the chase. You've been neutered."

"Wigwam looks like he's been neutered." Giggles nodded towards the door. The woman in the gold top was storming out. "He's standing there gaping like an electrocuted fish."

They all looked over at Wigwam. The speakers were now jangling a sprightly guitar and trumpet number. Some of the drunker customers were swaying to the music. The rest were easing into comfortable conversational grooves.

Bill smiled absently into his drink. Giggles stared at a group of office women who were laughing at some private anecdote. Wigwam unsuccessfully tried to catch the old barman's attention.

Tiffany turned her attention to Bill. Unlike Giggles, he looked older tonight. Older than thirty-five. His eyes were tired and red. The grey streaks in his hair gave him an aura, not of character, but of faded weariness. He seemed to be fed up with the game.

Tiffany had heard enough stories – many from Martha – to know that Bill's love life had now degenerated into a cycle of subtly demoralising defeats. He had ploughed on regardless, convinced that the wild carnival awaited him around the next dark corner.

Why the hell am I thinking so much about this gobshite? He's made his bed. Let him die in it.

Looking around the bar, Tiffany wondered if she should spend some time with the other guys there instead. Plenty of the guys were hot enough to be mildly distracting. Office drones glowing with the determination to forget about their problems and have a good time for the next few hours. Open-necked shirts. Ripped jeans and torn cuffs. Smart watches. Stupid grins. Frozen eyebrows. Complex runners and scuffed leather. Loud guffaws. Stroked goatees. Ironic earrings. Gentle smiles. Wandering fingers. Disturbing nose studs. Glowing phones and shadowy glances.

Sensing her stare, some of them cast puzzled glances at Tiffany.

But Tiffany knew she wouldn't make any moves. Not tonight. No matter how much she wanted Giggles to wrap his muscled arms around her and carry her to some secret dark sanctuary. Time enough for that some other night, maybe. But not for now.

Not with Bill watching the entire ritual.

"Here comes Wigwam," Giggles said, breaking Tiffany's reverie, "on his way back from Mission Impractical."

Wigwam sat beside them, placing his pint on the table. He gazed at the creamy froth for some seconds, a bewildered expression on his face.

"Well?" Giggles asked when it became apparent that Wigwam seemed to have no intention of saying anything. "What happened to the beginning of your beautiful friendship?"

"Women." He sighed. "I'll never understand a single inch of them. It's all a tumbleweed lost in last week's washing machine. One pointless cycle after another."

Bill, Giggles, and Tiffany raised several puzzled eyebrows as a piano boogie tingled from the speakers.

"You might," Joey suggested, "need to clarify that remark, Wigwam."

"Because," Bill added, "no one has a bloody clue what you're talking about."

Wigwam took a long drink, his face creased in a frown.

75

"It all just rolls by me." He shrugged. "Never makes a puddle of sense. One minute, we're yabbering away like two parrots on a foreign radio. The next, she's storming off into the sunset, six-shooter blazing. I'll never know what makes women happy."

Tiffany was beginning to tire of the silliness. She wasn't drunk enough to enjoy it. It was time to retreat.

She slipped back to Martha's table without saying a word to the guys.

A smooth guitar and organ riff oozed over the room as Tiffany squeezed her way through the crowd. Some handsome young men made eye contact with her, their sharp aftershave fleeting past. Some ignored her.

She didn't say a word to Martha as she sat down beside her. And Martha knew her well enough to know that conversation was unnecessary for now.

Tiffany needed time to reflect. She wanted to make a new start. Put Bill and the fiasco with the Turtle behind her. Find happiness again. And enjoy it.

It was time to make a new start. Time to start appreciating every day.

Time to start making changes too.

And she'd need the help of her guardian angel for that!

It's a new morning, baby. Time to clear the cobwebs from my head.

Wake up, it's a new morning, baby! Help me clear the cobwebs from my head.

Help me open up these eyes. Help me get out of this old bed.

4

The Merry Martyr Blues

Bless me, father, for I have sinned, I've sinned all over the place.
Wipe the tears from your eyes, baby, wipe that smile offa your face.
I'm eatin' the blues, and hungry for another race.

Tiffany prided herself on not being a procrastinator. When she moved, she moved! And when she decided to make changes, those changes came fast and furious. Usually furious.

And recently she had been making a few changes. She'd moved out of the manky studio and installed herself in Martha's spare room. It was only going to be a temporary arrangement, of course, to save up a bit of money and get some breathing space. A few weeks, at most. Certainly no more than a couple of months or so.

Another cost-cutting measure was selling the car. Martha's husband, George, could drive her anywhere she needed to go that wasn't within walking distance. However, living with Martha, she knew she'd want to do as much solitary walking as possible. So there were some health benefits to the new – *temporary* – arrangement.

Another benefit was how the tension in Martha's house

helped distract Tiffany from her own tensions. But some days, the atmosphere became a bit too fraught.

Like today, for example.

It had all kicked off with the traditional breakfast row at 8:00…

"Exactly what part of recession don't you understand, Robin?" His mother slammed down the burnt toast on the table.

"The part that says you have no money for my new runners," answered Robin, "but you have enough money to go out drinking with Tiffany three times already this week."

George buried his head further in his Sudoku puzzle.

"First of all, Tiffany is going through a difficult patch and I have to support her, whether I want to or not." Martha glanced at her sister while she formulated the rest of the argument. "Second of all, it's none of your business how we spend *our* money. Third of all, you're fifteen years old, so frankly, you're a bit too old to be throwing your rattle out of the pram. Fourth of all, shut up!"

"I never had a rattle to throw out of the pram. You wouldn't even buy me that!"

"Don't talk back! You're upsetting your father. Isn't he, George?"

"Hmmm?"

"See, he's speechless with despair."

"All the girls are making fun of me," Robin pleaded. "Do you not care what people think of me?"

"In fairness, Thrush," Tiffany said, "the runners probably aren't the only reason that girls are making fun of you."

"Even Lettuce was laughing at–"

"Enough!" Martha slapped her hand on the table. "Shut your mouth and eat your breakfast!"

Breakfast was the usual train wreck. Tiffany saw an opportunity to rescue Robin.

"Why have you given us roadkill, Martha?" she asked.

"It's not roadkill," her sister snapped, rubbing her stinging palm. "It's a strawberry pancake. It's very nice."

Tiffany gingerly smelled the meal. It didn't smell like it had died recently. That was encouraging. However, neither did it smell like strawberries. Nor pancakes. That wasn't encouraging.

But she was hungry, so she took a deep breath and tucked in.

She was surprised at how good the pancake tasted. The cashew nuts in it were a bit unexpected. As was the pineapple. But it was a marked improvement on the omelette tragedy that was served up yesterday morning.

The porridge, on the other hand, looked like an abandoned medical experiment, and the fruit juice tasted like the grapes of wrath.

Robin was obviously trying to think of a different approach as he liberally spread jam on what remained of the toast, a burnt sacrificial offering to the culinary gods. The jam almost made the cinder palatable.

"I've been doing well in school." Robin was discovering that palatable cinder was not necessarily digestible. *Cough cough cough.* "I'm getting good grades. Maybe it's time I got a small reward. Nothing fancy, just a pair–"

"Listen!" His mother flung the tea-towel on the table and rejoined the debate with gusto. "No one gets rewarded for doing what's *expected* of them. I don't get rewarded for keeping this house together. Your father doesn't get rewarded for doing his job. Do you, George?"

"Hmmm?"

"No, he doesn't. You're dead right, George! He goes in there every day and he... he... he does whatever the hell it is that he does. And he doesn't get rewarded. Not at all! Of course, the odd performance bonus wouldn't hurt. But then, he'd have to push himself a bit more and actually perform.

And sing his achievements from the rooftop. Instead of being the company doormat. And letting every fly-by-night knobhead walk over him in that place… But that's not the point. You haven't earned your runners, Robin. You spend most of the day with your head in the clouds, rather than doing your homework. Do *excellent* in school and then we might consider it."

Robin was old enough to know that there was absolutely no point arguing with his mother.

But he grimly carried on anyway.

"Listen, Ivan and Taku got new runners last month. I'll look like some Poverty Peter if I wear these ragged clogs another week. Even Scruffy Cedric is talking about getting a new pair. He remarked yesterday that mine were looking a bit ravaged."

"Everyone's entitled to an opinion," his mother agreed. "Even a stupid one. But for now, just finish your breakfast! Get your bag packed! And get off to school! I've got a headache from listening to Tiffany all last night. She's only realising now that love's not all it's cracked up to be."

"Don't try to blame this on me," Tiffany interjected.

Martha threw a dirty look towards her Sudoku-engrossed husband. She always threw dirty looks at George when the subject of life's disappointments came up. She often remarked that after her wedding, she should have kept the bouquet and thrown away the groom.

"It's only a pair of runners…"

Martha diverted her dirty look towards her son. Recoiling from the glare, Robin realised that it was time to retreat and reassess his tactics.

Tiffany knew that there was no chance that George would come to his son's defence during the breakfast battle.

George was born to be mild. His wife supplied enough combustion for the entire family.

Tiffany decided that her nephew needed someone fighting in his corner.

"You know what Thrush's problem is? You're not feeding him properly, Martha. He's getting no nutrition, so his little feathery brain has started to corrode and he can no longer tell the difference between what's important and what's trivial."

Oblivious to the explosion that was about to go off around him, George announced that it was time to go to work.

Tiffany, Robin, and George retreated to the car while Martha tidied up the kitchen and muttered dark curses about everyone.

Settling into the back seat of the car, Tiffany knew that the threats to life and limb had not yet evaporated for the morning.

Although George Mulcahy was one of life's mild-mannered doormats, there was one place he came alive: behind the wheel of his car. That was where he liked to give in to his darker nature.

"If you can't drive," he yelled at a battered SUV, "go back to bed. And now look at this clown over here. I've seen people with deaf guide dogs park their cars faster than this idiot!"

This man should not be allowed operate a cigarette lighter, never mind a car.

Mild George was a psychopath behind the wheel. All his pent-up frustrations exploded once he got the car out of the drive, and out of Martha's sight. He would scream and rant at other road users, and thump the steering wheel and curse with abandon. This morning, nothing was censored. By the time they got on to Harris Street, they already had the f-word, the c-word, the b-word, the t-word, the p-word, the w-word, and even the rarely launched h-word.

The only time George felt that he reigned supreme was when he got his beloved orange Škoda on the road. Here he was master. Here he was in control. Here *he* made all the decisions.

Unless Martha was with him, of course. She'd spend the entire journey pointing out in great detail why he was the worst driver "on this side of the solar system".

In fairness, Martha had a point. George was an abysmal driver. He took an á la carte approach to the rules of the road, those which he could remember. He never knew where the one-way streets were. And he navigated roundabouts through sheer force of will.

Tiffany began to suspect that George had his own guardian angel looking out for him. A guardian angel wearing a seat belt and a crash helmet, no doubt.

Like all abysmal drivers, George blamed his mistakes on everyone else.

"Who the hell taught these people how to drive? Inbred aliens?"

"There's no such thing as aliens, Dad."

"Hmmmm?"

"There's no such thing as aliens"

"Oh, there is, Robbie. There has to be a species more powerful than your mother." George shuddered suddenly. "Don't tell your mother if I run over some of these imbeciles. We don't want to upset her more than she already is."

"Ma does seem to be a bit… tense these days," Robin

ventured.

"She is, Robbie," agreed his father. "Your mother is like a complex chemical compound. She can become a little… unstable if disturbed. Oh, I don't believe this! Look at that Mazda over there. A jellyfish in a blender would have better co-ordination."

"Dad, please put your hands on the steering wheel!"

George had been so distracted by trying to scratch himself in three places simultaneously that he forgot he was driving the car. He hastily put one hand on the steering wheel while the other continued to scratch his earlobe.

"Aren't you supposed to indicate before you change lanes, George?" Tiffany remarked as a chorus of irate car horns blared all around them.

"There are a lot of things you're supposed to do in life. It's impossible to do all of them. Sometimes, you wonder if it's worth doing *any* of them at all."

Tiffany was glad to see the school gates at the end of the road.

"Who's that over there, Thrush?" Tiffany had noticed a fit, muscular young man standing near the school gates. Unlike Bruno, this man was able to elegantly fill out a tracksuit. And the goatee gave him a quirky, but appealing, air. "The stud in the green tracksuit."

"Oh, that's Mishmash. He's our PE teacher."

"Does he have a proper name?" Tiffany enquired, unable to take her eyes off the goatee.

"Mr Merriman, I think." Robin shrugged. "We all call him Mishmash because his fitness programme is just a mishmash of infographics downloaded from—"

"That's not important!" *What's important is what lies beneath that tracksuit.* "Go off to school now."

"I'll see you this evening, Robbie," George declared as he drove off – without indicating or looking.

In the back seat, Tiffany continued to enjoy the sight of Mr Merriman.

Let's get lost in the woods, honey, and see who's hanging around the trees.
A walk in the woods, honey, and then we'll hang out around the trees.
I'm eatin' the blues, and beggin' you on my knees.

Following the glorious sight of Robin's PE teacher, goatees were on Tiffany's mind for the rest of the morning. She found her mind wandering back to her college days with Oscar the Goatee. Yes, they were miserable, cold times in many ways. But she'd been happy with that self-righteous yahoo for a few months. He made her laugh, not always intentionally.

She also spent some time working, of course. There was the carpenters' conference to organise. There was some resistance to her intended hashtag #WoodenItBeNice, but she was sure she could wear down that resistance.

The way Oscar the Goatee used to wear down my resistance.

Enough work done for now, Tiffany decided that she deserved a break and it was almost time for her lunchtime escape from the office. Memories swirled around her as she lost herself in her afternoon walk. She was reaching a zen-like level of detachment from her surroundings. Her feet knew the way. Her mind was free to wander where it chose.

And it chose to keep wandering back to Robin's PE teacher. The sight of that fit – literally fit, indeed – goatee stirred up college memories she thought she'd buried. She assumed that her time with Bill has crushed any romantic yearnings for good. But now, those old yearnings were beginning to stir.

Perhaps the further I get away from Bill, the closer I can get to my true self. Every step I take away from him is a step closer to me. I can cast him aside and forever forget–

"Hey, Tiffs, is that you?"

Tiffany screeched to a halt. She didn't even have to look

around. She'd know that squawk anywhere.

"Jesus, Bill, can I never get away from you?"

"Great to see you," Bill enthused, ignoring her less-than-warm greeting. "I'd heard you'd taken up hillwalking. I've never seen the point of it myself. Walking and walking, never getting—"

"What do you want?" *Bastard can still annoy me within ten seconds.* "I'm in a hurry to get back to work."

Bill laughed out loud. He knew her too well to be fooled by that lie.

Tiffany ignored the laugh. She focused on her surroundings instead, breathing in the clear, fresh air. Listening to the gentle flap of the birds' wings. Feeling the warm embrace of the sun's rays. Inhaling the sweet scent of the flowers.

She focused on anything except her ex-boyfriend.

"You look really great, Tiffs," Bill said, realising that Tiffany had already abandoned the conversation. "I noticed that the night of the party. Did you have a good time, by the way?"

"I've already forgotten about that stupid party," Tiffany lied. "And, by the way, you looked like shit that night. Way older than your advancing years."

"I knew you were paying *very* close attention to me!"

"That's not the bloody point I was making." Even the flapping of the birds' wings was beginning to irritate Tiffany now. "I just wanted you to know that I—"

"Kylie thinks I look very young," Bill interrupted. "Remember her?"

"That pushy little featherhead slapper from your IT department?" Yes, Tiffany did indeed remember Kylie! "What's she got to do with anything?"

"Oh, nothing really. She just popped in to the party after you left. I'd invited her and she seemed glad to come along. She really enjoyed herself."

"Shouldn't you be at work, Bill?"

"Shouldn't you?"

They'd reached an impasse. Tiffany turned her attention back to the birds' wings. That didn't really help her mood.

"Anyway, turns out she'd broken up with her boyfriend." Bill was not going to let an impasse stop him. "She caught him having it off with a jockey. Or a horse. Something like that. The details aren't important."

"None of this is—"

"So we got talking and one thing led to another."

"It usually does." *Damn those bloody birds to hell!* "It's called a sequence."

"So, I hope you don't mind. I mean, you may have got the wrong message that evening at the party."

"Wrong message?" Tiffany couldn't decide whether to throttle the birds or Bill. "What the hell are you talking about now?"

"I saw the way you were looking at me all the time that night."

"I *wasn't* bloody–"

"And I still care for you too. Of course I do. We were good together. And Kylie understands that you'll always be an important person to me. And I'll always be an important person to you."

"You mean absolutely nothing to–"

"But we have to move on, don't we, Tiffany?" Bill now adopted his most infuriating, reasonable tone. "I've found someone new. And some day you might even find someone to replace me."

Tiffany never liked Kylie. She was always way too chirpy. A smile full of perfect teeth and a laugh as clear as a frosty morning. Not even Tiffany's most ferocious glare could douse Kylie's bright flame.

"Did you follow me all the way up here today just to tell

me this? You really are the worst stalker in the world!"

"It's just fair to let you know, Tiffs. I don't want you getting your hopes up, trying to swim in a river that has long since dried out."

"I want to drown you in a river, you dozy, self-centred gobshite! Now bugger off and let me get back to work."

"I can walk back with you if you—"

"Bugger off to hell and back to your poor demented slut!"

Bill sighed and gave her a patient, pitying look. And with a wise, world-weary shrug, he walked past her.

"If you ever need to talk, Tiffs, you can always—"

"Bugger off!"

Tiffany watched Bill walk down to the path back to the city.

She took a deep breath and listened to the silence for some seconds. Even the birds had gone quiet. No flapping wings now.

"So that's the famous Bill," a voice suddenly declared behind her.

Tiffany turned around to see Bruno devouring a cheesy quarter-pounder. His increasingly frayed tracksuit seemed to stretch closer to bursting point with each swallow.

"Why has everybody decided to come to this hill today?"

Tiffany asked.

"You think you can find enlightenment on this hill," Bruno said, between quick munches. "I thought it was time to enlighten you on some of the realities of life."

"Whatever happened to saints having to fast?" Tiffany flicked some flying bits of chewed meat off her dress. "I've seen sewer rats with better table manners than you!"

"You wouldn't want a fasting saint." Bruno shook the meat juice out of his beard. "They're the most miserable, hungry-looking dreary drips you could ever meet. They're all up there in heaven now, and still refusing the food. We all call them the bonies and run a mile from them."

"Anyone who ate my sister's cooking would be happy to go on a fast." Tiffany looked at Bruno's enormous girth. "You obviously didn't manage to fit in a hunger strike over your seven hundred years of martyrdom!"

"I had enough torture in my life." Bruno wiped his greasy hands on his greasier tracksuit bottoms. "I didn't need to add Martha's cooking to my plagues."

"Well, yes, that's true. I do often wonder how George can put up with her monstrosities."

"That's because he utterly adores her."

"George is incapable of–"

"You can't see that because you don't understand what love is." Bruno pointed to the path down to the city. "You're still in love with Bill, yet you've just let him walk away down that–"

"I am not in love with–"

"–path and continued on your own silent, bitter path. Whenever happiness crosses your path, you just have to push it away."

"The only thing I've wanted to push away today was Martha's farce of a breakfast." *Why does everything have to come back to Bill?* "Maybe it's time I did something nice for George. He does deserve a break from her cooking."

Tiffany remembered that there was something she needed to do between lunch and dinner. It was her job.

"Right, enough bullshitting with fat angels. Time to get back to work."

The only reply she heard was the flapping of unseen wings.

Sit down on my knee, sweetheart, this could be our last meal.
Let me read you the menu, let me tell you how I feel.
I'm eatin' the blues, getting ready for the final deal.

Tiffany knew that she'd need to keep George sweet while

staying with Martha, so she decided to treat the family to a meal out. As she'd pointed out to Bruno, the poor man deserved a break from Martha's cooking.

She was glad that the Maestro Bistro was so quiet this evening. There was already tension at their table. Martha was gently fuming over some secret slight that Tiffany couldn't be bothered investigating.

"Tell us about your day, George." Tiffany decided to focus on the least volatile member of the family. "Everything go okay?"

"Yes, I suppose." George was engrossed in the delights of the menu. "We managed to align our synergised parameters with value-added customer-focused deliverables."

Tiffany and Martha stared silently at George for some seconds.

Robin continued tapping absently on his phone.

"The food here is very nice." Tiffany decided that no other response was appropriate to George's update. "I'm looking forward to it."

"I swear to God," Martha said, putting down the menu with a disgusted headshake, "I think I'm going to murder someone before this meal this is over!"

Tiffany knew from experience that family meals in fancy

restaurants always had the potential to end in embarrassing catastrophe, if not arrests and court appearances. During the course of their last meal out to celebrate Tiffany's decision to move into the spare room, George had got locked in the toilets for an hour before anyone noticed that he was missing, and Martha had assaulted the piano player.

This evening was not shaping up to be much better. Everyone was on edge. Martha's powder kegs were even more primed than usual after what she would only describe as a "needlessly trying day". And George had to rush back into the office on the way to the bistro – something to do with "inconsistent throughput margins" – and, having thoroughly investigated the delights of the menu, was now busy consoling himself with a Sudoku extravaganza. Robin, of course, was busy texting his friends.

Starters were eaten in silence for some minutes.

"That's it, Robin!" Martha slammed down her soup spoon. "We take you out for a meal and all you can do is text your gobshite friends. Did we teach you no manners at all? Is a little bit of conversation too much to ask? George, take that phone off him."

"Hmmmm!" George looked up from his Sudoku book. "What's that, my sugar pumpkin?"

"George, take the phone off Robin. And then put that puzzle book away. Are we really *that* boring?"

Deciding it was safer not to answer that question, George took the phone from Robin and put it in his pocket.

"Now we can enjoy our soup in peace." Martha grimaced when she tasted it. "God almighty, the cat could produce better soup than this!"

Tiffany, scalded by the memory of the last soup that Martha had produced, decided to restrain her response. Instead, she looked across the room to the lobster tank. The lobsters seemed to be having a more enjoyable evening than she was.

"Finch, how was PE today?" she asked her nephew. The handsome goatee would take her mind off the misery about the table. "Did Mr Merriman give a good class?"

"Not really," Robin replied. "He yelled at us all and said we were obese layabouts. Except me. He said I look like a refugee. But other than that, he was–"

"Is he married, do you know?"

"How would I know?"

"Or seeing anyone, perhaps?"

"What's this sudden obsession with Robin's PE teacher?" Martha asked. "You're not going to take up jogging as well as hillwalking, are you? How many ways can you find to waste your time?"

Before Tiffany could snap back an answer, the waiter arrived and cleared away the soup bowls.

"Thank you, that soup was sublimely beautiful," said George, opening his Sudoku book under the table.

"Our pleasure, sir," the waiter replied.

"I've tasted nicer battery acid," said Martha as he took away her bowl.

"Our pleasure, madam," the waiter replied.

Tiffany decided to drop the subject of the PE teacher for now. It would be more fun to annoy her sister instead.

"Tell me, Finch, speaking about people seeing people and all that, how are things between you and the girls at school? You mentioned a Lettuce before, I believe."

"That's right. I messaged her earlier for some recommendations on new runners, but she hasn't replied yet." Robin looked over at his father. "And I can't check my phone now. So maybe I should call round to her house some evening and see if she's okay. Of course, I need a new pair of runners before I could even consider—"

"Robin, let me explain this to you just once," his mother said. "If you mention those bloody runners once more this evening, I'll feed you feet first to the lobsters in that tank. And, by the way, there's no need for you to go running after floozy girls from the school either, with or without runners! Do you understand me?"

Martha was very protective of her son, and was particularly determined to protect him from the pains of a broken teenage heart. Even if that meant murdering him in the process.

The main courses arrived before Robin could answer. George abandoned his Sudoku and attacked his steak with gusto. Martha delicately carved her lamb.

"Eat your burger, Robin," his mother said, "before people think you're on hunger strike. I must have a word with the PE teacher. I can't have him making smart comments about my son. I also need to warn him that my deranged sister has got him in her sights. George, try to chew your steak before you swallow. I don't want you choking again. You turn a most disagreeable colour when you choke."

The food was indeed delicious. Tiffany's penne pasta was a work of art. She couldn't remember the last time she'd tasted food so good. Probably the last time it wasn't cooked by her sister.

"This lamb tastes like asbestos, by the way," said Martha. "I don't know what's wrong with you all tonight. I cook beautiful meals for you and then Tiffany insists on dragging us to this chemical factory."

"You need a rest, lollipop," George said, pausing in his worship of the steak. "We can't have you cooking every night. It was very nice of Tiffany to take us here this evening."

"Oh, it's the very least she could do," Martha replied. "Not many would put up with her. Even Bill gave up, eventually."

"You should have chosen the steak, cutie socks," George said, gazing lovingly at his meal. "It's the nicest–"

"When we choose from the menu," Martha continued, looking pointedly at her husband, "we have to stick with our choice, no matter how *bland* the meal turns out to be."

"Your meals aren't bland, darling. It's just that you know your limits and stick to them. That's an admirable–"

"Waiter, some Scotch," Martha suddenly declared.

"Oh, I'm fine, dear."

"It's for me, George!"

Tiffany worked her way through the rest of the pasta, wondering if she'd ever find someone to replace Bill. Maybe she'd find someone here in this very bistro.

Seize the day! Live in the moment!

She looked up. And felt her blood turn cold.

Bill had just walked in with Kylie.

That bastard really is stalking me. And this time he's brought the spikey little dollybird with him!

But Bill didn't even glance over at Tiffany's table. His attention was solely devoted to Kylie, leading her gently to her table and pulling the chair out for her. She giggled at whatever remark he'd made as he sat down.

Tiffany noticed that, throughout his meal, Bill never once looked over at her, because never once did he take his eyes off the young woman sitting across the table from him.

It's all a bit of a giggle, it's all a bit of a joke.
I wanna fly you to the moon, but my engine gone broke.
I'm eatin' the blues, watchin' another martyr go up in smoke.

"My sister has such a martyr complex!"

Tiffany settled down on her bed.

"No matter what happens, she has to assume that it was designed solely to ruin her day."

"Don't get me started about martyrs!" Bruno was sitting on the edge of the bed, massaging his ripped-stockinged feet. "Constantly complaining. Even Jesus likes to go off on one about the crosses every now and then. You'd think we all hadn't already heard that story countless times for two thousand years!"

"Real martyrs did have a hard time of it, though," Tiffany conceded, fluffing her pillow with a vigorous thump. "At least your martyrs really did have something to complain about!"

"Of course they had a hard time," Bruno replied. "They wouldn't really be martyrs if they had it *easy*, would they? My favourite martyr was Archbishop Guido. He had his legs strapped into metal boots full of cooking oil and then had his legs slow cooked for three days before all the flesh fell off."

"This is a lovely conversation to have late in–"

"He's still hobbling around heaven." Bruno laughed. "We all call him Hot Legs."

"It's not as if Martha has anything to complain about, really." Tiffany now found herself slipping into the spirit of the conversation. "Not compared to what happened to your friends. Broken on wheels. Cooked alive in oil. Grilled in furnaces. Nailed upside down on crosses. Eaten by lions, tigers, rats, or sparrows. Impaled on red-hot spears. In comparison, her troubles are relatively painless."

"St Bridget was another one," continued Bruno, warming to his favourite theme. "Tore out her eye and fed it to the hens so she wouldn't be tempted by any handsome young men. A blindfold wouldn't do her. No danger of you tearing out your eyes. You're too fond of looking at hot young stud monkeys."

"I thought you were sent here to help me. Some guardian angel you are!"

"You're just as bad as the martyrs!" Bruno shuddered, giving his foot a good shake and unleashing an avalanche of mysterious dust. "They'd sicken you with their endless complaining. They think just because they've been disembowelled and quartered, no one else has suffered. Did I complain when that bastard of a duke was pan-frying my head? No, I didn't. I was too busy sizzling my way to eternity. Waiting for a choir of angels that never turned up, by the way. Seven hundred years later, and still no sign of the bastards."

"You seem to be a little bit inconsistent about how you died," Tiffany replied.

"That's not the point!"

"And what is your point?" Tiffany asked as she scanned her phone.

"My point is that you have a touch of the martyr about yourself too. I saw the way you were looking at Bill this–"

"I was *not* looking–"

"You need to lighten up a bit and drop this whole misunderstood martyr routine." Bruno shook a few bits of fungus out of his beard. "Every single person since the dawn of time has played that act. Even Jesus could be the most miserable, sanctimonious, dreary–"

Bruno's phone started ringing.

"Yes," he gruffly answered when he saw the incoming number. "Oh, what now? For heaven's sake, I was only... It was just to make a.... Yes, I know He is... Of course, I read it... Some of it, anyway... Fine, if you insist.... Will you just let me get on with it, please? Same to you..."

Bruno banged his phone on the bed a few times before slamming it back into his pocket.

"Okay, forget what I was saying about Jesus," Bruno said. "Seems there are some things I just can't joke about these days. Especially when some people upstairs have no sense of humour. Jesus was a lovely guy once you got to know him. Great fun to be around. Apparently." He glared briefly up at the ceiling. "Happy now?"

This time, it was Tiffany's phone that started ringing.

"If that's God," snapped Bruno, "tell Him I'm not here."

"Hi, Giggles," Tiffany said, answering the phone, relieved that she didn't have to lie to God. "What a nice surprise!"

Bruno raised a bushy eyebrow at this.

"Hey, Tiffany." Even at this late hour, Giggles was full of the joys of life. "How are you this evening?"

"I'm… okay overall. I got through the day without killing anyone."

"One less corpse for me to take care of then," Giggles replied, unconcerned about Tiffany's apparent willingness to commit random murder. "I was talking to Bill a while ago."

"Jesus, there's no escaping from *him* today!"

"Maybe you don't want to escape from him," Bruno interrupted, before returning his attention to his well-massaged feet. "You miss your martyr cage."

"Bill mentioned that he'd seen you at the restaurant," Giggles continued. "He thought that you looked sad. So I decided to give you a call to cheer you up. Or at least give you a little laugh."

"Well, that's very nice of you." *I didn't look sad, did I?* "It was just another normal evening out with Martha and her family. So just the usual level of sadness, I suppose."

"No worries. Cheering people up is part of this undertaker's box of tricks! I think Bill was worried that you might have been upset or something when you saw him with Kylie and—"

"Why the hell would I be upset about that skanky, bubbly little minger of a slut?" *Okay, that came out too loudly. Bruno nearly fell off the bed!* "She's welcome to him."

"I think that's what Martha said to her when you were all leaving." Giggles laughed loudly. "Martha is a very unique creature!"

Martha had indeed been delighted to see Kylie with Bill. Once she got over her initial revulsion at seeing Bill. As they'd left the bistro, Martha couldn't resist going over to his table and throwing a few conversational darts at him. Despite the onslaught, Bill had remained polite and infuriatingly affable. Martha had turned her attention to Kylie and begged her to hold on to Bill and not let him ever escape.

"I thought Martha was going to go up in flames when she saw him," Tiffany said, remembering the splash of outraged Scotch on the table, "but the sight of him with another woman seemed to calm her down. Relatively speaking."

"Does it hurt *you* to see him with another woman?" Giggles asked. "Or are you still glad to be rid of him?"

"He's moved on, and so have I! I've thrown out yesterday's rubbish."

"Oh, really? And who have you moved on to, Tiffany?"

"Oh, it could be anyone." Tiffany remembered how yummy Giggles had looked at Bill's party. It was the highlight of her night. "In fact, *anything* is possible."

"Good to hear you're okay." Giggles sounded greatly

relieved. "I was worried about you."

"Oh, I didn't realise I was so important to you, Giggles!" Tiffany indulged in a flirtatious laugh, ignoring the exasperated look Bruno was giving her. "I must add you to my list, ha ha ha."

"The only list I'm on these days," Giggles replied too quickly, "is the dead list. I'll be buried in work this week."

"Yes, we all love our work!" *Time to abandon this particular mission.* "Anyway, thanks for checking in. I'm okay."

Tiffany always felt a little bit more than okay after talking to Giggles.

"You take care of yourself, Tiffany." Giggles's voice was as bouncy as ever. "You'll find someone to replace Bill. You'll be back to normal again."

"Thanks, Giggles!" *What the hell does that mean? I've always been normal.* "Talk soon."

"That giggling tosser would drive anyone to martyrdom," Bruno remarked as he slipped his squeaky runners back on. "I think I got the easier mission after all."

Tiffany knew that maybe things weren't all that normal for her these days. After all, she was happily chatting away to an unkempt guardian angel in her bedroom. But Giggles had certainly put a smile on her face after the trauma of the bistro.

He had given her the enthusiasm to carry on.

She had her own mission now too!

Let's go in the forest, let's find that buried treasure.
I've got more riches for you than you can ever measure.
I'm eatin' the blues, but you want a brand new pleasure.

5

The Funny Uncle Blues

Morning has broken, put on my glasses and shoes.
The morning has broken down, put on them glasses and shoes.
Put in my new false teeth, take a bite of them endless blues.

Tiffany prided herself on understanding her nephew very well. Indeed, they had a special bond. He often declared that she was his *favourite* aunt. Of course, the only competition was George's sister, Muriel, a cocaine-addled exotic dancer who worked the corporate entertainment circuit and went by the name Juanita. By comparison, Tiffany was an eminently suitable role model for the boy.

She had a good grasp of what made him tick. And what made him thick. She knew that all he wanted from life was a few hours of peace every now and then, a girl who absolutely adored every single inch of him, and a new pair of runners. His needs were simple, and hopelessly unattainable.

Now that she was living in her sister's house, Tiffany looked for ways to make her nephew an ally – willing or otherwise – in her quest for a new partner in life.

When Martha and George had bought this house during

the Tiger Boom, the kitchen didn't really figure too much in their considerations. Although George was utterly smitten with Martha, he knew she was no goddess in the kitchen. A microwave, a functional cooker, and an electric tin opener were the only prerequisites for Martha's kitchen. Ever on the lookout for a bargain, she'd managed to buy all three at a fire sale at the local electrical store. Tiffany was the only person brave enough to voice the widely held suspicion that Martha was the arsonist who'd torched the store purely to force a reduction in prices. When it came to haggling, few actions were beyond her pale.

As her family well knew, Martha was also an arsonist in the kitchen. The walls and ceilings bore the scorch marks of many the abandoned meal over the years. A lingering smell of burnt toast and disinfectant pervaded the air.

Although Martha was no goddess in the kitchen, she was an absolute tyrant at the dinner table. She insisted people eat her food under her watchful glare, because the table was her fiefdom. The table – a "gift" from neighbours who'd abandoned their negative-equity hellhole down the road – was peppered with scratches and chips that bore testament to hastily eaten meals.

And sitting at this table, on a warm Sunday morning,

Tiffany plotted her next move.

Robin needed her help. And Tiffany needed Robin's help. So this was only going to end one way.

"We all have someone we like in this world, don't we, Pigeon?" Tiffany started off innocently enough. "Isn't there some girl that you're mooning about? Leadbelly, is it?"

"Leticia," Robin corrected his aunt. "But we all call her Lettuce."

"That's…" Tiffany couldn't think of anything nice to say. "Why on earth do they call her that?"

"Oh, you know what teenagers are like." Robin spoke with the weary wisdom of an ancient sage. And then scratched his acne. "They have to make a skit of everything. Just because Leticia isn't the liveliest person in the class. And doesn't always dress in the most colourful clothes. And walks around like a nun in an abandoned abbey… Look, I see something in her that they don't see."

"Hmmm, interesting." Tiffany had planted the seed. "Well, what I see is two lumps of coal on this table."

"That's not coal," Robin explained, as he rummaged in his schoolbag. "They're cookies. Or buns. Or fudge. Or whatever delicacy Ma attempted to cook last night."

"What are you digging for in that mangy bag?"

111

"I need to ask you something, T. It's about gym."

Tiffany knew that Robin hated gym class. His physique was more suited to the library. Or the mortuary. But Tiffany had to consider the wider picture. In particular, she had to consider the gym teacher.

"What about gym?" *What about that hot gym teacher?* "What's happened there now?"

"I don't want to go to gym class tomorrow." Robin rarely bothered lying to his aunt. He saved all his lies for his mother. "Can you write me a sick note?"

"You don't look very sick to me, no sicker than usual anyway. And why can't your mother write the note? Did she burn all the pens as well as the breakfast?"

"Can we not just keep it our little secret?" Robin handed Tiffany a sheet of paper and a well-chewed pen. "Why does Ma have to know everything?"

"I'm not very comfortable with lying to your mother," Tiffany lied. "Especially on a Sunday morning just before we go to mass."

"Why not? We all lie to her. That's the only way you can survive in this dungeon!"

Tiffany could empathise with this. After all, lying had been an integral part of her relationship with Bill. So she understood

Robin's situation. And in his problem, she saw her opportunity.

"You want me to write a note to Mr Merriman?"

"Yes. Finally! Will you do it?"

"Remind me. Is Mr Merriman married?"

"No, I don't think he is." Robin considered this. "I can't imagine anyone wanting to share their life with him. He just wants to share his time with the gym. He even gives yoga classes there in the evenings."

"Oh, I love yoga!" Tiffany despised yoga. She thought it an even greater waste of time than harmonica playing. "I should go to his class. See, everything works out. You have your Lettuce. I have my Merriman."

"Are you going to write the note or not?"

"Are you going to introduce me to Mr Merriman or not?"

They stared at each other, neither one willing to make the next move. Not just yet.

Robin picked up one of the mysterious burnt delicacies from the table and began chewing slowly, his eyes never leaving his aunt's.

Tiffany stood up and picked up one of the burnt offerings, maintaining steely eye contact with her nephew.

"If I don't write that note, Pigeon, you'll have to go to gym class." She sniffed the specimen and then flung it into the bin. "And you'll end up in a worst state than that poor cake! So are you ready to make a deal?"

"Why do I have to introduce you to Mishmash?" Robin asked, his mouth still full of burnt debris. "And he ever does is scream and yell at me and then–"

Robin suddenly stopped talking and began beating his chest.

"What's with this Tarzan routine?" Tiffany enquired. "Turning blue isn't going to convince me to write that note any faster."

Robin was desperately struggling to catch his breath as the chewed cake refused to dislodge itself from his throat. He grasped the side of the table, sweat pouring down his forehead.

"Oh, are you choking?" Tiffany knew enough about first aid to recognise the signs. First aid was another essential skill when she was living with Bill. "Good job I know the Heimlich manoeuvre."

Relief washed over Robin's face. He stared at his aunt, this angel who would use the Heimlich manoeuvre to dislodge the damn cake and stop him from choking to death.

Tiffany stared at her choking nephew.

I wonder why it's called the Heimlich manoeuvre. Heimlich must have been involved in it somewhere. Was he the guy who was choking? Or did he save the guy who was choking? Or did he play Martha's role and bake food that was destined to choke people?

"You're turning a very unusual colour, Pigeon," Tiffany remarked as she sat back down on the chair. "Why is that?"

Robin's eyes grew wider as he felt the grip of death begin to wrap around him. He tried to beg his aunt to hurry up. But all he could do was gasp desperately as his eyes watered up.

"Are you going to introduce me to Mr Merriman?" Tiffany asked, gazing nonchalantly out the window.

As he slid to his knees, Robin realised he'd never be the negotiator that his aunt was.

Mere seconds away from death, he nodded weakly, indicating his willingness to agree unconditionally to all of her terms.

"Thank you, Pigeon," Tiffany said, standing up. "Now, let's get rid of that monstrosity that your mother cooked."

Say your prayers, sister, it's time to pay the dues.
Say a few prayers for me, sister, I gotta pay these dues.
Gotta get my house in order, find a home for these endless blues.

Despite her recent encounter with an angel, Tiffany wasn't an overly religious person. Her constant battles with the nuns in primary school and her daily sparring with Jehovah at work had crushed any heavenly leanings she'd ever had.

Martha, on the other hand, still clung to her own á la carte blend of religion. She argued that she needed the help of all the heavenly hosts to get her through her days. She regarded George as the cross she had to bear through life, and Robin was her crown of thorns.

So every Sunday morning, the family found themselves listening to Fr Twitter in the local church. A social media fanatic, the local priest was determined to drag his dwindling congregation online. Endless updates – not always *appropriate* updates – were posted to multiple social media platforms. Whereas other priests meditated on rosary beads, Fr Twitter meditated on clickthrough rates and organic reach.

"We all go through life waiting for God to take our hand and lead us in the right direction." Fr Twitter waved his right hand across the church for dramatic emphasis. "Afraid to make our move, we sit quivering in the dark, playing with our iPads, reading Reddit, and watching other people live exciting lives on YouTube. And wondering when God is going to give us the push we need."

Sour faces seemed to be the fashion of the day in the church. George was sulking over Martha's failure to make edible porridge. Robin was sulking over being nearly choked to death. And Martha was sulking because it was Sunday and that was her favourite day to sulk. There was less to do, so there was more time to spend fuming.

The church did nothing to improve anyone's mood. Designed during World War II, it was constructed in a hurry, under the constant threat of invasion or bombing. As a result, it always had a slightly frantic and panicky air, even when it was empty. Some of the statues were chipped and scuffed, and the Stations of the Cross had a decidedly demented feel to them.

Today, Fr Twitter looked more distracted than demented. As usual, his mind seemed to be wandering elsewhere as he spoke.

"I used to wait for God to answer my prayers. But after so many years of waiting, you take the hint and seize the day yourself. No point looking for answers from someone else. Get on to Google or Wikipedia and start exploring. Make sure your internet connection is good, though. A good wireless router and a stable signal are essential. Of course, I'm not allowed to recommend any suppliers when I'm on the altar.

But if anyone would like some suggestions, you can talk to me after mass. I'll be in the confession box. I've got some brochures and cards and everything."

By now, everyone was wandering happily in their own thoughts.

"You see," Fr Twitter continued, "life is very short. While you're busy downloading the latest apps to your phone, the clock on the screen keeps ticking away relentlessly. Although it doesn't always update itself automatically when you go abroad. Rather annoying, that. I must find out how to do it… Anyway, while you're waiting for an exciting new app to download, your battery might die and the phone suddenly becomes useless. Even if you've only been using it for a few hours. Why on earth can't they manufacture sturdy batteries? Can anyone explain that to me?"

Fr Twitter patiently waited for a reply. His mobile chose that moment to chirp into life, and his "I Can't Take My Eyes off of You" ringtone resounded around the church.

Tiffany felt someone shoving her. She turned around and saw Bruno squeezing into the seat beside her. His right hand was a sizzling mass of singed flesh.

"What's happened to you now?" Tiffany asked. "Did you try to shake hands with Martha?"

"I just tried to fit in," Bruno grumbled, holding up his smoking hand. "I saw everyone else bless themselves. But as soon as I put my hand in that holy water, it started burning up!"

"Will you stop talking to yourself," Martha growled at Tiffany. "If you want to talk to yourself, enter the convent and become a nun."

"We're all waiting for God," Fr Twitter said, suddenly remembering that he had a sermon to deliver. "But He never returns our calls. His phone is for incoming calls only!"

A dramatic pause on the pulpit.

"I Can't Take My Eyes off of You" began chirping again.

"I'm really sorry!" Fr Twitter rejected the call and began typing a text message as he tried to find the point of his sermon. "We often forget that the future is in our own hands. We can make our own dreams come true if only we have the courage to grasp them… How many n's are in 'inappropriate'? Oh, it doesn't matter. She'll get the message… so to speak… Yes, don't wait for God, people."

"Is this man even a Christian?" Bruno asked no one in particular.

"Because we don't know what's going to happen tomorrow." Fr Twitter turned off his phone. "The Rapture could break out just when we think we've found the courage to ask the woman… courage to pursue our destiny, and then it's too late. The angels come sweeping down from the sky and start destroying the world."

"Don't hold your breath waiting for angels," Bruno said with a snort. "They always turn up when the danger's over!"

"The stars come falling from the sky," Fr Twitter continued, "and the oceans turn to fire and the mountains turn into toasted marshmallows, and the sun turns purple. And you're still sitting in your basement wondering why God hasn't answered the call. He's too busy unleashing the Rapture to care about your silly little indiscretions."

"What's this Rapture he's talking about?" Tiffany asked Bruno. "I don't want anything interfering with my yoga plans."

"It's a mad fairy tale told by a lunatic," Bruno replied. "I'm sure even God gets a good laugh out of that Rapture yarn. Well, the miserable old goat would do, if He had a sense of humour! Anyway, prophets have been predicting it for centuries, and they've never once got it right. Angels coming down from the sky breathing fire and brimstone? Don't make me laugh. They can hardly carry a tune, even after two thousand years in the celestial choir!"

Tiffany looked out the window at the gathering clouds. She couldn't see any angels up there. Or anything else, for that matter.

She didn't know yet whether that was a good thing or a bad thing.

There's a visitor coming, and he's got some exciting news.
Can't wait to see my visitor. Can't wait to hear his exciting news.
I'm gonna get the furnace ready, and burn away these endless blues.

Tiffany and Martha sat in silence in the café. Their thoughts were turning to their brother, Ernie.

Ernie was the funny uncle of the family. He lived life by his own rules, rules that he himself rarely followed anyway. A free spirit with boundless energy, he never cared what anyone thought about him.

Both of his sisters loved him and were very jealous of him.

He had announced that he was calling for dinner this evening. Both Tiffany and Martha were thinking of how they could impress him when he inevitably started asking about their love lives. He was always interested in other people's love lives, because his own was such a tragic farce.

"George seemed a bit sullen today," Tiffany remarked,

directing her thoughts to a man no one ever felt jealous of.

"Yes," Martha replied. "He's giving me the silent treatment."

"How do you know?" asked Tiffany. "I thought silence was his natural state."

"I asked him this morning how long he was going to keep up this charade and he just shrugged and muttered, '*Je ne veux pas parler!*'"

"I didn't know George could speak French!"

"Oh yes, he can bore people rigid in several languages." Martha glanced at her sister. "He's also worried about you, for some reason."

"Me?" Tiffany was amazed that George even thought about her. "Why on earth is he worried about me?"

"He thinks that you seem to be a bit lost, Tiffany. It's time to grab the reins and take control of your life. Just like that half-wit priest said this morning."

"And do you agree with his analysis?" *It's quite a shock to discover that you actually listen to that poor little man!* "Are you both going to gang up on me?"

"Well, yes, I can see his point, sort of." Martha shrugged. "Of course, I can't let him know that. If he thinks he's right about anything, he'll start getting all sorts of ridiculous ideas in his head!"

Tiffany looked over to the park. Some couples were walking hand in hand, or at least finger around finger. Some bored emo kids were throwing beer cans at squirrels. A few belligerent alcoholics were getting into a deep physical argument about economic theory. And some would-be poets were staring into the lonely clouds looking for inspiration or rain.

Tiffany watched the scenes unfold. Some would say it was life in its rich variety. Sure, there were alcoholics collapsing into a torrent of roaring fisticuffs on the grass. But there was always some beauty to be found in every scene. You just had to be mindful of every detail. Take a breath and look for the twinkle of light. Don't judge. Just observe. And smile a beatific smile, just like those stoner nuns.

The beauty was proving difficult to uncover, so Tiffany took another breath.

"Oh, shit!" Tiffany's gaze shot back to her cup of coffee.

"What's wrong with you now?" Martha asked.

But Tiffany wasn't listening.

She'd just seen Bill walking towards the café. Power-walking, to be exact, his speeding feet chopping the grass as effectively as a surgical scythe.

Suddenly, all the alcoholics and emos and lovers and squirrels disappeared as the only person in focus for Tiffany when she looked up again was Bill in his tight fluorescent tracksuit and elaborate runners.

"What madness has gotten into him now?" Tiffany muttered.

Martha followed Tiffany's stare. And started laughing uproariously.

Martha rarely laughed. Even smiles were a precious commodity for her.

But when she did laugh, she usually did so without thought of decorum or diplomacy. If she thought something was ridiculous, she'd let the entire building know it.

Soon tears were rolling down Martha's face.

Tiffany even permitted herself a little smile as she watched Bill's middle-age paunch jiggle beneath the dazzling fabric of his tracksuit.

"Oh my God, this makes up for *everything*!" Martha paused to try and catch her breath. "It has been worth knowing that tosser just so we could enjoy this sight."

Another explosion of laughter from Martha.

This time, the damage radius was wider. The laughter waves reached out to the street outside. And over to the park.

Bill suddenly stopped power-walking and looked around.

"Oh no!" Tiffany tried to hide her face. "Look what you've done now with that ignorant guffaw of yours!"

Bill looked towards the sound of the laughter. And then his face broke into a smile nearly as expansive as his stomach.

Before Tiffany could find an escape route, Bill strode over their table. A few customers shielded their eyes from the sudden burst of blinding light.

"Hello, Tiffs! How are you?"

"I'm here too, you ill-mannered pup," Martha shot back before Tiffany could answer. "Did you just not see me, or has that tracksuit blinded you?"

"Would you like me to get you some sugar for the coffee, Martha?" Bill replied. "It might help with the bitterness."

"What do you want, Bill?" Tiffany interrupted before a radiant brawl broke out in the café. "We're trying to have a quiet coffee here. And that stupid tracksuit is louder than the radio!"

"Do you like it?" Bill gave a twirl, oblivious to the looks of horror that flashed across the sisters' faces. "Kylie says it makes me look younger."

"Oh, how is Kylie?" Martha pounced on the chance to protect her sister from Bill. "I do hope she's keeping you. You deserve each other."

"Kylie and I are very happy," Bill replied, turning as solemn as he could while wearing a bright purple tracksuit. "I hope you don't mind me saying that, Tiffs."

"Why the hell would I–?"

"Take it easy, Tiffany," Martha interrupted, alert to the sudden shrill note of jealousy in her sister's voice. "Even the unfortunate are allowed some share of happiness."

"We complete each other, I suppose," Bill continued, brushing aside the insult. "She makes me feel younger and more carefree. And I get the chance to share with her my mature wisdom. And my various experiences and skills. Oh, sorry, Tiffs, I forgot how difficult it must be for you to hear this."

"Again, why the hell–?"

"But we all find happiness somewhere." Bill was beginning to get engrossed in his sermon. Even his tracksuit seemed to be glowing more brightly. "We all have to be patient and wait for our soulmate to come along and slot into place. It's like two atoms whirling around–"

"Why are you dressed like an inflated paedophile, Bill?" Martha asked, determined to stem the flow of Bill's oratory. "I'm surprised you didn't get arrested on your way over here."

"This is my new look." Another uncalled-for twirl. More gasps of horror around the café. "When you're bright on the outside, you feel brighter on the inside. That's what Kylie taught me. Don't be afraid to embrace the colour in your life. I like your dark-grey top, Martha, by the way!"

A series of beeps and buzzes erupted from Bill's tracksuit.

"Oh, my fitness tracker has noticed that I've stopped walking!" Bill started tapping a bracelet on his wrist. "Kylie wants me to complete ten thousand steps today. So I'd better run. Well, walk anyway."

Before either sister could respond, Bill walked out of the café with renewed, radiant vigour.

"At least technology is good for something," Martha remarked, looking at the departing high-vis blur. "I thought I was going to have to throw the coffee in his face in order to get rid of him."

"Why is Kylie so keen on getting him fit?"

Something in Tiffany's tone caused Martha to frown.

"I hope you're not still carrying a torch for him, Tiffany. He looks like he's on fire already."

"No, not at all." *Not too much, anyway.* "He's part of the past. I'm interested in the future now. That's why I was talking to Pigeon about his PE teacher."

"What's he's got to do with… ? Oh, I see!"

"What?" Tiffany couldn't make eye contact with her sister. "I'm just thinking of taking up yoga, that's all. He's looks like he'd be a good tutor. Really motivational."

"I'm sure it's his six-pack that's motivating you." Martha was delighted to focus Tiffany's attention on any man except Bill. "Poor George was always a bit of a disappointment in that department. And most others. You shouldn't let that stud slip out of your hands."

"Of course, he has a nice physique, no denying that." Tiffany smiled and looked back out at the park. "If I'm lucky, he has a nice personality too. He looks like someone who's at peace with himself."

"Peace with himself?" Martha snorted. "He's on his final warning at that school. There are volcanoes that are more stable than him. But I do think he'd be a good match for you."

Tiffany's phone started ringing. An unknown number.

"What?" Tiffany always assumed attack mode when answering an unknown number.

"You should listen to your sister," a sweet voice said, gentle celestial music playing in the background. "She speaks a lot of sense. Grab a chance of happiness when it comes along. God will guide you, but you can't always wait for Him.

He's a busy man."

"Who the hell is this?"

Before the voice could answer, an audible tussle seemed to have broken out on the other end of the call. After much growling and squealing, a more familiar voice came on the phone.

"Sorry about that." Bruno didn't sound the least bit sorry. "These bloody nuns have to interfere in everything. So much for vows of silence!"

"Who are you talking to?" Martha asked. "I didn't come here to watch you talking to people on the phone."

"It's just a friend." *Technically, not a lie.* "He seems to be in a bit of a state."

"I am not in a state," Bruno snapped back. "I just can't have holy drug addicts interfering with my mission."

"Do you have some parable you wish to share with me, Bruno?"

"Not a parable, exactly." Bruno took a deep, gaspy breath before lurching onwards. "You see, we all give in to hatred every now and then. And that's okay, so long as you don't get caught… I mean, that's okay so long as no one gets hurt. Pure hatred is one of the driving forces that hold life together. The kind your sister specialises in. With enough hatred in your

129

belly, you could become the ruler of the planet. You could control everyone. You wouldn't need God or that stupid priest to guide you. How amazing would that be? All you need to do is channel your hatred and turn it into a relentless force that can… Hold on a minute."

Tiffany could hear an unholy, muffled row develop between Bruno and the nuns. The more he roared at them, the gentler their replies.

Tiffany poured herself a glass of water as she waited for the theological storm to pass.

"Well, that's your opinion," Bruno was bellowing. "I'm just trying to highlight an alternative… You're not always right, you know… Just because I disagree with you doesn't mean I'm wrong… No, I don't want to go back… Okay, fine then, I'll tell her!"

"If you don't hang up soon," Martha said, "I'll leave you here with the bill!"

Martha was expert at finding excuses for not paying for coffee breaks.

Tiffany held up a pacifying hand before Martha could storm off.

"Okay, here's the story," Bruno was saying. "According to the boss, I was wrong about the whole hatred thing. Seems you have to love your enemies, not hate them. That's the word from upstairs."

"Love my enemies? Including that Kylie slapper?"

"Yes, apparently. Doesn't make much sense to me. But the new policy is to love your enemies… Unless your enemy is that bastard of a duke. In that case, it's perfectly acceptable to skin your enemy alive and bury him in a salt pit with some agitated scorpions… What now? Hold on a minute."

A further flurry of bellows and squeals.

"I'm telling her," Bruno roared. "I told her to love her enemies, even that Kylie bubble-brain… Well, I just thought I should qualify it with… I don't want her getting the wrong… Okay, I'll see you then!"

"Everything okay?" Tiffany asked.

"I've got to go meet the boss. Seems we need a little quality face time. Discuss missions and objectives. I feel a chronic headache coming on already. I knew I shouldn't have looked at Bill's tracksuit. It melted my brain. It seems to have melted yours too!"

Before Tiffany could answer, Bruno had hung up.

She looked up to face the silent fuming of her sister.

*

She said she'd make me dinner. All I got was a sandwich and a cigarette.
No lobsters for poor me. Just a sandwich and a cigarette.
I'll go to bed hungry 'cos these endless blues taste like death.

"You've made a right bluetit's arse out of this dinner, Mar!" Ernie tore his disgusted eyes away from the fried shambles in front of him. "Did you not even make sure the pig was dead before you fried those rashers?"

"I told you to eat before you came here," Martha mumbled, looking slightly chastened. "Your standards are too high because of Claude."

Following the choking incident, Robin had made his excuses and decided to spend the evening with some friends. So it was just Tiffany, George, Martha, and Ernie for dinner. George, as usual, was paying more attention to his Sudoku puzzle than the meal in front of him.

Ernie was that rare creature: a man who could stand up to Martha and live to tell the tale. Perhaps this was because he was three years older than she was, and she'd always grown up in his shadow. Maybe it was because he always looked out for her when they were at school. Or perhaps it was because Ernie was the only person who ever stood up to their mother, the formidable and inaccurately named Agnes Angelina.

The real reason was probably that Ernie was the only person for whom Martha felt unconditional affection. Not even George was granted that privilege. For all Ernie's faults – and they were legion – Martha felt a deep fondness for him and regarded him as a staunch ally in any of life's fights.

"I couldn't eat before I came here." Ernie shook his head sadly. "Claude isn't cooking for me anymore. In fact, he's doing *nothing* for me anymore."

"Oh, really?" asked Martha, taking her usual relish in someone else's misfortunes. "What's happened between you two now? Did someone hide the moisturiser?"

"You know how it is, Mar. Claude doesn't get his way in something. And then the Great Sourness descends on our castle for a few days. Most of my conversations are with Bono these days."

Bono was Ernie's musically gifted budgie. Whenever Claude was giving Ernie the silent treatment, Ernie resorted to long chats and singalongs with the ever-eager budgie. They once spent an entire month discussing Yeats and Beckett and singing Aslan songs while Claude fumed in silent fury over an escalated disagreement over which film to see.

"And despite all that," Tiffany remarked, "the only person to find a good man in this family was Ernie."

"George!" Martha shook her husband's shoulder. "Are you going to let her insult you like that?"

"Hmmm?"

"Actually, Tiffany does have a point." Ernie pushed the plate away from him. "For all his many, *many* faults, Claude is indeed a good man. And a very good cook."

"That's very true," George piped up. "We must go visit them again some evening, sugar cup."

"Shut up, George, and drink your juice."

All eyes watched George obediently drink the juice.

"My orange juice tastes like prune juice, darling."

"That's because it *is* prune juice, George. It was on sale."

"You know what prune juice does to my bowel movements, dear." George put his glass back on the table with a shudder. "It turns me into a power hose."

"Oh, don't talk about your bowel movements during dinner!" Ernie wailed. "They're like your work projects. No one cares about them but you!"

"We'll all call around to you some evening for dinner," George replied. "I can't wait to try Claude's–"

"Why the hell would we want to do that?" Martha asked. "I'm perfectly capable of cooking a–"

"You need a break, dear. You're always complaining that

you never get a chance to—"

"I never complain, George!"

"You're always *remarking* that you work like a slave in this house—"

"She certainly cooks like a slave," Tiffany added.

"—and I think it would be nice for us all to go around to Ernie's and have a meal together as a family. A nice edible meal for us all. Cooked by Claude."

Tiffany realised that George's chances of getting through the dinner alive were diminishing by the second.

However, it was Ernie who came to George's rescue by shifting the focus to Tiffany.

"I hear you're thinking of taking up yoga, Tiffany. That will be good for you. Channel your happy vibes." He examined his sister as if she were a washed-up corpse. "You know, your face would look a lot less like a decayed lemon if you thought happy thoughts every now and then. Imagine giddy lambs frolicking in a field, for example."

"I prefer to imagine them under the grill. Unless Martha is cooking them, of course!"

"George," shouted Martha, letting her pent-up fires roam around the room for a while, "are you actually just going to sit there while all and sundry walk in off the street and insult your long-suffering wife like that?"

"Hmmm?" George had already retreated to the sanctuary of his Sudoku puzzles. "Oh, of course, it should be four in that cell, not five. So silly of me... Oh, sorry, what was that, peach bubble?"

Martha sipped her tea with the twitching intensity of a damaged incendiary device.

"Don't worry about it." Ernie laughed. "Everything can be made better if you just smile to yourself every now and then. Of course, that isn't easy when you're living in a hornets' nest like this place, but try your best."

Tiffany wished she could have Ernie's attitude to life. Recklessly optimistic, irrepressible, and somewhat dangerously irresponsible. Ernie seemed to have inherited the family's entire supply of happy genes, leaving all the anger and bitterness to be divided equally between his two sisters.

"But do I notice a tiny smile on Tiffany's lips now?" Ernie asked. "Have the hounds of happiness managed to climb over her barbed-wire fences?"

"He's right!" Martha scrutinised her sister. "You have been a little bit less acidic lately."

"We all deserve a little bit of happiness now and then," Tiffany said, nodding her head. "Sometimes someone crosses your path and completely changes the journey of your life. Maybe I've been given a second chance at happiness."

"*Second* chance?" Martha pointed at her sister. "You've had at least fifty chances in your life, you brazen, wanton—"

"Mar, not in front of the children," Ernie cautioned, nodding to George.

"I just want to see where this… yoga thing leads," Tiffany continued, ignoring her sister. "Bill's got his fingers all tangled up in Kylie… I swear to God, if I ever get my hands on that treacherous little tart, I'll tear off her arms and beat her up with them!"

"You really should start those yoga classes as soon as possible," Ernie remarked.

"So why shouldn't I explore new waters too?" Tiffany leaned forward defiantly. "We're not all trapped in the marriage cell like Martha."

"My marriage isn't a cell! Can you believe she said that, George?"

"Hmmm?"

"Marriage is sacred." Martha already seemed unsure about her debating strategy. "Do you think I'd stick with that… thing over there if I didn't think our vows were sacred? Don't you think I often fantasise about being with someone else, *anyone else?* Every single day! But I don't act on it."

"Your sister's right," Ernie said. "You should perhaps dampen down your enthusiasm for exploring every new nook and–"

"Oh dear Jesus, spare me from another preacher," Tiffany snapped back. "Just because you've finally managed to give up the drink and found the Lord doesn't give you the right to go interfering in my life! You're all the same, you shower of self-righteous whiskey whiners. Torn between Jesus and the bottle!"

An awkward silence descended on the table. It was well-known that one of Ernie's countless faults was a lifelong fondness for alcohol. A few months ago, Claude gave him an ultimatum. He had to choose between his partner or the cocktails. It took Ernie three weeks to come to a decision.

After one last blowout, drunk beyond belief, Ernie found Jesus before he found his way home. Soon the bottles were being poured down the toilet and the Bible was being dusted off. Bottles of whiskey were suddenly being replaced with bottles of holy water.

Claude indulged it all as another of Ernie's passing fancies, like the windsurfing, the salsa dancing, and the communist activism. However, six months in, Ernie was still relatively sober most of the time and holding on tentatively to his new-found faith.

"You should try one of those breathing exercises you're so fond of," Ernie said, trying to force some levity into his voice. "Are you still looking for Jesus in raindrops? The secrets of existence in a fallen leaf?"

"At least I wasn't looking for them at the bottom of a bottle!" Tiffany's engine was beginning to warm up as her face got redder. "Who are you to start lecturing us on who we should and shouldn't spend our time with?"

George devoted all his attention to his Sudoku as the temperature around the table descended a few more degrees.

"Anyway, enough about Tiffany," Ernie said. "What about my hopeless nephew? Why hasn't he come along to the ritualistic slaughter this evening?"

"I'm sure he's too busy," Tiffany said, eager to avoid any forensic examination of Robin's absence. "Maybe he's gone off somewhere else to find something to eat."

"That boy worries me," Martha suddenly declared. "He spends too much time on that computer. I'd nearly be happier if he spent his time on drugs instead. He looks so gaunt and frail."

"Certainly, I've seen healthier creatures hanging on

butchers' hooks," Ernie agreed. "Maybe you should just give up on him before it's too late. Can't you put something in his porridge to put him to sleep?"

"I'm not going to poison my child!" Martha carefully considered that plan for a few more seconds. "No, I don't want to go to jail.

"He definitely needs beefing up a bit." Ernie considered the options. "I've got an idea! Let's do George's suggestion. Why don't you all come over to us some afternoon for lunch? George has already made it clear how much he craves edible food. I'm sure Claude will be talking to me again soon. He's beginning to get jealous of all the attention I'm giving Bono. I'll get him to cook up something spectacular. At least he knows how to not make a bishop's bollocks out of a meal, Mar!"

"That would be wonderful!" George's voice quivered with heartfelt gratitude. "Claude is such a wonderful, amazing, normal cook."

"What exactly is wrong with my cooking, George?" Martha toyed with her knife. "Be careful how you answer."

"And perhaps Tiffany might like to bring somebody along with her," Ernie said, once again saving George from serious injury.

Tiffany decided to ignore all the eyes that had now turned to her.

You better clear the table, honey. My head is gettin' ready to explode.
Clear up that table, honey. See my head getting' ready to explode.
Endless blues snapping at my feet, following me on up the road.

6

Jehovah Done Given Me the Blues

We break this day our daily bread, but we end up breaking our vows.
It begins with the breaking of bread, it ends with the breaking of vows.
I'd have a nicer time having dinner with the slaughterhouse cows.

Although George was forever destined to be one of life's spare parts, he did in his own way bring joy to Tiffany's life. Seeing him gradually lose the plot as he screeched through the early morning traffic was a sight to behold.

"If you're still asleep, you shouldn't be driving!" George pounded the horn, glaring at the car in front of him. It had stalled at the traffic lights, and the sound of a blaring horn was doing nothing to ease the driver's panic. "Some of us try to wake up before we start driving."

"To be fair, I think he's a learner driver," Robin suggested from the back seat. "Everyone has to learn to–"

"Is he crying? Good God, man, get it together! Put the car into first gear, ease off the clutch, gently press the petrol pedal... And then get the hell off the road!"

"He's moving, George," Tiffany said. She never liked to see a grown man cry. She found it disturbingly pathetic. Unless the man was Bill. Then she found it hilarious. "Just give him a chance to dry his eyes."

George's temper gradually dissolved as the car in front began crawling ahead. Eager to make up lost time, he decided to ignore the fact that the lights had turned red again. And ignore the roar of horns around him.

"Dad, why don't you let Ma drive me to school some days?" Robin tried to hide his face from the other drivers. "Maybe she'd find it less—"

"Because she's banned from driving," Tiffany replied.

"Exactly," George agreed, as he swerved to avoid knocking down the elderly lollipop man. "Forever. Anywhere on this planet. And if we colonise the moon as planned, she'll be banned from there too. She always has to go beyond the bounds of acceptable behaviour!"

As George slipped into fraught reverie about his marriage, Tiffany found herself thinking about Robin's PE teacher. She'd dreamed about him again last night. When she woke up, her pillow was on the floor and her head was in the clouds.

"Do you think that dreams ever come true?" she asked George.

"Hmmm?"

"I was just wondering if dreams ever come true."

"No." George sullenly watched a three-legged poodle limp in front of him. "Never. That poodle's life is more of a dream than what I've—"

"That's not very encouraging, is it?" Robin piped up. "We're always being told at school to follow our dreams. Seize the day. *Is feidir linn.*"

"Oh well, that's different." George turned around to look his son in the eyes. "Opportunities are different from dreams. You must grab your opportunities, son. Don't let the earth swallow up all your hopes. Otherwise, you spend the rest of your life in regret, wondering why you're married to—"

"You're driving on the footpath!"

"You know, someday I'm going to drive to work in a tank." The car shuddered as it slammed back down off the kerb. "That'll show them who owns the road!"

"We have to hold on to our dreams." Tiffany had decided that she was going to get to know the PE teacher, by any means, legal or ambiguous. "When an old dream dies or decides to hook up with a chipper blonde-headed bimbo slut, you just have to grab the next dream that—"

"I hate every single driver on this road." George ripped the scented hedgehog from the mirror in frustration and threw it out the window. "I want to kill them all."

"Were you bullied a lot at school, Dad?"

"No… the bullying didn't start until I got married." George turned to look at his son again. "Beware of bullies, Robbie. They'll take your hope and slowly crush it without—"

"Keep your eyes on the road, Dad! Please!"

"You're still being bullied at school, are you, Starling?" Tiffany knew all about Robin's bully problems at school. A brute called Neville had taken a particular dislike to Robin this year. Of course, Robin hadn't spoken to his mother about this. If he had, Neville would have long ago been dismembered in a bath of acid. "Maybe you could talk your PE teacher about it. Or, if you prefer, *I* could have a word with him."

"Don't worry about it." Robin glanced nervously in the rear-view mirror. "I can handle it myself."

A headless octopus was better equipped to deal with life than Robin was. But Tiffany decided not to argue the point. If her nephew was being bullied, this gave her an opportunity to get closer to the PE teacher.

Even though he was doing 95 kilometres in a 50-kilometre zone, George still had enough concentration to spare to notice Robin's tragic gaze.

"What's wrong with you now, Robbie? Why do you have a condemned man's stare?"

"Nothing!" Robin dragged his eyes away from the street. "I was just thinking about how all the girls seem to–"

"Don't let yourself get distracted by pretty skirts, son." George let the words hang in the air for a few seconds before realising that he should probably elaborate before the next set of traffic lights. "I mean, you should concentrate on your studies and your football and–"

"I don't play football."

"Really? I could have sworn I saw you playing football a few years ago."

Please, lights, stay green. Don't let him stop. Don't give him time for this sermon.

The lights turned red.

"Better not break another red light, I suppose. I've got too many penalty points already... Oh, don't tell your mother about the penalty points, Robbie. No sense in infuriating her... I mean, worrying her..." George palely shuddered as they waited for the lights to change. "You know, I was once madly in love with a girl."

"Really? You mean Ma?"

"Er... yes... your mother. Of course."

"I must tell her."

"No, don't!" George yelped. "Oh great, the lights are

green again. Away we go"

Tiffany noticed that George's face was swinging alarmingly between scarlet blushes and ashen terror.

"Are you having a heart attack, George?"

"Love is complicated." George sighed, ramming the car noisily from first into fifth gear. "So's life. It's just like Sudoku, really. You get my drift, Robbie?"

"I don't play Sudoku. Or football."

"You never forget the one you love, Robbie." George smiled wistfully as he sped up the bus lane. "Her china-blue eyes... Those burgundy lips... That gentle ivory skin... The tingle of her soft ginger hair..."

"Martha has black hair," Tiffany pointed out.

"Hmmm?"

"Ma has black hair," Robin reiterated.

"Oh... Yeah, right... I'm sure she had ginger hair back then." George swerved off the bus lane then tried to manoeuvre out of the path of an oncoming ambulance. "It turned black when she got older. When she had you, actually. Let's not think too much about that."

"You've gone straight past the school again, Dad."

Tiffany tried to drown out the sound of the screeching brakes, the ambulance siren, and the screaming seagulls as

George brought the car to a halt in the disabled parking spot.

"I'll make you eat your words," she said, "I'll make you eat your rotten teeth."
"You're gonna eat your words and you're gonna eat your rotten teeth.
You won't get very far, walking out of here without your stinkin' feet."

After the drama of the drive to work, breakfast in the canteen was a relatively sedate affair. Tiffany liked to be alone whenever she breakfasted at work. It gave her a chance to enjoy the taste of the food without being distracted by the need to engage in pointless banter with her colleagues.

I mindfully taste the jam on my toast. I savour the texture as I slowly chew. I let a feeling of blissful contentment fill my... Oh Christ, what the hell does he want?

Tiffany noticed Jehovah walking over to her table.

"Good morning, Tiffany," he said, with his usual icy politeness. "Enjoying your breakfast?"

"I was until you—"

"I guessed you were," Jehovah continued, sitting down at the table beside her, "because you've been taking so long eating it."

"You don't have to sit beside me, Jehovah." *Go bugger off, you obnoxious little creep!* "In fact, I'd even prefer if—"

"I know how much you enjoy company," Jehovah said, undeterred. He sipped his coffee for some seconds. "You really hate being on your own. You much prefer the company of… the company of many, *many* men."

"I make some exceptions," Tiffany replied, glaring at him. She tried to concentrate on her toast, but it now tasted liked sour gunpowder in her mouth. "What the hell do you want, Jehovah? You know how busy I am with this new—"

"Funny you should mention that!" A humourless smile spread across Jehovah's face. "Is the project going well?"

"I think so." Tiffany couldn't remember how her project was going. She hadn't thought about it since she'd left the office yesterday afternoon. She wasn't even sure which project he was referring to. "We're all working together on the same team and delivering value to our stakeholders. Making everyone part of the conversation and… all that shite."

"Are you delivering value to Gordon too? After all, if he delivers CDs to you, it's only polite for you to deliver… *something*… to him in return."

"What the hell does the Seagull have to do with anything?" Tiffany didn't like this swerve in the conversation, especially when she noticed how Jehovah's sanctimonious eyebrows shot up. "Nobody cares what he thinks. And anyway, who the hell gives CDs to someone these days? Does he think I'm some Boomer?"

Jehovah said nothing, drinking his coffee and gazing into the middle distance, an indecipherable look on his face.

Tiffany found the silence as unnerving as Jehovah's aftershave.

"What are you trying to tell me? Has the Seagull been complaining about me? I'm sick of the incompetent bastard flapping about over the least—"

"No, he's not *complaining*." Another dead smile from Jehovah. "No complaints from him."

"Well, at least that's—"

"In fact, quite the opposite." The eyebrows were visibly quivering now. "He's very *happy* with your... performance, shall we say."

Tiffany pushed her plate away. All thoughts of enjoying her breakfast had been shattered by Jehovah's cryptic rambling.

The only thing she wanted to do mindfully right now was strangle him.

"I know you're trying to deliver some parable to me. But I don't speak whatever obscure biblical code you're so fond of. So just spit out whatever you want to get off your chest."

"I agree with you there. You're certainly very unfamiliar with the Bible. That's why you're always so sour and grumpy."

Tiffany stood up. Going to her desk was a less horrific option that sitting here listening to Jehovah.

"If only there was somebody who could cheer you up." Jehovah spoke slightly louder as Tiffany walked away from him. "Someone who *really* wanted to cheer you up."

Tiffany pretended that she couldn't hear him.

But, as she walked out of the canteen, she could still hear him. And she didn't like what he was hearing.

"Walk with me," she said, "and tell me what's on your mind.
"Come along and walk with me and tell me what's on your silly little mind.
"Do you like what you see today, or do you think you'd be better off blind?"

Tiffany spent the morning checking and replying to her emails, even spam ones. It was exactly the sort of mindless task she needed after her uncomfortable encounter with Jehovah. Mercifully, he was in meetings all morning, so she was free from his innuendo for a few hours.

By lunchtime, however, she had a full-blown case of cubicle fever and decided to go for a long, soothing walk in the park. She hadn't decided yet whether she'd return to the office in the afternoon.

As soon as she entered the park, Tiffany could feel most of her tension dissolve in the cool afternoon breeze. She took a few deep, cleansing breaths and savoured the moment.

I breathe in the energy. I breathe out the bullshit. I breathe in the promise of the future. I breathe out the memory of Bill. I breathe in sunshine. I breathe out the Seagull.

As she walked around the park, Tiffany felt grateful for her health. Despite taking at best a token interest in her own physical wellbeing – usually when her doctor begged her to – Tiffany was in excellent condition overall. And she knew this was something to be appreciated, because she'd seen how others had weathered the storms.

But now, ever since seeing Robin's PE teacher, Tiffany had determined to make an extra effort to stay fit and in shape. Biscuit consumption was scaled back. Water consumption was scaled up. And walks in the park were more than just an excuse to flee her cubicle.

Indeed, looking at some of the other people in the park, Tiffany felt a dash of smug pity.

How did these people let themselves go like that? The guy over there in the skinny jeans isn't much older than me. Skinny jeans, what the hell was he thinking? The only thing skinny about him is hair. And as for that thing walking with him, I've seen healthier overdose victims. It really isn't that hard to take care of yourself, is it? After all, I can manage it.

"Judge not, lest ye be judged," a voice suddenly declared beside her.

Tiffany looked around and saw another specimen of man gone to seed.

The unfortunate choice of tracksuit today was light grey, with innumerable varieties of stains dabbled around the creases. On the plus side, it did go well with his grey hair.

Bruno's idea of a healthy lunch was a chocolate bar in one hand and a creamy mocha in the other. Despite the bracing breeze, he was sweating with abandon.

"I wasn't judging anyone," Tiffany lied, taking her eyes off the alarming insects holding a lively conference in Bruno's beard. "I just think that people should take care of themselves. Otherwise they end up looking wrecked and bitter, just like Martha."

"Why are you walking so fast?" Bruno panted through half-chewed chocolate and slushing mocha. "Are you in a hurry to get back to work? Or to the Seagull, perhaps?"

"Of course not." Tiffany slowed down. The last thing she wanted was to get back to the office too soon. "It's not my fault you can't stir a cup of coffee without breaking out in a sweat and turning a whiter shade of purple."

Slowing down helped Tiffany better enjoy the park. Slowing her pace helped to slow her mind. She looked at the delicate leaves shivering in the bright breeze. She could smell recently cut grass and the last gasps of the fading flowers. All her senses came alive as she absorbed nature's embrace. The beauty in the air was like a symphony rushing through her ears.

Except for the incessant chewing and slurping and panting beside her.

"My God, I'd hate to be in a restaurant with you! The lobsters would have better table manners."

"Don't talk to me about lobsters," Bruno replied with a shudder, dislodging some of the insects from their conference. "It reminds me of when that bastard of a duke tried to boil me alive."

"You'd think after all these years you'd have forgiven that duke," Tiffany said. "After all, I thought forgiveness was a big thing with you guys."

"Yes, Jesus was a great one for coming up with the big ideas," Bruno grumbled, mid-chew, "but it's us who have to put his words into action. He made the bullets, but we had to fire them! He never had to put himself under any pressure."

"Didn't he get himself crucified?" Tiffany remembered

little of what the nuns had screamed at her when she was in school, but she was reasonably sure about this point. "That sounds like enough pressure for anyone."

"Yeah, that was another big mistake! Since then, everyone's queuing up to be a martyr, always looking for some cross to climb up on. Don't they realise all they're doing is wasting wood?"

"I learn enough about martyrdom from my sister."

Bruno's phone started ringing.

"Yes?" His face clouded over immediately. "Now how the hell is *that* blasphemy? I was only making the point that… Yes, we all know what he went through, you never stop reminding us… Well, everyone thinks their son is perfect… Oh, I'm sure it was very unpleasant… My own martyrdom was no teddy bears' picnic, I can tell you. More like a raging lions' picnic. Where that bastard of a duke got the lions from I don't– Okay, fair enough, I'm listening."

Bruno nodded and grumbled and occasionally glanced at Tiffany as his boss explained what was needed.

Growing slightly disgusted by the puffing walker beside her, Tiffany turned her attention back to the other walkers in the park. A young couple caught her attention. They were clearly not walking for the good of their health. Their sunken cheeks and dead eyes told a story of addiction and neglect. They clung to each other as they made their way to some rendezvous, scruffy tracksuits fluttering around their skeletal frames.

Mindfulness wouldn't be much help to that pair. If they breathed in too deeply, they'd probably disintegrate. Wait, what the hell is Bruno saying about me now?

"Well, we all know she's a bit of a featherhead," Bruno was explaining over the phone, glancing not too furtively at Tiffany. "But I don't think she'll do too much damage. It's not the Seagull I'm worried about. It's this poser PE teacher... It's just another desperate crush. She'll soon realise that he has no interest in her."

"What are you saying about–?"

"Yes, I agree with you, for once," Bruno continued with exaggerated patience. "She has absolutely no self-control. If a man smiles at her, she assumes he's going to spend the rest of his life devoted to her. She doesn't understand what a cynical age this is. Who worships anyone nowadays? Well, I'm glad you think people worship you. How's that working out for you?"

Before his boss could answer, Bruno put the phone back in his tracksuit.

"I'm not a featherhead!" Tiffany glowered at Bruno. "You're some guardian angel!"

"Oh, right." Bruno shrugged, as if remembering his responsibilities to Tiffany and not really caring about them. "Well, maybe that was too strong. It's just that you lack a certain... acceptance of reality. By the way, why are you staring at that pair of corpses over there?"

"I'm not staring at anything!" Tiffany didn't realise she was being so obvious. "I was just thinking that–"

"You pick the strangest people to be jealous of." Bruno shook his head sadly, dislodging some more fleas. "Maybe someday you'll find a man who loves you as much as that skeleton loves his mate. Look how tightly they're clinging to each other. That's true love."

"That's not love." Tiffany tried to suppress the jealousy she'd felt when she saw how tenderly the junkie looked at the woman clinging to him. "That's heroin!"

Bruno finished his mocha and flung the plastic cup into the grass.

"Didn't they teach you any manners up in heaven?" Tiffany asked. "We're all trying to save the planet down here. The last thing we need is defective angels dropping in and littering the place."

"Your planet is already doomed," Bruno explained matter-of-factly. "Not by water next time, but by fire. You've lit your own funeral pyre. That's what happens when you idolise a misguided nutcase such as Joan of Arc. You start thinking that burning yourself alive is a good thing!"

"I'm not going to be lectured by a—"

"I hope the Seagull doesn't set himself on fire over you," Bruno remarked, as he tossed the chocolate wrapper after the coffee cup. "The smell of burning feathers lingers in the nostrils for ages."

"Why would the Seagull want to do that?" Tiffany felt another pang of jealousy as she saw the skeleton guffawing at some remark the skeletonette had made. "That incompetent tosser wouldn't know how to start a fire."

"Well, you've certainly started a fire deep inside of him," Bruno replied, rummaging for more snacks in the folds of his tracksuit. "That's what Jehovah was trying to tell you earlier. Of course, you weren't listening to him. In fairness, it's hard to listen to sanctimonious shites. They're all so bloody dreary."

"Why does it have to be the Seagull who has a crush on me?"

"We saints are experts on crushes. Take Margaret of York, for example. Her life ended because of a giant crush. They pressed her under her own door. Put rocks on the door until she wasn't going to be able to open any doors anymore. Sadly, they opened the pearly gates for her and we had to listen to her sermons for centuries up there. Honestly, you'd think she was the only one to be martyred!"

"I don't really see what this has to do with me and the Seagull."

Tiffany wasn't ready to deal with the Seagull's feelings for her, so she turned her attention back to the tracksuit couple. Their lives were scarred and broken, but despite it all they were holding each other up. Tiffany and Bill barely survived a few big rows. Then again, perhaps heroin was less of a problem than living with Bill was.

"Did I ever tell you about my crush?" Bruno asked, frowning at the young couple. "She wasn't really a crush. More of a stalker."

Tiffany found it hard to imagine any woman stalking the sweating mass beside her.

"She was an abbess at the local convent. Like all nuns, she had no personality and all the charm of discarded dishwater. She could suck the light out of an entire parish."

"Bill must be a descendant then." Tiffany allowed herself a brief smile. It would explain a lot if Bill had some ancient nun DNA sloshing around his system. "I wish he'd told me about her when I first met him."

"She followed me around the village like a lapdog. Thankfully, she'd taken a vow of silence, so at least I didn't have to listen to her. But she made up for that with the most alarming grunts and sighs. The sound of a moaning nun has no place in polite society."

"The sound of a panting saint isn't very welcome either," Tiffany remarked, recoiling slightly from Bruno. "What happened to the abbess in the end? Did she break her habit and run off with you?"

"She followed me right to the end." If Bruno thought that Tiffany's little joke was hilarious, he gave no indication. "While they were flaying me alive with rusty swords–"

"I thought you were boiled–"

"–she just stood there in the crowd, watching it all without a word. Stuck to her vows to the end. I did hear rumours that she used some of the… leftovers… from my martyrdom as parchment for her prayer books. That's devotion!"

"I suppose we can't control who or what we fall in love with," Tiffany agreed, looking at her watch. It was time to start thinking about maybe beginning to return to the office. "That's what happens when somebody gets under your skin."

"You could have used a better expression!" Bruno shuddered. "You've no idea how many years it took me to grow back this pelt. Anyway, it's clear that you've got under the Seagull's skin. But you're too busy looking to get under somebody else's skin. No wonder you're walking so fast! Anything to impress him."

"What the hell is that supposed to mean?"

Tiffany turned around but Bruno was gone. The only sound was the laughter of the tracksuit couple.

I've got you in my head, I've got you under my skin.
I've got you right inside my head, and you're down there under my skin.
I gave you my rusty heart, and you threw it in the bin.

Love was clearly in the air today. Robin came home with a bruised heart and a split lip.

As usual, he couldn't confide in his mother. So he turned to the lesser of two evils, his aunt Tiffany. Being the sympathetic aunt didn't come naturally to Tiffany, of course. But she usually could turn these confidential chats to her advantage.

Fingers Flaherty's "Broken Bread Blues" provided a suitably dour backdrop for the encounter. Like Robin, his heart was bruised. So were his eyes, shoulders, knees, and toes. He wailed about the broken bread and broken teeth that plagued his life.

"I hope she was worth all the hassle," Tiffany remarked, dabbing a damp tissue on Robin's lips. "It looks like your teeth survived the encounter. So you've no excuse for not eating your mother's dinner, I'm afraid. But, with any luck, your tongue won't be able to taste the horror."

"I've tasted enough horror today," Robin wailed. "I thought she liked me. But she just glided away like an angel going back to heaven."

"You've got great eyesight. You see things that aren't there!" Tiffany knew well what it was like to get lost in the blurry haze of love. And she knew well the disappointment when the haze lifted. So did Fingers, as he bawled about his woman who had run away with the local vet and left him with a mangy dog and bald budgie. She wanted to protect her nephew from similar trauma. "What you have to understand, Ostrich, is that—"

"I feel so sorry for the others," Robin declared, oblivious to his aunt's musings. "Every day, an angel walks among them, and all they see is this grey, dowdy, slightly dusty bundle of misery."

"Don't get me started about angels!"

"But she doesn't really see me either." Another weary sigh. Another scratching of acne. "When she sees me, she just sees a lonely, confused, scruffy, awkward, pimply guy with a million hang-ups."

"Well, at least we don't need to bring Lettuce to the optician!" Tiffany adored her nephew, but was ruthlessly aware of his shortcomings. "You need to give these things time, Ostrich. Or hope you grow out of them."

"I don't have time. The years are passing us all by. Look how old you are already... Ouch, don't pinch my lip so hard! And if I don't move fast, she'll drift off with Neville."

"Ah yes, the guy who is bullying you this year?" Like his father, Robin was destined to be bullied through life. "You really don't stand a chance if that's who you're up against."

"Exactly!" Robin wiped some blood from his lips. "So I decided on another strategy."

"And what went wrong?"

"Why do you have to assume that it went wrong?" Robin's teenage hormones began to assert all their self-righteous rage. "Just because I come up with an idea by myself doesn't mean it's a bad one. You're just like my mother. Everything I do has to be a disaster. You all think that I'm incapable of working

163

things out for myself!"

"What went wrong, Ostrich?"

"*Everything!*" Robin shrugged. "It wasn't my fault."

"What did *you* do wrong, Ostrich?"

"I knew I couldn't beat Neville if he's my enemy. So I decided to try and make him my friend."

"I see." Tiffany shook her head in pity. "So instead of trying to triumph over him, you decided to surrender to him? You get more like your pathetic father every day. I thought this Lettuce was worth fighting for."

"She is!" Robin's voice quivered with confused passion. "But I made the mistake of listening to Fr Twitter…"

"That's always a mistake. Nearly as bad as listening to your mother."

"He's always going on about peace and love and all that stuff that you hate. So I thought that if I extended the hand of friendship to Neville, Lettuce might think better of me. She'd be impressed by my self-control and dignity."

There wasn't much dignity coming from the speakers. The mangy dog had stolen Flaherty's breakfast and run off the budgie. And the vet had sent him a bill for the dog's vaccination shot. And his woman's new dress. Just when he thought things couldn't get worse, Flaherty realised that he now had mange too.

"I see." Tiffany nodded. "Well, they do say that the best fighters are the ones who know when to give up and walk–"

"Who said anything about giving up?"

"Oh, I thought that was the point." Tiffany's face furrowed in confusion. "I assumed you'd finally realised that she has absolutely no interest in you and that you decided to become friends with Neville instead."

"No, I'm never going to give up on love."

"That's the spirit, Ostrich!" Tiffany felt some vague obligation that she should try to encourage Robin, no matter how misguided she thought he was. She slapped him too hard on the back, setting off another spurt of lip bleeding. "You've got nothing to fear except fear itself… And maybe agonising pain… And gut-wrenching despair… Yes, and heart-breaking betrayal."

"And my mother's cooking," Robin added, entering into the spirit of the discussion as he tried to lick away the blood. "Anyway, speaking of food…"

"I thought we were speaking of your mother's cooking!"

"Speaking of food, do you remember my friend Lavender?"

"Isn't he the one who smells like a sewage plant?"

"Yes, that's him. Great guy! Anyway, he arrived on the scene when I was thinking of offering the hand of friendship to Neville. He had a big bag of biscuits that his mother had baked."

"I know his mother. A toxic little razor blade."

"That's the one. But a great cook. Not just in comparison to my mother. By *any* standard. So I ate one of the biscuits." Robin sighed ecstatically at the memory. "Oh, you should have felt how the biscuit slowly massaged its way down into my stomach. That must be what angels taste like."

"Remind me to talk to you someday about angels, Ostrich. They really aren't all that great!"

"Anyway, after eating seven of the angel biscuits, I was full of peace and love and understanding!"

"And sugar," Tiffany added.

"I would have offered the hand of friendship to Satan himself. But he doesn't work at our school anymore. Anyway, I look up and see Neville approaching me. Which was a bit strange, because he wasn't due to beat me up until Friday this week... But anyway, I decided to offer him more than the hand of friendship. I offered him one of the biscuits! I knew this was my chance. As they say, the greatest tragedy in your life would be if you don't reach your potential."

"Actually," Tiffany countered, "your greatest tragedy would be if you've *already* reached your potential."

"Whatever! Anyway, I saw Neville coming up the stairs and decided to offer him a biscuit. If I wanted to kill him, I'd have offered him one of my mother's. But today was all about friendship and forgiveness. Because those are the most important things in the world."

"You have so much to learn about the world, Ostrich. Even Fingers Flaherty would agree with that."

"Why do we have to listen to that moany old shite anyway? How am I supposed to recover with that racket banging on in the background? I thought we'd finished with all that once you finished with Bill."

"We're listening to it because a… a… because someone gave it to me. It's only polite to listen to presents that people are kind enough to give you. No matter what you exactly think of those people. Or the present."

"Who gave it to you?"

"You were telling me about Neville!"

"Oh yes." Like any teenager, Robin could always be easily guided to focus on his own problems. "Neville sees me and says, 'What the hell do you want, titweed?' He always calls me 'titweed'. It's a thing between us. And he reaches out for the biscuit with one paw. And I get my sermon about brotherly love ready."

Tiffany knew that she'd have to sit down with her nephew someday to talk about the true meaning of love. She'd enlist Flaherty's help with the discussion. He was currently complaining that the woman he loved had hidden scorpions in his pillowcase.

"So how did Neville react to this stupid… to this sweet gesture?"

"He snatched the biscuit with one paw. And punched me in the stomach with the other."

"I'm sure your stomach is tough enough to survive a small punch every now and then, after all these years of your mother's cooking." Tiffany almost felt sorry for her bewildered nephew. "What you have to understand, Ostrich, is that in this world, some people are just so irredeemably awful that you really can't waste your time trying to improve them. You just have to wipe them off your boots and move on. That's what Jesus said. I think."

"I did move on!" Robin stretched himself proudly to his full height, still sadly short for his age. "But not before I taught that bastard a lesson."

"Oh God! Don't tell me you made another mistake."

"Why do you have to assume that? Once I recovered from the shock, I picked myself up off the floor. My lip was bleeding. My head was spinning. And my stomach was in agony."

"Just like the time Martha made prawn curry for us. The only ones who survived that meal intact were the prawns!"

"I was hurt. But I wasn't destroyed." Robin's voice began to take on a worrying Thatcherite shrillness. "To hell with peace and love. To hell with forgiveness. Lettuce was nowhere to be seen, so I didn't have to pretend to be normal anymore. I was going to give Neville a piece of my mind."

Flaherty was giving his woman a piece of his mind too. As well as some pieces of his broken teeth. He declared that if she wouldn't come to him, he'd hang himself. The next day, a noose arrived in his mailbox. Along with another bill from the vet.

"So I stormed up to him. Well, not stormed. It's hard to storm when you're bent over in agony. But I marched… I went up to him and grabbed him by the shoulder."

"I almost admire your bravery, Ostrich. It would be noble if it wasn't so stupid. And all this grief for a girl who looks like a dried-out nun."

"By then, my rage was drowning out my other emotions."

"Such as your panic, for example."

"I grabbed him by the shoulder and I swung him around. And then… And then things didn't go so well."

"I see." Tiffany searched for some encouraging words for her nephew. None came. "So what stupid thing did you do next?"

"It seems I caught Neville off guard. He swung around to pulverise me, but his big gammy feet tangled beneath him just long enough to completely throw him off balance. Before any of us knew what was happening, he was tumbling back down the stairs. Some of the students tried to help him. Most didn't."

"You must have felt terrible."

"I felt *wonderful!* Pure hatred is a powerful buzz. It was the most amazing feeling in the world to see that bastard bouncing from stair to stair. I kept waiting for his head to shatter. But then, the worst possible thing in the world happened."

"He broke his leg?"

"No! Lettuce appeared at the bottom of the stairs. She ran straight over to him. Of course, she wasn't there when I was being all noble and offering biscuits to him. But as soon as I flung him down–"

"Well, you didn't exactly *fling* anyone down–"

"She suddenly appears. The last thing I saw was her helping him up. And the two of them walking away, holding hands."

Tiffany threw her arms around her besotted nephew and embraced him close to her. That way, she could laugh without him seeing it.

"My poor Ostrich," she said, mastering her composure again. "Someday, you'll learn that love never works out as you'd expect it. Just ask your mother. Maybe your chance will come another day. Or maybe you've had a very lucky escape. Let's face it, it could go either way."

It was a beautiful moment. Aunt and nephew embracing each other. Consoling each other as they struggled, in their own ways, with the unpredictable currents of love, floating one day, sinking the next.

Then Martha entered the kitchen.

"Tiffany, stop manhandling my child!" Martha surveyed the scene. "What's wrong with your lip, Robin? Have you been chewing yourself to death again?"

Robin struggled free from his aunt's painful embrace and shook himself.

"Your son is in love," Tiffany declared, before Robin could explain himself. "I've been trying to enlighten him that love's no picnic. It's more like a dose of food poisoning."

"Don't pollute my son with your bitterness," Martha replied, scrutinising and poking at Robin's face, oblivious to his winces and moans. "Just because you never found love doesn't mean no one can find love. After all, I managed to… I became quite… Anyway, Robin, you have to find your own path to love. Don't follow your aunt's path. It's full of nettles and potholes."

"Stop fussing," Robin yelped as his mother's finger prodded his lip. "It's just a small cut. I get worse during PE class and you never even notice that!"

"That reminds me," Tiffany interjected. "You said you'd introduce me to your PE teacher, Mr Merriman."

"Haven't you got stung by enough nettles?" Martha said. "Stop fidgeting, Robin. I nearly poked your eye out there."

"I'm just interested in doing some yoga classes," Tiffany lied. "Ostrich mentioned that he gives classes in the evenings."

"I've long since given up caring what you do in the evenings, Tiffany. If yoga helps you relax, then there might be a bit more peace in this house."

"He usually does his shopping on a Thursday evening," Robin said. "If you go down to the supermarket later, you might meet him there."

"How do you know this?" Martha asked. "Have you got nothing better to do than sneak around after your psychopath PE teacher? And speaking of psychopaths, can we please throw that CD in the bin?"

"Blondie followed him to the supermarket a few times," Robin explained. "He was trying to get him arrested for shoplifting. It's a long—"

"Stop encouraging your bitter aunt to go stalking your teachers!" Martha shook her son, causing him to bite his lip and unleash another flow of blood. "God almighty, you're as a fragile as an icicle! And just about as useless!"

Tiffany went over to the CD player. Flaherty was in the process of being neutered by the vet. Another large bill was on its way to him. It seemed like a good point at which to turn off the CD.

"I think we need some milk," Tiffany said. "I'll go down to the supermarket and get some."

Tiffany was out the door before either Robin or Martha could reply.

The tea's gone cold, and the stupid milk's gone sour.
Honey, this tea is cold, and this milk ain't nothing no more but sour.
I don't taste your love no more, just bitterness every single hour.

"This is absolute insanity," Bruno whispered in Tiffany's ear as they skulked around the frozen vegetables. "That bag of sprouts has more common sense than you!"

"Shut up!" Tiffany scanned the next aisle. "All I'm doing is buying some milk."

No sign of Mr Merriman in the biscuit aisle. No surprise there, really.

"You certainly wouldn't live by bread alone in this town," Bruno remarked, greedily eying the delightful variety of crackers and biscuits on the shelves. "There's enough here to satisfy a hungry monk. Those ancient martyrs wouldn't have been so eager to starve themselves if they could treat themselves to this selection of sugary heaven. It's easy to give up eating when your dinner usually just consists of stale, tasteless bread and mouldy, half-gnawed cheese."

"Put those cream crackers back on the shelf," Tiffany snapped. "And the Jammie Dodgers. And the Jaffa Cakes. Not even you could eat that much junk in one sitting."

"I'll just hold on to the chocolate chips." Bruno put the other packs of biscuits back on the shelves. "No point making a martyr of myself. I did that once for the bastard of a duke, and once was enough. So just the chocolate chips. And the peppermint squares."

They moved on to the next aisle. A dizzying array of scents, lotions, creams, and toiletries. But no PE teachers.

Tiffany pushed Bruno to the next aisle, interrupting his study of beard-grooming solutions.

No Merriman in the dairy aisle either. Tiffany was about to move on when she realised that she'd need a carton of milk to maintain a cover story that nobody believed anyway.

She was about to give up the hunt when she spied him in the stationery section.

"Gotcha!" she exclaimed, too loudly. "You stay here, Bruno, and play with the erasers while I go talk to him."

Tiffany's heart was racing as she approached him. Under the harsh fluorescent lights, he still looked radiant. Casual and confident in his sleek, grey tracksuit, he was studying a book, oblivious to her approach.

Finally, a man who knows how to wear a tracksuit. And read a book!

"Oh, is that you, Mr Merriman?" she said as soon as she was within earshot. "How are you?"

Merriman looked up, puzzled but friendly. He gave her a dazzling, non-committal smile.

This man is no stranger to his dentist. You could hold an ice-skating tournament on those teeth.

"Yes?" Merriman clearly had no idea who she was. But seemed keen to find out. "Can I help you?"

"I believe you work in my nephew's school." Tiffany covered the remaining distance between her and the teacher in seconds. "PE, perhaps?"

"That's true," he replied, not hiding his pride in his work. His goatee practically bristled. "Who's your nephew?"

"Oh, that doesn't matter," Tiffany replied, laughing. "I recognised you from when we drop him off at school in the morning. I'm Tiffany."

"I'm Karl." He extended an eager hand. Another blinding smile. "I hope your nephew enjoys the classes. Whoever he is."

"Oh, he's a lost cause! Gets himself into fights that he can't finish. But we all appreciate your efforts."

"Oh, it's Robin! Yes, I do try to teach him. I believe Fr Twitter is going to have a word with his mother about that unfortunate incident on the stairs. So anyway, how are you?"

Tiffany was too busy admiring his expertly crafted buzz cut to register the question. Just enough flecks of grey to indicate aspirations of maturity. But a cut trendy enough to indicate someone who likes to stay contemporary. The goatee managed to be individualistic without being pretentious.

"Sorry. What?" *Jesus, get a grip!* "I was just looking at... What book are you reading there?"

"This is really interesting," Karl said, holding up a fitness book. "Some excellent workouts in it. I'm thinking of incorporating some of the routines in the pre-class warm-ups with the children. But of course it's difficult to..."

Tiffany's attention was already wandering from the delights of the latest fitness fad. She was studying Karl's shopping basket. An inevitable supply of fresh fruit and vegetables. Bottles of sparkling water. Esoteric tea blends. The moisturiser was a bit of a worry, but otherwise nothing to raise alarm bells.

"...teenagers crave variety and stimulation. Don't you agree?"

"Of course." *What the hell was he saying?* "I try to keep in shape myself too. There's no time limit on being healthy, I say. Just because we get older– Just because we get *a little* older doesn't mean we have to let ourselves go."

"Absolutely." Karl's eyes gave Tiffany an approving full-body scan. "I can see that you value healthy living. Though you should consider switching to low-fat milk. It's much better for you."

"Oh, very true." *Damn it! What's the point of having a bloody guardian angel if he can't even guide you to the right carton of milk? Too busy licking the cheese, the fat bastard!* "But this isn't for me. It's for my sister. She's kind of given up on herself. It's very sad to see. I keep telling her if she consumes crap, she'll look like crap. But that's her life choice."

"Well, hopefully your nephew won't follow the same path. I'll see to that."

"Yes, anything you can do to help us make it through the... to help him stay on the healthy path. That'd be very much appreciated."

Tiffany glanced at Karl's hands. No engagement or wedding rings. Even his fingers were perfectly sculpted and manicured. Rugged but well maintained, like a soulful marine.

"Well, it was very nice to meet you," Karl said. "I'd better get going because—"

"It's very stressful worrying about young people these days, isn't it?" Tiffany wasn't going to let him escape that easily. "I do find life quite a handful sometimes. As I said, my sister isn't really up to the task of looking after her family. Or herself. So I find myself stepping into the breach often. Of course, one doesn't hesitate to do whatever good one can for one's family. But being good can be something of its own burden, can't it?"

"Robin is certainly lucky to have such a… a caring aunt. Maybe I'll see you–"

"Actually, he mentioned to me that you do evening yoga classes in the school. Perhaps that's something that would help me become more… flexible in my engagement with difficult family members."

"Yes, every Tuesday night." Karl suddenly became engaged with the conversation again. "We do a unique combination of body stretches and mind stretches in order to expand our limits of being."

"That's exactly what I need!" *Expand our limits of being?* "A chance to explore boundaries, but in safe hands, if you know what I mean, ha ha ha."

"We begin with some abdominal chants, and engage in mindful explorations of our inner psyche before integrating our physical realities with our subconscious drives. In that way, the body becomes a holistic expression of our mutual beings, to put it simply."

"Absolutely." *Where the hell is Bruno?* "I'll be sure to sign up for a class. It's been a while since I've enjoyed the pleasure of expanding my… of engaging in mutual… of having a chance to calm the hell down."

"Excellent. Well, Robin will be able to show you where the

classes are. We'll have an extra cup of green tea ready for you!"

"I look forward to it." Tiffany decided not to reveal that green tea usually triggered her migraines. The sacrifice would be worth it. "I'm sure I'll be a better student than my useless lump of a nephew."

"See you then."

With that, Karl strode off to the checkout with the calm, self-confidence of a renaissance prince.

"What an insufferable, self-absorbed tool!" Bruno had suddenly reappeared beside Tiffany. "I heard enough of that sanctimonious bullshit during the weekly meetings in heaven. Why are you wasting your time on that poser?"

As she watched the tracksuit disappear into the distance, Tiffany could already feel some niggling doubts about Karl's absolute perfection. She'd noticed the fundamentalist glint in his eye when he talked about his classes. And she'd heard the rumours of psychotic tantrums in the school gym.

However, she had plenty of time to waste. And this could be a fun way to waste it.

She gets up and sniffs the roses. I stay in bed and sniff the cocaine.
She's up sniffing the roses, I'm down here sniffing the cocaine.
The stink of this affair will always linger in my brain.

7

The Jogging Jesus Blues

Lead us not into temptation, baby, every day is another race.
Walk me not into temptation, baby, I can't go another race.
You'll find your map back home in the wrinkles in my face.

Fr Twitter was choosing his words carefully, aware that one slip would detonate the unstable bomb in the room.

"So, you see, Mrs Mulcahy, we really can't have boys pushing other boys down the stairs." Fr Twitter tried to remain calm in the face of Martha's savage glower. "People get injured. Tiles get stained. The banister gets chipped. It's just not acceptable."

Tiffany could see that Martha didn't like having Fr Twitter invade her inner sanctum. In fairness, he was hard to warm to, with his smug smile and neatly parted hair. A peacock prelate. And Martha took great pleasure in turning peacocks into feather dusters.

However, Martha's fury was divided between the pompous priest and her agitated son. Unable to decide where to direct her fire, she chose the third way.

"George, have you got *nothing* to say about any of this?"

"Hmmm?"

"George, your son is being accused of nearly murdering someone. Do you think you could stir yourself to contribute to the discussion?"

"Oh…" George added a few more numbers to his Sudoku. "Well… obviously, cherry blossom, murder is wrong…" He glanced over at Tiffany. "In *most* cases."

"This has nothing to do with whether murder is right or wrong." Martha gave her husband the death stare. "We all know that murder is justified in certain trying circumstances."

"If I could just interject," Fr Twitter ventured. "Murder is actually always–"

"But I know my son," Martha continued, oblivious and indifferent to the priest's views, "and I know he's incapable of murder. In fact, he's incapable of anything useful. He's capable of a lot of useless things, of course."

"Perhaps, dear… But maybe Robbie was pushed too far and just lost control. It can happen to the best of us." Some passion finally stirred in George. "A man can be pushed too far and then–"

"Have you actually forgotten your marriage vows, George? Don't you know that your job is to *unconditionally* support me to the hilt no matter what?"

"Whatever you say, pumpkin." George blanched as he returned to the safe comforts of his Sudoku. "I'll leave it in your capable... hands."

"I'd just like to reiterate," Fr Twitter intervened tentatively, "that murder is *always* wrong. No matter what. The app... the book... the Bible is very clear on that... It's one of those commandment things that Jesus found in the temple under a bush... These are lovely carrot sandwiches, Mrs Mulcahy, by the way. Very unusual tang to them."

"That's because," Tiffany pointed out, "they're apparently supposed to be salmon sandwiches."

"Oh... my goodness..." Fr Twitter chewed cautiously for some seconds. "Anyway, I just wanted to be clear with you all that our school doesn't condone mindless violence. The pupils will see enough of that in the real world. We try to make our school a haven of tranquillity... Oh, by the way, Robin, Mr O'Shea asked me to remind you that your geography assignment is now three weeks overdue."

"You haven't finished that bloody assignment yet?" Martha erupted before Robin could mount a reasonable defence. "What have you been doing up in your bedroom every night? Dancing with angels?"

"Is there no privacy in this house?" Robin protested.

"Of course not!" George finally found a topic that interested him. "You know, the other morning I was in the shower and your aunt waltzed right in and–"

"Go back to your book, George. I don't want to have to murder you in front of Fr Twitter here! Can't you see we have guests? Some welcome." She smiled at Fr Twitter, who'd used the distraction to check his email on his phone. Then she stared at Tiffany. "And some becoming less welcome."

"I'm just pointing out, sugar pie, that a man needs–"

"Shut up, George! Shut up, Robin!" Martha nearly told Fr Twitter to shut up too, but stopped herself in time. "We've got company so we should all pretend to be nice. And that means shutting up and listening to what our guest has to say."

Not expecting to be offered the floor so graciously, Fr Twitter found himself lost for words as everyone stared at him.

"I suppose what I'm trying to say," Fr Twitter finally began, "is that we want our students to appreciate the value of love and peace and friendship. There's too much hatred in the world. No thanks, I won't have another cup of... of... that, Mrs Mulcahy.... Yes, I'm absolutely certain... You see, love is much important than hatred. It's the light that shines through the darkness–"

"Love is certainly blind," Tiffany agreed, completely missing Fr Twitter's point.

"And marriage is a real eye opener," Martha remarked, looking over at her oblivious husband.

"I'm not talking about marriage, I'm talking about love," Fr Twitter continued. "There's a difference."

"There certainly is," Martha vehemently agreed. "You have to look hard to find any love in marriage. It's the first flower to wither away!"

"That's not really my point, Mrs Mulcahy." Ft Twitter was becoming more unsure of his point by the second. "Our students have to realise that they can't go through life hating each other. Otherwise, everyone is climbing over everyone else trying to put each other's eyes out. We'll have enough of that carry-on once the Rapture starts. That's why Miss Spindle is so happy that *Romeo and Juliet* is on the curriculum this term. She's such an excellent teacher and that play will teach them what love really–"

"And what exactly," asked Martha, "would that decrepit stick insect know about love? I'd say, the last time she was kissed, old Ronald Reagan was nodding off in the White House."

"Miss Spindle is a wonderful woman!" Realising that he'd

spoken too forcefully, Fr Twitter tried to climb out of the hole. "*All* our teachers are wonderful."

"I'm sure you're right, Father." Martha wasn't going to let someone who openly disagreed with her stay in her house a moment longer. "Anyway, I have my hands somewhat full with this shower here. I'll take on board… whatever it was you were saying. And I'll pray to God for the strength to do the right thing."

"Prayer is very important." Fr Twitter hadn't taken the hint. "But remember, sometimes God answers our prayers by saying no."

"Well, that's not much use to anyone, is it?" Martha decided to use a more direct approach. "Anyway, the door is just at the end of the hall, Father."

"Oh… Okay… Well, I won't take up any more of your time…"

Martha began escorting him down the hall before he changed his mind.

Tiffany thought about Fr Twitter's staunch defence of Miss Spindle. Martha was right, of course. She was a particularly decrepit form of stick insect. Yet, she obviously aroused some dormant passion in the bewildered priest.

Tiffany felt hints of that passion whenever she talked to

Giggles. She felt a static electric surge of it when she saw Karl in the supermarket aisle. Indeed, a few years back, she used to feel it whenever she talked to Bill. That was before he aroused more powerful passions in her, such as hatred, disgust, and despair.

Would her guardian angel be able to lead her back to that passion some day?

We run over the mountains, we run over the hills,
Every night, we run over the mountains and the hills.
Every morning we wake up, and swallow a great big pile of pills.

"So now you're jealous of a self-absorbed idiot priest?" Bruno shook his head in frustration. "Every time someone meets a priest, bad things happen!"

"I'm not jealous of him," Tiffany clarified. "I just noticed that even *he* has more passion for life than I do."

Tiffany was enjoying the fresh mountain air. The sharp breeze helped to scatter the toxic aftermath of Martha's conversation with the priest. Martha's post-priest fury had been directed wantonly at everyone in the house, so Tiffany knew it was time to get out for a while.

Whenever she came to the mountain, her senses

reawakened. The suffocating stupor that would often engulf her when inside lifted like smoke once she had a chance to breathe in some clean, refreshing air.

It was time to get her blood pumping again.

"Come on, Bruno!" Tiffany broke into a brisk jog. "Let's give that rusty old heart of yours a good workout!"

She didn't wait for Bruno to gather his thoughts.

"Slow down," he grumbled through a mouthful of barely chewed chocolate cake. "What's the rush?"

"Run faster, you fat bastard!"

Bruno was having a hard time keeping up as he panted beside her in his sweaty tracksuit.

"No matter how fast you run," Bruno said, shaking the sweat from his beard, "you'll never outrun your problems."

"Maybe if you'd been fit enough to run away from that bastard of a duke," Tiffany replied, "you wouldn't have been burnt at the stake or eaten alive or whatever the hell happened to you."

Despite his enormous girth, Bruno managed to get into a puffing, creaking, fluttering rhythm beside Tiffany.

"And anyway, I'm not running away from anything." *Why do I have to explain myself to him?* "I'm running towards something. Running towards happiness. Towards a new start."

"Be careful what you wish for. Back in the day, the Spanish colonisers wished for gold, so the natives poured molten gold down their throats."

Tiffany didn't want to dwell on Spanish colonisers. She didn't want to dwell on timid priests and fraught sisters.

She wanted to dwell on the cool breeze that embraced her as she jogged along the mountain path. She wanted to dwell on the crunch of the small pebbles beneath her feet. She wanted to dwell on the music of the birds in the trees.

She wanted nothing to distract her from her temporary bliss.

Oh my yummy goodness! Look who it is!

In the distance, she could see Karl jogging towards her.

"What's lit your fire now?" Bruno glanced at her suspiciously. "Someone else stirring the embers?"

"How the hell did you know what–?"

"Your eyes widened. Your breathing got faster. You mercifully slowed down your jogging pace. You licked your lower lip. Do I need to go on?"

"I just noticed someone ahead. No one special."

Someone very special! Sweet Jogging Jesus, he was built to wear those shorts.

Karl had seen her and slowed down.

Stay calm. Don't make a tool of yourself.

"Hi there again!" Tiffany's wave was so wide, she nearly knocked Bruno's eye out. She also noted that her voice was much shriller than she'd intended it to be. "We meet again, ha ha ha ha ha."

Karl's face was creased in momentary bewilderment as he came to a graceful stop.

"Tiffany," Tiffany clarified. "Robin's aunt. His *young* aunt, ha ha ha."

"Of course!" Karl unleashed a perfectly sculpted grin. Despite the jog, there wasn't a hint of sweat on his face. "I knew I recognised you. What brings you up here?"

"Oh, I like to come up here for a jog most days." Tiffany tried to ignore the derisive snort from Bruno. "It's very important to keep fit in these stressful modern times, isn't it?"

"Indeed." Karl nodded enthusiastically. "And it becomes even more important for people as they get older."

Tiffany recoiled slightly from the perceived insult. But she noticed that Karl was oblivious to having caused any offence.

"I must remember that advice when I get old, Karl. Fail to prepare when you're young, prepare to fail when you're old."

Tiffany noticed that Karl was studying her closely. Bruno was also studying her closely, but she ignored that.

"Jogging is great for the soul," Karl continued, after a spartan sip from his designer water bottle. "We run away from our negativity and into the arms of our positivity."

"Absolutely." *Jesus, I'd murder him to get my hands on that bottle of water. Why do I always forget to bring mine when I come up here?* "I'm positive something good has come from this jog today."

Tiffany hoped he'd picked up the hint.

"Yoga is also good!" Karl seemed to have found a subject that excited him. "There's a class tonight. Why don't you come along and try it out?"

"Of course, I'd love to." *Did he just ask me out on a date?* "If you'd like me to come."

"Yes, absolutely. Yoga is a great help for people as they get older. It keeps them flexible, both physically and mentally."

"Something else for me to remember *when* I get old." Tiffany worked hard to make her laugh sound natural. "What time shall we meet, Karl?"

"The class starts at eight this evening. Just pay for a one-night class and see how you get on."

"It's been a while since I've done a one-night anything."

"Speaking of time, I'd better get going." Karl started jogging before waiting for a reply. "Remember, eight this evening."

Tiffany watched him jog away, admiring the ballet of his muscles as the dust kicked up around him.

Such rhythm. Such grace. Such sculpted muscles. Such–

"Such a poser!" Bruno snorted. "You'll never come between that guy and his mirror!"

Tiffany felt an adolescent urge to jog after Karl. But she wanted to retain at least some dignity.

"Come on, you fat, sweaty bastard," she said to Bruno as she started to jog back home. "I need you to tell me all you know about yoga."

You're the sugar in my coffee, you're the spice in my curry.
You're the sugar in my coffee, babe. You always spice up my curry.
You came to me like an angel, but you sure flew away in a hurry.

"God must be having a hard time recruiting if that sanctimonious, twittering git is all He could find," Martha declared as they walked to the café. "He's enough to turn any Christian into an atheist."

"You were an atheist two weeks ago, after you lost your bracelet in the church," Tiffany reminded her. "You're always walking out on God and then going back to church as if nothing has happened."

"Just like you and Bill for many years, if I remember right," Martha reminded her.

Tiffany decided to let that one pass. A cinnamon bun and sweet coffee would give her the energy she needed for the yoga class this evening. And she had gone jogging this afternoon, so she deserved a treat.

Another treat, if you count meeting Karl. Two yummy treats in one day!

While most people prayed to God, Martha preferred to *negotiate* with Him, and negotiate from a position of strength and superiority. She regarded herself as being more infallible than the Pope.

"I just don't think Fr Twitter will be able to guide Robin on the right path," Martha continued, as she assaulted a slice of apple pie. "He's too cautious and uncertain about everything. Constantly seeking approval, like some pathetic little puppy."

"Oh, that reminds me," said Tiffany, "I must buy George some chocolates to thank him for driving me to work."

"No, not chocolate. Don't over-stimulate the man."

I don't think poor George has been over-stimulated in twenty years! A man who spends that much time wrapped up in Sudoku has clearly given up on walking on the wild side.

Tiffany felt sorry for George. However, she could see that he and Martha had developed a sort of workable co-dependency that enabled them to both survive, just like a shark and pilot fish.

"Don't be too hard on Fr Twitter," Tiffany remarked. "No one really knows what the right path is anyway."

"I suppose," Martha grudgingly conceded. "But at least I don't waste my time galloping up pointless paths to lunacy. So many people latch on to crazy fads and childish games, thinking they're the true roads to enlightenment. It's so pathetic... Anyway, why are you so interested in yoga all of a sudden?"

"I knew that missile would finally find its way to me!" Tiffany was used to her sister's barbs. "Anyway, it's not a fad. Cats have been practising yoga since the dawn of time."

"You expect cats to lead you to nirvana now?" Martha started laughing, unleashing her full indiscreet guffaw with abandon. "That's the first step to spinsterhood!"

Tiffany decided to disengage. Martha was clearly still agitated from the priest's visit and needed somewhere to direct her aggression. Tiffany shifted her attention to the other people in the café. Maybe she could find some enlightenment among the lattes and cappuccinos.

Before any coffee-scented, zen-like calm could envelop her, Tiffany saw Bill and Kylie walk in.

Kylie was dressed in a body-hugging pink tracksuit with silver stripes. She lifted her bottle of water to her lips as if she were in a sultry music video for a jaded rock star with some dodgy medical issues. Kylie always acted as if all the eyes in the room were on her. Because they usually were.

Bill was aiming for boho-chic today. Aiming, and missing. The torn jeans spoke more of a rottweiler encounter than edgy fashion. And the tie-dyed shirt had the air of a tragic laundry mishap. The tartan baseball cap was as faded as his stubble.

Despite looking like an air-crash survivor, Bill seemed to be making a great effort to convince himself that he was happy. Only for some seconds did his smile waver.

Then he saw Tiffany and he gathered his smile back together again.

"Hey, Tiffs!"

Bill's smile always irritated Tiffany. Because it stirred something deep inside her that she wasn't comfortable acknowledging.

"Hello, Kylie," Tiffany replied, ignoring Bill. Her icy politeness almost made her teeth hurt. "You're looking as *radiant* as ever."

"You always make such an effort to look good, Kylie," Martha agreed. "It's like you're trying to impress every single man on the street."

"Yes, indeed," Tiffany elaborated. "Like you're trying to catch the attention of *absolutely* every single available man on the street."

"You guys are so sweet," Kylie enthused, flashing a dazzling smile. "When you look good, you feel good."

"Well then, you must be feeling pretty awful, Bill," Martha noted, "given how you look."

"I'm just trying something new," Bill replied, trying to look unruffled as he glanced at Kylie. "My clothes are making a statement."

"More like a cry for help," Martha said, gnawing on the conversational bone. "They look like they're trying to escape from you."

Kylie looked away, unsuccessfully suppressing a giggle.

"Pay no attention to Martha, Kyles," Bill said. "She finds it very hard to say nice things to people. Probably because she'd find it hard to say anything nice about herself."

"Anyway, Bill," Tiffany said, feeling no obligation to defend her sister, "we came here for a quiet chat, so there's no need for you to keep hanging around. We'll see you again sometime."

"That's okay, Tiffs." Bill nodded wisely. "I totally understand."

"Understand *what?*"

"Look, you're going to have to get used to seeing the two of us together." Bill placed his hand on Kylie's shoulder, causing her to instinctively recoil. "We're moving on together to a new phase in our lives. And you should move on too."

"Bill, I moved on as soon as—"

"The only people who should live in the past are historians, Tiffs."

"What about archaeologists?" Martha asked. "People like Kylie, who like digging up old fossils."

"Actually, I studied philosophy at college," Kylie pointed out.

"Then you're used to dealing with the meaningless and absurd," Martha replied. "That'll come in useful when living with Bill!"

"Oh, we're not living together," Kylie said quickly.

"Not yet," Bill clarified, with a hopeful smile.

"We're *not* living together," Kylie reiterated to the café in general.

Tiffany could see the storm clouds gathering around the

sylvan idyll that Bill had conjured up in his mind. She could also see that Bill was gloriously unaware of the doubts that had crept into Kylie's heart.

That was when she felt something in her own heart that made her feel uncomfortable. Another emotion that she didn't want to acknowledge.

Do I feel sorry for Bill?

"See, look, Tiffs has drifted off again to the happier times when we were together. And it's great that she has those memories. But that's all they are, babe. Memories."

And as quickly as it surfaced, Tiffany's pity for Bill evaporated.

"Babe?" Kylie asked sharply.

"That's all they are, Tiffs." Bill hastily reformulated his philosophy. "Memories."

Tiffany tried to navigate her way out of the conversational minefield.

"So, Kylie," she said, "you look like you're going for a run."

"Yes, Tiffany." It was now Kylie's turn to be icily polite. "It's great to get out in the fresh air and away from all the… away from things."

"It's been great for us," Bill agreed, a little too eagerly. "I feel much better these days. I look much better too… Oh, sorry, Tiffs! That was thoughtless of me."

"Tiffany is trying out new things too," Martha said, before Tiffany could throw her coffee in Bill's face. "She's now decided that yoga is the key to lifelong happiness!"

"Oh, really?" Kylie jumped enthusiastically back on to familiar territory. "That's so awesome. I love yoga!"

"I guessed you would," Martha replied, glancing at Tiffany. "It definitely attracts… a certain type of person. Tiffany starts her first, and maybe last, class tonight."

"Oh, do you go to Karl's class, Tiffany?" Kylie had forgotten all about her storm clouds. "He's amazing. He takes such good care of us all. The really *personal* touch, if you know what I mean."

Tiffany now felt her third uncomfortable sensation: jealousy of Kylie.

"I've heard he's very good," Tiffany said, looking away. "Anyway, it's just something new I'm trying out. Not reason to get excited about it."

"Tiffany said she's very impressed with Karl," Martha added, gleefully adding some static electricity to the storm clouds. "That's why she's so keen to try something new."

"You should go too, Martha," Kylie continued. "He's

amazing. You'd be butter in his hands."

"She'd be rather bitter butter," Bill said. "Don't let her ruin the lovely mood of your class, Kylie. I know how much you enjoy it. You spend so much time there."

"Anyway, Bill," said Kylie, blushing slightly, "let's leave them to their coffee and chat. There's a free table over there. Order me a kale juice and some tofu salad."

"Okay, Kylie." Bill turned his full smile on Tiffany. "Remember what I said, Tiffs. Don't live in the past. Walk towards the happy future."

Tiffany watched Bill walk over to Kylie's table.

"Kylie has changed," Tiffany whispered to Martha. "She's started to lose that childish innocence that she used to always radiate."

"You mean her stupidity?"

"It's amazing how being with Bill changes people. And never for the better."

However, it wasn't pity for Kylie that Tiffany felt.

It was pity for Bill.

You fell into my life, like an angel falling from the sky.
You fell right on top of me, just like an angel falling from the sky.
But now you just walk all over me, kicking the dirt into my eye.

The last person Tiffany wanted to meet on her way to yoga was Jehovah.

So, of course, he was the first person she met.

It was bad enough having to listen to Bruno's snarky comments about her new-found enthusiasm for yoga.

"Your bitter sister is right, you know," Bruno said, as he wolfed down the last of his second cheeseburger. "You have no more interest in yoga than you have in advanced quantum physics. The only physics you're interested in relate to the self-absorbed gym monkey giving the class."

"Look, just because *you've* never found love in all the centuries you've been gallivanting around the heavens doesn't mean that some of us are incapable of finding love on our own. Indeed, I know Martha is praying that I'll find love soon."

"Does she often pray to God?" Bruno asked. "That might explain why He's always so grumpy."

"Every morning and every night," Tiffany said. "Optimistically in the morning. Menacingly in the evening. At the moment, she's praying for the patience of a saint to help her get through the week."

"Oh, she shouldn't pray to be a saint!" Bruno laughed. "I could tell you things about saints that'd make your hair stand up and walk away from your head."

"Anyway," Tiffany continued, increasing her pace to get to Karl's yoga class, "I'm just looking to have a nice, fun evening. I'm not searching for the meaning of life."

"If you were looking for the meaning of life, you'd need to ask the man upstairs. Not that He'll answer you. That's His great trick. Generations talking to Him, and He never once answers anyone."

Never the most helpful of guardian angels, Bruno was in a particularly foul mood today because his boss had given him another telling off about his evident failure to keep Tiffany from hurting herself.

Tiffany had stopped listening to Bruno's tirade. Another voice had caught her attention. A voice even more annoying than that of a disgruntled saint.

"And when that glorious day comes and we are all lifted on high, above the swamp of sinful humanity, we will disappear into the light, safe forever from the barbs of vicious, deceitful humanity."

A small crowd applauded. They were beaming, all eyes on the street-corner preacher.

Jehovah acknowledged their applause with a smug smile that was almost as annoying as the chirpy, uplifting gospel muzak playing on a tinny speaker in the background. He was totally enraptured in his sermon.

"Look at the state of him," Tiffany said to Bruno. "He should be locked up in a seminary."

"You know what smell always reminds me of a seminary?" Bruno replied. "The smell of hypocrisy and self-righteous bullshit. Back when I was in the seminary, my colleagues were all degenerates. Gamblers. Arsonists. Alcoholics. Mushroom munchers. Nettle fondlers. And then every night, they used to whip themselves into a frenzy to atone for their sins."

"What happened them when they left seminary?" Tiffany asked, trying not to think about whipping Jehovah in the street.

"Some of them became bishops. Some of them became nuns. Some of them became both. And some of them became fishermen. They soon discovered that there was more money to be made becoming fishers of fish rather than fishers of men! I tell you, the best thing that bastard of a duke ever did was to burn that seminary to the ground. Unfortunately, most of them escaped the flames. Well, they escaped the flames there. I don't think they escaped the flames down below, if you know what I mean."

Listening to Jehovah condemn the wanton indulgence of

fallen humanity made Tiffany want to indulge in some sparring with her sanctimonious nemesis. Battling with Jehovah always made her feel better.

"I think I'll go over there and drown him in a bucket of holy water," she said. "Put an end to his endless preaching and judging."

"It might seem like a good idea now," Bruno warned, "but good ideas often descend into pointless savagery when the preachy brigade get involved. Just look at the bloody crusades!"

Oblivious to how close he'd just come to being drowned, Jehovah was working himself up into a sweat-and-spittle froth of pious passion. He prayed for the day when the angels would descend and wrap the righteous in their arms, protecting them from the rapturous judgement that would burn away the sins of corrupt humanity.

"Well, if an angel invasion happens," Bruno remarked, with a dismissive snort, "it'll be the biggest surprise since you-know-who managed to sneak out of the tomb that Sunday morning when nobody was looking. And no one will be more shocked than the boss."

"Everyone seems to be obsessed with this Rapture these days!" Tiffany checked her watch. "I hope it's not going to interfere with my yoga class."

"Well, just like your yoga, the Rapture is a mad fairy tale told by a lunatic," Bruno replied. He allowed himself a hearty laugh. "Even the boss gets a good laugh out of that Rapture yarn. Prophets have been predicting it for centuries, and they've never once got it right. Angels coming down from the sky breathing fire and brimstone? Don't make me laugh."

"You're just bitter," Tiffany said, "because no angels turned up when you were being nibbled to death by gummy sheep, or whatever the hell happened to you."

"The boss is very proud of this mess of a world that He's created," Bruno continued, ignoring Tiffany. "Do you seriously think he'd destroy it? He'd sooner suck out his own teeth."

The small crowd was now singing a high-pitched invocation of the Rapture, clapping their hands so fervently that Tiffany predicted broken wrists by the end of the song.

"Okay, I've heard enough of this nonsense," she said to Bruno. "I'm off to find some rapture of my own."

Tiffany made her way to the school gym, thinking of the angel that she wanted to descend from the sky and carry her off to a better world.

You can bend me, shake me, you can even wake me.

You can bend me or shake me, babe. Some mornings, you can even wake me.

But when you look at me with those eyes, all you do is break me.

No matter how hard she tried, Tiffany couldn't get comfortable on the yoga mat.

Maybe it was the mat. Or maybe it was her pants.

Or maybe it was Kylie.

After going home, Kylie had changed into a light purple tracksuit.

She'd also done up her hair. And she was wearing just a little bit too much lipstick for a yoga class.

She was a good student of yoga, however. She never took her eyes off Karl.

Neither did Tiffany.

Yummy yummy, mister!

Karl was explaining the importance of deep breathing to the class.

"I know you all know how to breathe," Karl explained slowly. "Otherwise, you wouldn't have made it to the class tonight. But how many of you know how to breathe *properly*?"

There was some nervous giggling in the class. Everyone assumed this was a trick question.

Tiffany began to have the first stirrings of regret, as she suspected that coming to the class was a mistake.

"I suppose," said Kylie, gleefully sure of her supposition, "that we need to breathe from deep inside ourselves."

"Exactly!" Karl smiled his effortless smile at Kylie. "We must reach down deep inside ourselves to find the source of our spirit. That way, we bring the positive energy of the universe deep into our very being, and we expel the most ingrained negative energy, pulling it up by the roots and casting it on to the dung pile."

Karl paused, allowing the profundity of his words to sink in.

The class stared back at him, lost.

"Breathing is a lot like sex," Karl elaborated, latching on to a subject that everyone could relate to. "We all do it every day, but very few of us are really good at it."

Everyone laughed.

Except Tiffany.

Every day? Who's he kidding?! And who the hell is Kylie kidding? The only thing you get every day with Bill is a headache!

"So let's start with some deep-breathing exercises," Karl said, shaking himself loose. "Close your eyes and take a deep, cleansing breath. In through the nose, out through mouth.

Good air in. Bad air out."

Initially, Tiffany found the sound of the deep breathing around her very irritating. It reminded her of when Bill used to practise his harmonica. Heavy breathing, leading to self-indulgent wheezing.

However, as she found her own breathing rhythm, she felt a gentle calm begin to wrap itself around her. Breathing deeper and more slowly, she could sense that she was gradually dissolving into her own breath, becoming as immaterial as the air around her. Feeling a oneness with the universe that felt irresistibly exciting and reassuringly familiar. She could feel her entire being transporting itself to an alternative realm of consciousness.

She breathed in.

She breathed out.

Good air iiiiiiiiiinnnnnnnnnnnnnn.

Bad air ooooooouuuuuuuuuuttttttt.

Oh shit! I'm falling asleep!

Tiffany jolted with a start, managing to stop her body lurching forward on to the floor.

She thought that maybe no one had noticed. Then she noticed Kylie giggling and looking guiltily away.

Karl hadn't noticed, though. He was already warming up

for the first few rounds of body stretches.

"If you feel pain," he cautioned, "remember to stop. We all have different levels of fitness. And we are in a safe space. Our very own circle of comfort. We don't make fun of people who aren't fit. There is no fat-shaming here. Sometimes, people are simply comfortable with the body they've been given. Or they've allowed to grow. Now, follow my lead."

Tiffany knew she was fit. And she knew she wasn't fat. One of the advantages of living with Martha was that there was no temptation to overeat!

However, as she stretched and swung her body, following the movement of Karl's graceful and finely toned limbs, Tiffany could feel her body creak and crack in protest. Unfamiliar aches and stabs suddenly asserted their presence.

When did that part of my body decide it wanted some attention?

Tiffany also noticed how supple Kylie was. Like most of the class, Kylie never took her eyes off Karl, seemingly mesmerised by his rhythmic gestures.

Tiffany felt her jealousy of Kylie begin to stir again. In a way, Kylie reminded Tiffany of who she herself once was. Flexible, excited, positive, and eager to please. All the things Tiffany was before she met Bill. Or at least that was the easiest way for Tiffany to rationalise how her cynicism had hardened over the years.

Why the hell am I jealous of her? She's with Bill! Why be jealous of anyone in a sinking boat? A few years with Bill, and all that flexibility will be gone. She'll be as hard and bitter as Martha. Or as me...

Tiffany didn't like where her thoughts were taking her. She decided to focus on her nagging physical pains to take her mind off the emotional twinges that were beginning to make her uncomfortable.

The class wore on, stretch by stretch, roll by roll, twist by twist, breath by breath.

Finally, Karl seemed to be slowing down.

"You've all done very well tonight," he was saying. "Even those of you who've let yourself get out of shape in recent years. Remember, you have to believe in yourself if you want anyone else to believe you. Well done, Kylie, by the way. You didn't miss a beat tonight."

"Oh, thank you, Karl!" Kylie's face was bright red. Perhaps from the physical strain of the exercises. Perhaps from something else. "It's great to have a good teacher to watch very closely."

"And it's great to have a good student to watch closely too." Karl's smile this time was reserved exclusively for Kylie. "I hope you enjoyed the class as much as I did... Anyway, thanks everybody! I look forward to seeing you all next week."

Tiffany got up as fast as her reluctant body would allow her. She wanted to slip out quickly and get away from this room, with its overpowering aura of judgemental self-righteousness.

"Did you enjoy that, Tiffany?" Kylie suddenly appeared beside her. It had clearly taken her a lot less time to gather herself back together. "Isn't Karl totally awesome?"

"He's certainly unique." *Very unique to look at, in fairness.* "You seem to really like him."

"Oh, yeah! We're very close. We're always egging each other on during class. That's why I enjoy coming here so much. He always gives me a good laugh."

"I can understand your need to grasp any laughs you can these days." *I wonder if they've reached the harmonica horrors yet.* "When you're with lemons, you have to go out and find lemonade somewhere. That's what the philosophers say."

"Exactly, taste all the sweet goodness in life," Kylie replied, apparently missing Tiffany's point entirely. "Did you enjoy the class? You seemed to be struggling a bit – well, quite a bit – at times there this evening."

"Not at all," Tiffany lied. "How difficult can breathing and moving be? I've been doing it since I was a baby."

"I really admired your bravery coming here tonight." Kylie's smile didn't waver for a second. "You prove that people are never too old to start something new. And, of course, self-improvement gets even more important as we... as a person gets older."

"Yes, it's good to try new things." Tiffany rolled up her yoga mat with exceptional force. "Anyway, Kylie, I'd better–"

"As Bill said earlier, it's time for you to move on." Kylie placed a sympathetic hand on Tiffany's shoulder. "I know it was difficult for you to see the two of us today. But I'm so glad we can be friends and all grown up about it!"

"Nothing difficult about it." Tiffany shrugged her shoulders violently, dislodging Kylie's sympathetic hand in the process. "Anyway, I'll probably see you here next week."

"Oh, you're coming back?" Kylie patted Tiffany's shoulder this time. "I really do admire your *bravery*. You're an inspiration. I love people who don't accept defeat. See you next week!"

Before Tiffany could get any final barbs in, Kylie bounced away out of the class, throwing a merry wave in Karl's direction on the way.

Karl grinned at her and waved back.

Then he smiled to himself.

That smile decided it for Tiffany.

She walked up to Karl.

"Hi," she said. "Can I ask you something?"

"Of course." Karl adjusted his mouth into a wise, patient smile. "I was thinking you'd have some questions. I could see you were struggling in the class."

"Oh no, that's not it." Tiffany's determination to return to the class next week dropped yet another notch. "No, I just wanted to ask if you'd like to meet up for a coffee some time?"

"Coffee?" Karl sounded aghast. "Have you any idea what caffeine can–?"

"Or maybe a beer?"

"Beer?" Karl looked at her in horrified disbelief. "Too much alcohol can have very serious–"

"Let's just meet up for a drink." Tiffany was determined to salvage something from the evening. "We can discuss how I can integrate all this positivity into other areas of my life. We all need a good shot of calm now and then, don't we?"

"Oh, I see." Karl's smile reasserted itself. "Of course, Tiffany. I'd be delighted to discuss how you can improve yourself."

"Okay, I'll be in touch." Tiffany knew that if she stayed too long in this conversation, it'd end badly. "Bye for now."

Before Karl could reply, Tiffany strode out of the room, almost certain that she'd made the right decision.

Despite his perfect looks, Karl wasn't perfect. But Tiffany knew that she couldn't afford to wait for some other angel to come along and lift her into the heavens.

I see you in my dreams, and the whole bed starts shakin'.
I see you in my dreams, babe, and this ol' bed starts into shakin'.
I wake up on the floor, with my poor ol' heart a-breakin'.

8

Like a Seagull (The Blues Flew in)

Ev'ry single night with you, I sing a song of praise.
Ev'ry single night with ya, babe, you make me sing a song of praise.
But on the mornin' after, I'm rockin' in a seasick haze.

There were many things that Tiffany hated about her job.

She hated the mindless tedium of most of her work. She hated many of her colleagues, and some of them with a passion. She hated the canteen food, which always had the texture of washed-up plastic. She hated her boss.

Most of all, she hated the annual performance review.

In fairness to the Seagull, he didn't take performance reviews entirely seriously either. However, a change in the moss at the top of the company meant that all layers of meaningless middle-management now had to engage in this ritual.

To keep things informal, the Seagull insisted on having the meeting in the local café. Tiffany tried to convince him to have it in the boardroom. Or the carpark. Or the toilets. Anywhere but the café. That was where she came to relax and vent with Martha. She didn't want its sacred atmosphere being

215

corrupted by the Seagull's breath.

However, the Seagull insisted on the café.

And Tiffany soon realised why.

"It's so nice to get the chance to *relax* with you, Tiffany," he said, his hand reaching across the table towards her. "Away from the clinical vibe of the office. We can just kick back here and chill together like old friends."

"Let's focus on the review," Tiffany replied, strategically placing the condiments and napkins in the path of the wandering hand. She wondered if there were any mousetraps handy. "It's best not to compromise the professionalism of the meeting."

Tiffany knew she'd have to engage her corporate persona for the next while. This was a rarely used mask that she took out for emergencies. She'd absorbed enough corporate buzz talk over the years to be able to induce a self-hypnotic trance to get her through the most trying of encounters at work. She'd read somewhere that serial killers used a similar tactic.

"Well, sometimes it's fun to compromise!" The Seagull arched his eyebrows so high that they nearly took flight. "So did you enjoy that little gift I gave you a while back?"

"What gift?" Tiffany was genuinely puzzled. Had she repressed some horrific memory? "I don't recall getting *anything* ever from you."

"The blues CD! You told me how much you loved blues music. I like to take an interest in my staff. Get to know them as humans, not just employees. Find out what hearts beat beneath the façade of –"

"Did you give Geoff any gifts?"

Geoff was a fifty-year-old divorcé with the personality of a vengeful toothache. He'd joined the department last year. Even the cobwebs tried to avoid him. His fatalistic sighs sent graveyard chills through the cubicles most afternoons. He was taciturn, argumentative, manipulative, and petty.

Tiffany really liked him.

"Jesus wept! Of course I didn't give Geoff any gifts!" The Seagull sounded aghast. "I've been trying to exorcise that dreary plague out of the department ever since he joined! No, what I mean is that when I think an employee is special, I make a *special* effort to get to know her better."

Tiffany remained as silent as a glacier and gave the Seagull her iciest of stares, a stare that would make a wasp contemplate suicide.

The Seagull barrelled on.

"You've changed your hair, Tiffany. It looks nice."

"No, I haven't," Tiffany lied. She *had* changed her hair

colour slightly, but not for the Seagull's benefit. For someone else's benefit. "Let's talk about something else that hasn't changed. My salary."

"Oh, there's plenty of time for that," the Seagull breezed along. "We should see this as an opportunity to get to know each other on a more personal–"

"I'm really interested in the new HR guidelines on personal space. I need to talk to Jehovah about them. He makes me uncomfortable."

"His desk is six feet away from yours!"

"I wish it was six feet under me! He just makes me uncomfortable whenever he's on the same planet– I mean, whenever he's in the same room as me."

"Well, I'll see what I can do. Is there anything else I can do to make you feel more comfortable? *Anything* at all?"

Much as Tiffany hated her job, she really didn't want to lose it either. After all, she needed money. She had long since become expert in the art of strategic incompetence, doing the bare minimum to get by, safe in the knowledge that someone, usually the Seagull, would be happy to pick up her slack and correct her mistakes. However, there were limits to how far she could push him. So she decided that a diplomatic silence was the best response to the Seagull's question.

The Seagull pretended to look through some documents.

Tiffany pretended to think of innovative ways to boost the company's social media presence.

The waitress pretended to care whether they were enjoying their coffee.

"Actually, can we get two more cups?" the Seagull asked. "We'll probably be here for a long while."

"Why would we be here for a long while?" *Jesus, this meeting has already gone on much longer than I wanted.* "We have enough coffee."

"Yes, maybe you're right." The Seagull shooed the waitress away. "We can get something stronger after the meeting. I know this nice cosy place over by–"

"I'll need to get back to the office soon." Tiffany found it hard to keep a straight face. "Those videos of our new stationery won't trend all by themselves."

"Okay, then, let's focus on your work." The Seagull visibly deflated. "Let's first look at the targets we agreed last year..."

Tiffany's mind instantly began to wander.

I really need to get my shit in order. I made so many promises to myself after I left Bill. Time to meet my own targets. And Karl, babe, you are dead centre in my sight! Time to do my own performance review.

Tiffany gazed longingly at the café door, as the Seagull

fluttered on. She prayed that Karl would walk through it and rescue her. An angel descended from heaven to lift her up to rapture. She didn't really believe in God, but she prayed for that one small miracle.

You owe me, God!

A shadow fell across the doorway.

Tiffany's heart raced.

And then stopped dead.

In walked Bill.

Bill's tracksuit looked unwashed and faded today. So did Bill.

His face brightened when he saw Tiffany. And darkened again when he saw the Seagull.

Okay, God. Another miracle instead. Take him out of here. Heart attack. Spontaneous combustion. Fatal diarrhoea. Whatever works for you.

Bill walked over to them.

"Hiya, Tiffs," he said, gathering as much bonhomie as he could muster in his fragile state. He gave a curt nod towards the Seagull. "Gordon."

"William." The Seagull gave a curt nod back.

With any luck, their heads will collide. Can I have that miracle instead, God?

"What brings you here, Bill?" Tiffany asked. "Don't you ever go to work any more?"

"We're here *together*," the Seagull said, as quickly as he could.

"For work," Tiffany clarified, as quickly as she could.

"I understand." Bill nodded, as slowly as he could. "I understand and it's okay. I've moved on, and it's okay for you to move on too."

"What the hell are you talking about now, Bill?" *He's more deluded than ever!* "The Sea– Gordon and I are just here to–"

"Actually, we were having a *private* conversation," the Seagull said. "So maybe you should go... maybe you should go get yourself a coffee and *leave*, William."

"I'll leave when I'm ready to leave." Bill tried to give the Seagull a hard stare. The best he could manage was a blinking gaze. "Tiffs and I have no secrets. In fact, Gordon, I know her better than *anyone* knows her."

Tiffany clutched her coffee cup, wanting to throw it at Bill.

But she hesitated, because she realised that Bill was jealous. She found that pathetic. And hilarious.

She relaxed her grip on the cup.

"Okay, Bill," she said, with an exaggerated sigh, "you're right. I can't hide *anything* from you. To be honest, Gordon and I aren't really here for work. But you could always see right through me."

"I knew it!" Bill declared. His confused eyes quivered. "No one knows you better than I do."

"Jesus wept, Tiffany!" The Seagull sounded even more confused than Bill. "Maybe we should continue this meeting back at the office."

"Oh, Gordon," she replied, grabbing his hand, "it's okay. We have to be truthful to Bill."

"Um, okay." The Seagull sounded like he was gearing up for a heart attack. "If that's what you want."

"We all have to be adults here," Tiffany said, nodding with determination. "Bill has moved on. He's found Kylie. And I've moved on. I've found Gordon. Oh, how is Kylie, Bill?"

"Who?"

"Kylie," Tiffany clarified, "your girlfriend."

"Oh, her." Bill shrugged, eyes darting from Tiffany to the Seagull. "She's… I must admit, Tiffs, I'm surprised you've managed to pull yourself back together so quickly after the huge loss when we went our separate—"

"I'm delighted to hear you and Kylie are still so happy together," Tiffany interrupted. "There's hope for all of us!"

"Now, I never said we were *happy*. Look, Tiffs, are you sure this is a good idea? I mean – and no offence, Gordon – you really could do better."

The Seagull was too busy preparing to have a heart attack to respond.

"Anyway, Bill," Tiffany said, standing up, "give my love to Kylie. She's one in a million."

"She's certainly something else," Bill said, with a sudden frown. "Where are you going?"

"Goodbye, Bill." Tiffany blew a kiss to the Seagull. "See you later, darling!"

Before either man could respond, Tiffany walked out of the café.

Bill was not an angel sent from heaven.

But at least he'd given her a pathway out of the performance appraisal.

God did indeed work in mysterious ways.

When I look at you, my tongue ties itself in knots.
When I look at you, darlin', my tongue gets itself all up into knots.
My ears fall offa my head, and my poor ol' brain just rots.

Tiffany carefully examined Letitia.

She usually made snap judgements about people and then

refused to change those initial impressions, no matter how much evidence to the contrary accumulated.

However, Letitia Ferguson was something of a conundrum. It was difficult to form a concrete first impression of someone who failed to make much of an impression.

As Robin had already explained to Tiffany, everyone in the school called Letitia Lettuce because of her less-than-compelling personality. Steady, reliable, and efficient in a crisis, but something of a drag at all other times. Even if Lettuce were a bunny boiler, she'd probably have eminently practical (and boring) reasons for her dinner choices.

She's something of a bland bombshell!

Tiffany hadn't got around to going back to the office yet after bolting from the performance review. She guessed that the Seagull would be in shock for the rest of the day and wouldn't notice her absence.

Her ramblings took her by Robin's school, and she noticed that students were beginning to pour out of the gates, a smelly, guffawing, hormone-fuelled mass of pimply teenage humanity. She decided to catch up with her nephew and walk home with him.

That's when she saw Lettuce.

Robin and Lettuce were engaged in a thought-provoking discussion on cutting-edge fashion trends when Tiffany joined them.

"I really like your socks," Lettuce was saying, with an excess of enthusiasm.

Tiffany glanced down at Robin's feet. What once were quirky and vibrant Spider-man stocks had, under Martha's secret laundry regime, disintegrated into frayed, off-orange tatters.

"Glad you like them," Robin replied. "I… um… My feet are pretty awesome too."

And with that, the sparkling conversation juddered to an awkward halt before the engine had even got warm.

What a complete tool! I should rescue him from himself.

But Tiffany decided to stay silent and monitor the unfolding verbal joust.

"What bus are you getting home?" Lettuce tried to give the conversation a push to get it moving again.

"Dad's picking me up. You should hear him screeching into the car park around 11:00 tonight."

"Oh, okay."

Lettuce didn't try to mask her disappointment.

"I was just thinking," she persisted, "I could share the bus home with you. Don't worry about it. It's fine."

Oh, pick up a hint, you clueless cabbage! She's obviously realised that Neville was a hopeless case. Did your mother teach you nothing about girls?

Robin's supply of words had been exhausted, and he just shrugged at Lettuce.

"Well, I'll talk to you later then." Lettuce walked off, barely noticed.

Robin stared after her, confused and helpless.

"Hello, Parrot!" Tiffany walked over to her nephew. "You look as useless as zips on a parachute."

"Oh, hi!" Robin jumped back in shock and instinctively reached to protect his throat. "Why aren't you at work?"

"I had my performance review today."

"Oh, did you get fired?"

"Of course I didn't get fired!" Tiffany decided not to confuse Robin any further with details about the café debacle. "I wouldn't be that lucky."

"Do you want a lift home? Dad will be picking me up some time this evening."

"Let's walk home, Parrot. Stretch those feet you're so proud of!"

"Okay, let me phone Dad."

"There's no need. He'll eventually work it out himself when he sees you're not here."

Tiffany always enjoyed making George's life a little bit more difficult.

"So tell me, Parrot," Tiffany said, after they'd walked in silence for five minutes and Robin was still lost in his own haze, "what is it about Lettuce that excites you?"

"She's amazing, isn't she?" Robin suddenly came back to life. "I've never met anybody like her."

"Neither have I," Tiffany admitted. "She's certainly uniquely… generic."

"Exactly," Robin agreed enthusiastically, "one of a kind."

"You don't seem to know what 'generic' means," Tiffany pointed out. "And you don't seem to know when a girl is giving you a hint."

"Oh, I know her very well. I've been studying her for a long time."

"Okay…" Tiffany didn't want to analyse that particular revelation too deeply. "Did you not hear her asking you to go on the bus with her?"

"Why would I go on the bus? Dad was supposed to be collecting me."

"I can't think of a better reason for getting on a bus.

Anyway, forget about your father. Just like your mother does. And let's think about you. Something your mother never does."

"I can work things out myself, you know."

"No, you can't, Parrot. You're just a man. And you're George's son. You're doubly cursed. So when you find a girl who you like – for whatever reason, no matter how watery and dull she is – you should do your best to be with her as much as possible. Get to know her. Get to enjoy her company. Pick up on the hints that are blindingly obvious to everyone else."

"Like the way you want to spend time with Karl?"

"Something like that." *The little cabbage is sharper than I thought.* "Anyway, this isn't about me. It's about–"

"So if you spend a lot of time with him, you can decide whether he's better than Bill?"

"Everybody is better than Bill." Except maybe the Seagull, Tiffany conceded. "I made one bad choice. I just want to make sure you don't make bad choices too. Get to know the lettuce and see if she really is to your taste. Assuming she has any taste in her."

"Karl mentioned today that you're meeting him for drinks later."

"Really? What did he say about me?"

"I thought we weren't talking about *you*."

Before Tiffany could strangle her nephew, her phone started ringing.

Giggles's number displayed on her screen.

"Hey, Giggles!" All thoughts of strangulation of family members temporarily vanished. "How are you? How are the corpses?"

"Oh, you know, they're all dead on!" Giggles guffawed at his joke. "How are you?"

"I'm good." Tiffany thought of Karl. And she thought of Giggles. She felt super good, actually. "I had my performance review today. And Bill turned up in the middle of it. So you can imagine what a total shitstorm that whole experience was. But at least it was a good laugh."

"Yeah, we all need a good laugh." Giggles treated himself to a good laugh there and then. "Actually, I was wondering if you're doing anything tonight."

"Um… I'm not sure yet." *It depends on where Karl wants to take me.* "Why?"

"There's a new blues club opening in town. I was thinking of checking it out. I always like to try somewhere new. Do you fancy coming to it with me?"

"Ummm… Let me get back to you." Tiffany tried to

ignore the quizzical stare Robin was giving her. "I might not be in the mood for late-night blues dreariness."

"That's close enough to a yes for me." Boundless optimism was clearly one of Giggles's coping mechanisms. "I'll check in with you later. I have to get back to my deadbeats now."

Tiffany was still smiling as she put the phone back in her pocket.

"Exactly how many men are you trying to get to know better these days?" Robin asked.

Tiffany didn't want to admit to Robin that she didn't know.

He was confused enough already.

Wine warms the soul, whiskey sets fire to the heart.
Good ol' wine warms the soul, good ol' whiskey lights up the heart.
It took two glasses with you to totally blow my world apart.

"You're just another one of those á la carte, wishy-washy religious drips." Bruno sniffed contemptuously. "You would have been no use to me when my holy jewels were slowly turning from rare to well done!"

Tiffany was starving, and all Bruno's words did was make

her mouth water in anticipation of a large steak. With some fries and onions. And a chilled sparkling water, just to keep Karl interested.

Speaking of whom, Tiffany realised she'd probably be late for the date with Karl. She picked up the pace, ignoring the agonised gasping of the overweight angel plodding beside her.

"You're going on a date with Karl this evening!" Bruno declared. He started to wave his arm in the air in a grand oratorical gesture, but apparently decided it wasn't worth the effort when he felt this close to having another angelic heart attack. "And after that, you're going on a date with that giggling clown tonight. Do you have anyone lined up for the wee small hours?"

"I still don't see what my social calendar has to do with your roasted holy jewels!"

Maybe some roast potatoes, glazed with gravy. Jesus, I'll be drooling like Pavlov's dog any minute now...

"You're completely incapable of committing to anything." Bruno shook the sweat out of his hair, an exertion that caused his face to turn a stormy purple. "Except yourself, of course!"

"What are you wheezing about now?" *Would a dessert be too indulgent? Maybe just a small Black Forest gateau... Oh, who the hell ever heard of a small Black Forest?* "I'm trying to concentrate on

231

how I can make a good impression on Karl whilst also maintaining a sparkling conversation."

Tiffany began to wonder what wine she should have with the sparkling water. How many glasses would be socially appropriate when trying to seduce a gym teacher? She wanted to get nice and relaxed and convivial… without getting shitfaced.

"As soon as you order from the menu, you start doubting yourself. Total fear of commitment. Always afraid of making a mistake or ordering the wrong thing."

"Well, I made one massive mistake in my life already." *Two if I include letting you be my spiritual guru.* "I'm allowed to be cautious from time to time. I don't want to end up like Martha."

"And what is wrong with Martha?" Bruno stopped walking in order to catch his breath and reframe his question. His face slowly faded back to a less alarming shade of overcooked salmon and his left arm stopped quivering. "She's got a better handle on her life than you do."

"She made a terrible mistake when she married George. And now she must live with that mistake. Literally!"

"Can't she just divorce him?" Bruno argued. "Or murder him? No one would really notice that he's no longer there."

"She'll never divorce him. That would be like publicly admitting that she'd made a mistake. Never gonna to happen! And she's against murder because she doesn't want to go to jail. And then there's poor Chicken to consider. He has enough instability in his life already."

Maybe chicken Kiev instead of steak. I'd have to go easy on the garlic butter, of course. Make some token gestures in the direction of healthy living.

"You're the one who's not willing to admit you're making a mistake!" Bruno reluctantly started to walk again. "Just because you've made terrible mistakes, you think that everyone else is also making terrible mistakes."

"For someone who has lived for six hundred years," Tiffany retorted, picking up the pace, just to punish Bruno, "you've learnt remarkably very little. Maybe that duke was right to roast you alive after all."

"He didn't roast me… Anyway, that's not important at this particular moment. We don't have time to talk about the endless crimes of that bastard of a duke. Back to Martha. Isn't it clear to you that Martha utterly adores George? Why else would she be spending her life with a hopeless cretin who could bore a leaf of kale to death?"

"Martha is incapable of adoring anyone!" *I should order a*

kale salad on the side, just for show. I don't have to eat the bloody thing. "She's too bitter about everything to feel any other emotions."

Tiffany was glad to see that they were near the café. She wasn't enjoying this line of exploration.

"When you see something that doesn't agree with your sour worldview, you simply ignore it," Bruno declared. "You turn a blind eye, in the easy sense."

Tiffany was thinking about how hard she'd find it to turn a blind eye to a large bowl of chicken wings.

"You just see what your jaundiced eyes want to see," Bruno continued. "You'd make a great TV evangelist, if you had the looks for it."

"Well, what I want to see right now is Karl." *Someone who is nice and easy on the eyes.* "So goodbye."

Tiffany strode into the café before Bruno could develop his argument any further.

She was glad Karl had chosen the Loose Leaf Café. They could enjoy some food and a chat without it feeling like they were on a proper date. No candles or nosy waiters to give the wrong impression. Just food and chat. Especially food!

With slight irritation, Tiffany noticed that Karl was already seated at a table. That didn't give her time to compose herself or shake off the insults Bruno had hurled at her. She made a promise to herself to be early the next time she met Karl.

Will there be a next time with Karl?

Ah yes, Karl! He did look particularly perfect this evening. He was very well groomed. (Perhaps a little bit *too well* groomed.) Neatly parted gelled hair sat confidently atop precisely shorn back-and-sides. Just the slightest hint of grey here and there, to add a dash of wise ruggedness. His well-shaven face exuded the fresh glow of healthy living, or expensive moisturiser. The goatee looked trimmed and blow-dried. Tiffany knew how difficult it could be to sculpt a presentable goatee. When Bill tried to grow a goatee, he looked like he was walking around with a lethargic rodent gnawing on his chin.

Karl smiled a Tom Cruise beam when he saw Tiffany. And Tiffany tried to reciprocate with a Julia Roberts dazzler, but it felt stiff and awkward on her lips, and soon collapsed in a confused, lippy heap.

Shit! He'll think I'm on day release!

"Sorry I'm late." *I'm not really that late, am I?* "I ran into an old... friend."

"No problem at all." Karl continued to grin as he looked at his wristwatch-slash-health monitor. Tiffany wasn't sure whether he was trying to ascertain exactly how late she was or just checking his heartbeat. "We can relax now."

Tiffany noticed that Karl somehow made the word "relax" sound like hard work, a goal that had to be pursued with single-minded determination.

Tiffany sat down, trying to *relax* and marshal her scattered thoughts. She glanced at the menu.

And then she glanced at Karl.

With his bicep-hugging light top and sleek running pants, Karl looked like he'd come straight from the gym. But he smelled like he'd come straight from an exotic spa retreat. Whenever Bill used to go to the gym – an occurrence comparable to a solar eclipse in its rarity – it could take four showers to finally flush away the reek of his sundry body odours.

Thinking of Bill's body odours risked putting Tiffany off her food. Her stomach reminded her why she was here.

"Shall we order?" Tiffany asked, noticing Karl now tapping complex diagrams on his watch. Looking at the menu, Tiffany realised that this was a health food café. "I'm in the mood for something nice."

Tiffany searched in vain for something nice on the menu.

"I hope you don't mind," Karl replied, unleashing another blinding grin that allowed no room for minding one way or the other. "I've already ordered."

"Oh, really?" *That fat bastard Bruno must have delayed me more than I realised.* "Sorry I'm so late."

"Not a problem." The grin never faltered. He was very polite. (Okay, perhaps a bit *too* polite.) "I know the menu very well here, so I took a chance."

"What did you order?" Tiffany was curious to find out how he'd found *anything* appetising on this menu. "I'm still looking for... anything."

"I ordered a Mediterranean salad and sparkling water. With a slice of lemon." The grin reached its climax. "Because I was in the mood to treat myself."

Tiffany was in the mood for a double cheeseburger with garlic chips and a side order of pizza. However, she resigned herself to some vague faux-soup dish. It appeared to be as organic and self-righteous as an early morning farmers' market. She could sneak off to the takeaway on the way home anyway. She prayed that, in the meantime, her starving stomach wouldn't roar in protest.

Tiffany gave her order – "No, of course a glass of sparkling water is absolutely fine for me too" – and looked for ways to fill the silence before their food arrived.

Looking for a neutral subject, and looking to avoid staring

into the Caribbean depths of Karl's eyes in rapt devotion, Tiffany mentioned that she'd been talking to Robin earlier that day.

"How is he?" Karl asked. "We really need to find some ways to build up his muscles. His frame is rather delicate."

"Yes, I've seen sturdier jellyfish," Tiffany agreed. "His brain is rather delicate too. Of course, he's slowly being starved to death because his mother can't cook anything. She could burn an ice cube."

"I must talk to him about nutrition. He needs to be eating proper food."

"He'd be delighted if he even got a chance to eat properly cooked food!"

"We have to be extremely careful about what we eat," Karl persisted. "No matter how many times a week we go to the gym, it can be hard to undo the damage caused by poor food choices."

"So you think he's a lost cause." Tiffany nodded sagely. "I've been trying to find a diplomatic way to explain that to his mother. But sadly, Martha is stubbornly deaf when it comes to listening to advice on how to correctly raise her son."

"No, he's not a lost cause at all!" Karl's voice was beginning to quiver with passion. "We can all change at any time, no matter how far we have let ourselves go."

Tiffany recoiled slightly from the implication. However, Karl's smile was as perfectly curled as ever, so she had to assume no malice in his words.

For now.

"Actually, I think he'll be taking a bit more care of himself from now on," Tiffany said, shifting the focus from her own failings to her nephew's failings. "Some girl in the school seems to have fallen for him."

"Really?" Karl's precisely trimmed eyebrows shot up. "That's... well, it's extraordinary."

"Unbelievable, I know," Tiffany enthusiastically agreed. "After all, he looks like a discarded scarecrow. How could any girl feel anything except pity for him?"

"Well, they do say that there's a special someone out there for everyone. But still—"

"A special someone for a special case, I suppose. Although, to be honest, his special someone isn't all that special. You probably know her. Leticia, or Lettuce as they call her. She's about as exciting as a shopping trolley."

"Yes, I know her. A very steady, non-disruptive student. Remarkably unremarkable, you could say."

"Exactly! As dry as dust. However, they might find

239

happiness together, if they don't bore each other to death."

"I suppose," Karl ventured, "we shouldn't judge books by their covers."

How come only people who look perfect say that? It's like millionaires always pontificating that money doesn't bring happiness. Boy, his book cover does look perfect today, though.

The food finally arrived. Tiffany didn't think her dish looked perfect. The "soup" appeared to be a lukewarm, muddy liquid with a sprinkling of indeterminate vegetable slices, seeds, bulbs, pips, and plastic. She sniffed it, searching in vain for an aroma.

"That looks amazing!" Karl nodded to the soup. "Tasty and nutritious. What more could you ask for?"

Some food with it maybe…

"It tastes really good," Tiffany lied, repressing the sudden urge to vomit as she swallowed the first tentative spoon of soup. "I don't think I've ever tasted anything quite like it!"

"It's really interesting," Karl explained, between enthusiastic munches of multi-green Mediterranean salad, "how our bodies instinctively like the tastes of foods that are good for us. It's as if we're programmed to like healthy food!"

"Indeed," Tiffany agreed, still battling her increasingly demanding urge to vomit. "I must get the recipe for this…

um… soup. I couldn't trust Martha to cook it. She'd turn it into a chemical weapon. The most frequent visitors to her dinner table are UN inspectors."

"You don't even need recipes," Karl continued, clearly delighted to have such an easy opening into his favourite topic of conversation. "Sometimes, you just have to listen to your body. When we mindfully prepare food, our bodies react to the potential nourishment and almost automatically guide us to the right ingredients to satisfy our… well, not quite our hunger. To satisfy our biological needs for good food. That's why animals in the wild almost never eat anything that's bad for them. They know that in order to survive, they must eat healthy food."

"That's a really interesting– "

"We used to be the same, of course," Karl plunged on, "before we started poisoning ourselves with processed food and fizzy drinks and… Are you full already? You've stopped eating."

"I'm just taking a moment to savour the taste." *And fantasise about lasagne.* "It is difficult to eat healthily all the time, though, isn't it?"

"Not at all!" The pitch in Karl's voice crept up a notch. "It's easy if we make the *proper* effort. We must try hard if we

241

want to succeed at anything in life. If we get lazy or careless, of course we'll fail. It's the complacent antelope, the one that can't resist one small Irish breakfast, that gets eaten by the lion because it's too fat to run away."

A few other diners glanced over at Karl in bemusement as his sermon reached a climax.

Oh dear God, now he's got me thinking about Irish breakfasts! I would gladly murder every diner in this café for a few sausages and a slab of black pudding.

Karl had paused in his speech in order to focus on his salad again. He chewed carefully, not letting any leaves or stalks protrude from his lips.

Nevertheless, Tiffany had to avert her eyes. She always found the sight of someone eating to be vaguely distasteful. It reminded her that humans – even perfectly formed, beautiful Adonis-esque specimens like Karl – had biological urges that had to be satisfied one way or another.

She turned her gaze to the liquid catastrophe in the bowl in front of her for some seconds, before assuming that it was now safe to look back up again. To her chagrin, she saw that Karl was still chewing contentedly, lost in the munchy moment.

"Are you chewing the cud?" she enquired, with as much

levity as her unease would allow.

Karl took the hint and swallowed his salad in a smooth, burp-free motion. "I like to eat mindfully," he explained. "It's important to thoroughly savour the taste and chew the food before swallowing it. Take time to appreciate every nuance in the experience."

"I see." *Exactly what taste is there to savour in a salad?* "If you lived with my sister, you wouldn't linger over your food. You'd try to fast-track it to your stomach before the taste registered."

"You should try cooking your own meals," Karl replied enthusiastically. "It could become a communal sharing experience, along with Robin and his father!"

"George couldn't find his way around a frying pan," Tiffany explained. "And I sort of got out of the habit of cooking after I left Bill. I started treating myself to meals out instead, and that soon became the new habit."

Tiffany had hated eating in the flat on her own. The silence and the bland aromas from her plate would depress her. Bill was the better cook in the relationship. Indeed, his meals were one of the few things that she really missed about him. Glancing at her alleged soup, Tiffany felt a sudden craving for one of Bill's korma surprises.

Thinking about Bill made it difficult for Tiffany to enjoy

her time with Karl. So she banished Bill back to the dark torture dungeons of her mind by focusing her attention again on the man sitting across the table from her.

He really was an immaculately groomed (perhaps *too* immaculately groomed) specimen. Each individual hair on his head seem to politely complement all the others in a graceful, stylish symphony. His neatly tended goatee gave him just the right hint of edginess without any of the smelliness. And his aftershave hinted at the dizzying scents of a citrus billionaires' exotic conference.

"Are you not going to finish your soup?" Karl enquired.

"Oh, maybe not." *Shit! I need to stop gawping at him.* "I find that I fill up quickly when the food is this good."

"This salad tastes out of this world!"

"It certainly does bring to mind scary little green men!"

Karl didn't seem to see the hilarity in Tiffany's remark.

"You know," Karl continued, having finally chewed and swallowed the last of the extra-terrestrial salad leaves, "I could help you with your nutrition problems."

"My... *what?*" Tiffany tried to regain control of her offended eyebrows. "Martha's cooking is the problem."

Karl took a slow contemplative sip of water before proceeding, with due caution.

"It's easy to make excuses, I know." His smile was a mix of sympathy and pity. "However, each of us has to take responsibility for our own choices."

Tiffany began to suspect that she'd made a bad choice when she agreed to meet Karl.

"We're all responsible for our own choices." Karl was developing his pitch. "But we often need some guidance to help us make the right choices. A bit of direction. A mentor, even…"

"Not all of my choices have been catastrophic." Tiffany again tried to bundle Bill back into the dungeon. "I walk regularly in the hills, for example."

"That's a good start," Karl amiably conceded. "But you need a regular exercise routine with regular nutrition."

"It's a hill." Tiffany wasn't sure why she felt so defensive. "It's hard work. My friends have a hard time keeping up when they come with me."

"Hard work makes us stronger." Karl was beginning to get evangelical again, oblivious to the annoyed glances from other diners. "Tell you what. I could put together a health regime for you, incorporating fitness, nutrition, and of course some meditation to smooth out the sharp edges of your emotions. I do that for a lot of my clients!"

Tiffany suddenly wasn't sure whether this was a date or a sales pitch.

"That's a… um… very… interesting, I suppose, offer." *Clients?* "I'm not sure I'm ready to take that sort of plunge."

She could almost hear Bruno laughing at her in the background.

"If you want to change your life," Karl insisted, staring straight into her eyes, "you must commit to change. We can't find fulfilment without commitment. So, Tiffany, are you ready to commit?"

Tiffany smiled and sipped her water.

She knew right then that she certainly wasn't ready to commit to Karl. Maybe it was time to commit to Giggles.

You pluck the strings, baby, you send a shiver up my heart.
When you pluck my strings, you send them shivers right up my heart.
You shatter my spine, baby, you blow my mind apart.

Deep down, Tiffany knew that this was bad.

Really bad!

Two sort-of dates in the one day could give people the wrong impression of her. It gave Bruno such a bad impression that he refused to come along with her (much to her relief), muttering darkly about the fall of Babylon.

She'd told Giggles that she'd meet him inside the Weeping Willow club. Looking at the club's grubby exterior – all cracked windows, chipped paint, and strident cobwebs – she again found herself marvelling at how anyone could actually enjoy blues music.

The aficionados were out in force, of course. Pampered students in second-hand clothes, trying to look poor and authentic despite their expensive haircuts and complicated smartphones. Middle-aged businessmen with bloodshot eyes, sad stubble, and beer bellies, looking for verification that there were actually some people even more miserable than they. Pious music critics with anguished goatees and distressed jackets.

The club's grunginess reminded Tiffany of her student days and Oscar the Goatee. The warm fuzzy embrace of hash, when every care in the world seemed to dissolve into oblivion for a few hours. And then the haze would clear, and reality would come back into focus.

Tiffany just hoped that she wouldn't bump into anyone who knew her. She wanted to have Giggles to herself, albeit in the safe confines of a crowd of strangers.

"Well, hello again, dear," a familiar friendly voice chirped beside her. "Fancy seeing you here."

Tiffany turned around to see who was going to ruin her evening with poetic couplets.

The two nuns from St Peter's church were standing apart from the crowd, enjoying a smoke break before heading into the club.

"What are you two doing here?" *And what the hell are you smoking?* "Has the entire heavenly brigade been unleashed to interfere with my life today?"

The nuns were in civilian clothes this evening, wearing surprisingly stylish black leather jackets and even more surprisingly tight blue jeans. Their faces were as beatific as ever, despite the aromatic smoke swirling around them.

"You know our job," the taller one said. "We focus on saving lost souls."

"And where better to find lost souls," the other nun expanded, "than a blues club?"

Tiffany could spot a few lost souls queuing up to go into the club, their expressions as shabby as their suits.

"The more important question," the taller nun said, "is what are *you* doing here?"

"I'm here because I want to listen to some blues music, obviously!"

"You're here because you don't know what you want," the nun corrected her. "You're here because you want to keep your options open. Still surveying the menu!"

"And anyway," the smaller nun asked, "what exactly was wrong with the hot young gym monkey you were with earlier? Apart from his droopy ears, of course."

"There was nothing really wrong with him." *What droopy ears?* "He was perfect in many ways. Not every way, but many ways."

"I see." The taller nun took a deep drag on the joint before handing it back to her companion. "That's exactly what was wrong with him. There was nothing wrong with him apart from the ears."

"What are you mumbling about now?" *I wish she'd pass that rollie to me!* "Why do nuns never talk any sense?"

"His perfection, specifically his raw physical perfection, makes you too aware of your own imperfections," the smaller nun persisted, undeterred, smiling through the insult and the smoke. "You can't fix him, so you have no project to distract you from your own flaws."

"And that's why you stayed with Bill for so long," the taller nun added. "His innumerable flaws would keep you busy for decades!"

The two nuns smiled their infuriatingly sympathetic smiles at Tiffany.

"You know nothing about me," Tiffany replied, resisting the urge to grab the joint from the nun's beautifully manicured hand. "Just because you're stoned off your faces doesn't mean that you're talking any sense."

Tiffany stormed into the club before the nuns could reply. She had enough of righteous interfering in her life for one day. For the rest of the evening, she was going to enjoy herself, listening to depressing music, drinking warm, over-priced cocktails, and laughing at Giggles's jokes.

A wall of heat, sweat, and mushy blues hit her when she entered the club. The dim lighting added to the abandoned graveyard vibe, whilst also hiding the most alarming of the stains on the walls and chairs. The place was crammed with the usual opening-night crowd, all desperately seeking the next hot spot.

The club was certainly hot, with no ventilation to be felt anywhere. Tiffany doubted she'd last more than an hour in the place. She was already craving the fresh, hash-infused air outside.

On stage, the Wonky Donkeys were making their ponderous, oh-so-earnest way through their set. They seemed to have got themselves lost in some discordant blues riff that coiled menacingly around their instruments, like a hungover alligator with a persistent earache. The lead singer was resting his vocal cords as he tried to find a chord sequence that would guide them to the song's ragged conclusion, a jazz-inspired improvisation that looked about to degenerate into shambolic amateurism.

She looked around for Giggles. Only he could lighten the dour mood.

"I love this band," a raspy voice declared beside her. "They could play cabaret night in purgatory."

Something in the timbre of the voice raised Tiffany's hackles.

It couldn't be him, could it?

She glanced around and, sure enough, there stood Jehovah. Not *stood*, exactly. He swayed uncertainly, his feet unsure of where of the floor was. Workplace Jehovah had been inflicted on her over the years. This was her first encounter with Casual Jehovah. It was no improvement.

"What the hell is a sanctimonious knob like you," she asked, astonished, "doing in a dump like this? Shouldn't you be listening to some uptight choir down by the river? What happened to your conversion?"

"I love blues music!" Jehovah declared, a bit too loudly. "It's really grown on me ever since Gordon introduced me to Toenails Flaherty."

Jehovah closed his eyes in rapture as the Wonky Donkeys began to crank out a graveyard riff that the singer unsuccessfully tried to sing along to.

"Who's your friend?" another voice suddenly asked.

Tiffany jumped.

Why the hell is everyone sneaking up on me tonight? If I go to the toilet, Bill will probably pop up out of the crapper.

Tiffany's attention was so riveted on the stoned colleague in front of her that she hadn't noticed Giggles come into the club. She'd even momentarily forgotten why he was there.

"Oh, there you are!" Tiffany tried to recover her composure. "Okay, first of all, he's not my friend. He's a work colleague. And even that's stretching the truth a bit, considering the amount of backstabbing he does. He should make pin cushions for a living."

Giggles nodded, patiently waiting for Tiffany to introduce him. However, Tiffany appeared to have got stuck in a furious reverie about some work-related slight that she blamed Jehovah for. And Jehovah was busy smiling to himself as he drifted off into a bluesy haze of three-chord oblivion.

"I'm Ray," Giggles finally declared, with a surprising amount of pride. "Though my friends call me Giggles. I'm not entirely sure why, ha ha ha."

Giggles enthusiastically extended his hand to Jehovah, where it hovered in mid-air as Jehovah struggled to bring the hand into focus.

After a few aborted attempts, he grasped the extended hand of friendship and then grimly held on to it as he tried to retain his balance.

"I work with Tiffany," Jehovah explained, trying to engage his slightly numb tongue. "I work hard, and she hardly works."

Giggles laughed fulsomely at this, until he realised that it wasn't a joke.

"I'm a friend of Tiffany's too," Giggles explained. "Well, first I was a friend of her ex, but now I'm *her* friend. And still her ex's friend. But I'm not yet her ex-friend. Actually, this is getting quite complicated!"

"Again, Jehovah is not my friend," Tiffany clarified through clenched teeth.

"Tiffany and I have been friends," Jehovah explained, "ever since she started working with... pretending to work with me a few years back."

"Yes. In fact he's been working against me for around

three years now," Tiffany added.

"So, do you like blues music?" Giggles asked, as Tiffany glared at Jehovah and he gaped back at her, still holding on to Giggles's hand for support and protection. "It's not really my groove. I much prefer Estonian death metal."

"Well... I suppose it's a rich... and complex musical form." Jehovah was struggling to find the right words. On stage, the singer was also struggling to find words as he got lost in the song's unnecessarily complex narrative. "I suppose it celebrates the resilience of the human spirit while, at the same time, simultaneously accepting the nihilist impermanence of–"

"Oh, Christ on a scooter!" Tiffany interrupted. "The only reason he's here is because he thinks the Seagull will be here. Even though he's stoned off his tiny nuts, he's still trying to climb the career ladder. You're impressing no one, Jehovah!"

"In fairness, I don't think *anyone* impresses you, Tiffany," Giggles remarked while Jehovah searched in vain for a suitably robust response.

"The crazy thing is," Tiffany continued, settling herself into a roll now, "the feathery shite doesn't even like blues music. He only listens to it because he thinks *I* like it. And I hate it because it reminds me of Bill. In fact, the only person

254

who likes blues music is Bill, and his brain was already donated to medical science when he was born."

"When Bill likes something, he really likes it," Giggles said, as Jehovah struggled to follow the chain of Tiffany's logic. "He seems to have completely fallen down the well for Kylie, for example."

"What exactly does that little grinning bimbo slagheap have to do with anything?" Tiffany swung her glare on Giggles. "And how come we still have empty hands? It's hard enough to listen to this dreary shite when you're wrecked, but it's totally impossible when you're stone cold sober!"

"Oh yeah!" Giggles took the hint. "It was nice to meet you, Jeremiah… Umm, you can let go of my hand now, by the way."

Jehovah's puzzled gaze was fixated on the lead guitarist's fingers, as he tried to untangle his thoughts. Giggles, meanwhile, tried to untangle his fingers from Jehovah's.

Tiffany frogmarched Giggles away, scanning the club to make sure Bill hadn't crept out from any dark corner while she'd been distracted by Jehovah.

"What would you like to drink?" Giggles asked, when they'd carved their way to the disconcertingly sticky bar.

"Anything that helps me to forget about that pious

gobshite! Gin and lemon, for now."

"Gin to make you sin… Oh Jesus, did I say that out loud? Sorry! Obviously, I have no intention of–"

"It's just a drink, Giggles!" Tiffany laughed. "Relax and enjoy the evening."

Tiffany studied Giggles as he tried desperately to get the barman's attention. His skinny jeans emphasised his well-toned legs, she noted with pleasure.

They also emphasised the middle-age curve of his beer gut, she noted with displeasure.

Oh well, not every guy can look as perfect as Karl.

Karl's flawless body – droopy ears aside – could make up for his other flaws, maybe.

The Wonky Donkeys were trying to lighten the mood with a jangly instrumental that reminded Tiffany of a dentist's drill.

The crowd, now well lubricated, seemed to like it though, admiring the piece's searing commentary on the dour seriousness of blues purists. Or something.

"You never used to drink gin" Giggles said, finally passing her drink to her. "It this another post-Bill change?"

"A new drink, a new me," Tiffany replied, forcing a laugh. "What was it you said? Gin to make you sin, lemon to make you bitter."

"I never said you were bitter... Oh Good God, don't tell me I said that out loud too!"

"What?" Storm clouds descended on Tiffany's face.

"Bill's all about change these days." The grim lighting couldn't hide Giggles's flustered blush. "What with Kylie and all."

"Her again?" *Now I am beginning to feel bitter!* "I thought you wanted to spend the evening me."

"I wonder what Kylie drinks," Giggles pondered, after a long drink of beer.

"Poison, hopefully." *Did I say that out loud? I'm getting as bad as him!* "I mean–"

"Something fizzy and fun, just like her." Giggles smiled off into the hazy distance, until Tiffany's aggressive throat-clearing brought him back to the here and now. "Sorry, what?"

"How is your work going these days? This dump must remind you of the undertaker's place. It's about as lively!"

"It's all deadly." There was the Giggles laugh that Tiffany needed! "The working hours are flexible, even though many of the customers are stiff."

"Is Bill one of your customers now?" Tiffany asked, after the obligatory laugh. "It'd be the only time anyone got him to shut up!"

"If he ends up on our slab, it'd be a grave situation indeed. But that would free up Kylie for... Oh, look, here comes your friend Abraham."

Before Tiffany could correct Giggles again, she turned around to see Jehovah edging his uncertain way towards them.

"Are you having a good time with your new, ahem, friend?" Jehovah asked, steadying himself at the bar.

"I'm not her new, ahem, friend," Giggles clarified. "As I said, we've been friends for years. Ever since she was going out with Bill."

"Which one was Bill again?" Jehovah asked with an exaggerated, bloodshot frown. "It's hard to keep up with *all* of Tiffany's men, of course. I'm never sure which are the steady ones and which are the unsteady ones."

"You're looking pretty unsteady yourself there, Jehovah," Tiffany remarked. "And if you don't stop with the snide jabs, you'll be stoned in more ways than one."

"We're not exactly steady," Giggles explained, after another long draught of beer. "Although I'm not too unstable either, I don't think, ha ha ha."

Jehovah joined politely in the laughter, and then seemed unable to stop for some seconds.

While the giggle fit unfolded, Tiffany turned her attention to the band. They had locked into a slow-burning riff that grumbled with swampy menace. Tiffany wondered if it would put her to sleep. The singer was signalling excitedly to someone in the audience.

"Come on up, sister," he shouted. "Let's show these heathen hippies how we do things at Bible school!"

There was an excited commotion around the stage as the smaller nun scrambled up to join the singer, her denim legs getting tangled up in the cables and mic stands. Once on stage, she took something out of her leather jacket and turned around to the crowd to bless them with a sign of the cross.

Is that a crucifix she's holding?

Closer inspection revealed it to be a blues harmonica. The sister brought it to her lips with more passion than Tiffany believed nuns were capable of.

"Sister Misty, everyone!" The singer applauded along with the ecstatic crowd. "Blow me away, sister!"

Sister Misty began to blow a slow, smoky riff more at home in Parisian brothels than Irish convents. Each provocative wheeze was answered by a searing guitar lick, while the lead singer moaned in tongues – or slipped into a stroke.

"Didn't Bill play the harmonica?" Giggles asked. "It used to be his party piece. That and limbo dancing. Neither ever ended well, come to think of it."

"Yes, indeed." Tiffany shuddered at the memory of Bill in his Donald Duck outfit, blaring into his harmonica in the worst seduction rite in human history. The disconcerting thing was that the seduction worked. Tiffany didn't want to dwell on any of that. "And why are we talking about Bill now?"

"Bill is going steady with Kylie now, Joshua," Giggles explained to Jehovah, who was now transfixed by the vision of the writhing nun on the stage. "He and Kylie are playing the same tune and hitting all–"

"And why are we talking about Kylie again?"

"Why are you all here tonight?" Sister Misty was suddenly launching into a sermon as the guitars wriggled around her. "I said, what brings you all here tonight?"

She swooped into another bordello vamp as the crowd roared its approval.

"So, is Kylie the replacement Tiffany?" Jehovah asked. "A new model, so to speak?"

"Do they still burn sanctimonious trouble-makers in this part of town?" Tiffany replied. "We can arrange some matches and–"

"To be fair to Bill," Giggles said, deftly coming to Jehovah's rescue before Tiffany's glare could start to singe his hair, "he did wait until he was finished with the old model before slipping into a new model."

"Old model?" *I'd like to roast the two of them at stake. Kill two clowns with the one fire.* "You're clomping on very thin ice, Giggles!"

"Of course, it took him a while to realise that the old model… the previous model was gone." Giggles was oblivious to Tiffany's death rays. "Took him a few months, in fact."

"You're here because you want to find salvation, sinners," Sister Misty shouted to the gyrating crowd. "Someone to wash you clean so you can start afresh. Lord have mercy!"

"A few months?" Tiffany asked. "What the hell is wrong with that idiot? Why did it take him so long? I knew the next morning that things were over between us!"

"Probably because you had a new man in the bed beside you," Jehovah suggested.

"There'll be a new man sitting at your desk at work next week, Jehovah, if you're not careful."

"Fresh water always tastes sweeter!" Sister Misty was still testifying from the stage as the band beat out an orgasmic throb. Suddenly, she turned to look directly at Tiffany. "We spend our days looking for those cool, clear crystal waters."

Why's that self-righteous, interfering bitch staring at me now?

"But sometimes we don't realise that we're already swimming in them!" Sister Misty threw her hands up to heaven, and the crowd, assuming this to be the latest dance move, did the same. "We don't realise that we already have salvation right in front of us! We are so busy looking for someone to rescue us that we don't realise that we've already been saved. Amen! Hallelujah!"

"Hallelujah!" Jehovah shouted, caught up in the moment.

"You're beyond rescue!" *Maybe I am too.* "You're just like Bill."

"Well, Kylie rescued Bill anyway," Giggles suggested, stopping as he felt the intensity of Tiffany's glare. "He's as devoted to her now as a shelter puppy."

Tiffany had never worried about Bill being unfaithful. She'd always assumed that no other woman – nor man, nor animal, mineral, nor vegetable – would be interested in him. He was her project, hers to fix and then send on his way.

On stage, Sister Misty continued to preach the good word about salvation, as the crowd gleefully hollered its approval.

Maybe Giggles was right. Maybe Kylie did rescue Bill.

But who is going to rescue me?

Could it be Giggles, with his breezy attitude that always – nearly always – made her laugh? Could it be Karl, with his perfect – almost perfect – body? Ears could always be fixed, after all.

Or was Bruno, with his sweaty gasps and apocalyptic odours, her saviour? Would he teach her to rescue herself?

You're telling me I'm wrong, sister, even before I've spoken.
How can I be wrong, sister, when I haven't even spoken?
How can I say a word when this ol' pen's already broken?

9

Boiled Blues for Dinner

Holy Mary, mother of God, it's time to give up this cross.
Listen to me, mother of God, I gotta give up this ol' cross.
I been carryin' it so long, it's covered in moss.

"Jesus told us to love our neighbours," Fr Twitter announced from the altar. "Of course, that's not always easy to do. Especially if they play techno until five in the morning and then throw beer cans at you when you politely ask them to turn it down. I think they were all on drugs or something. The smell of marijuana from that flat would floor an elephant. Brought me right back to my days in the seminary. Funny how smells can play tricks on the mind... Now, where was I?"

The aimless throat-clearing that greeted this opening salvo indicated how much attention people were paying to the sermon.

"A famous philosopher – Harpo Marx, I think it was – once said that hell is other people," Twitter continued, having given up his search for the thread of his sermon. "But I know that philosopher was wrong. Hell isn't other people. Do you know what hell is?"

More aimless throat-clearing from the seats.

"I'll tell you," continued Twitter, having waited an embarrassingly long time for a response. "Hell is having no other people. Hell is being alone in this world. We all need companions. God didn't create us to be alone."

"Oh dear God," Martha said to George. "The man has finally lost the plot. Has no one told him that priests are supposed to be celibate? There are two types of men who should be left alone: priests and idiots. Of course, that takes care of ninety-five percent of the male population, but such is life. George, stop playing Sudoku on your phone!"

"Hmmm."

Martha grabbed the phone and stuffed it in her handbag.

Despite what Fr Twitter said, Tiffany was rather enjoying being single, for now. It was nice to have solitude and not be disturbed.

She glanced down when her phone pinged. Ignoring Martha's exasperated gasp, she checked the message.

Let me know when suits for a consultation. K

Tiffany suspected this wouldn't be a consultation in the biblical sense. Thinking about Karl tingled her deep inside herself in ways that she admitted weren't entirely suitable in a chapel.

"We never know who is going to wander in our garden," Twitter was saying. "Our garden may be blooming. It may be full of weeds. It may be... Has anyone seen Mr D'Arcy lately, by the way? It really is time he weeded the church garden. You could hide a baby giraffe in the nettles out there. I got a terrible sting the other evening when I was sleepwalking... Anyway, such is life. We never know what it has in store for us."

Tiffany found herself idly nodding in agreement. She thought she'd have a bright, shiny path ahead of her once she'd left Bill. However, that path proved to be strewn with as many weeds as Fr Twitter's garden.

Another phone ping. Another exasperated sigh from her sister.

Bumped into Kylie in town. We're having a coffee at Maestro Bistro. She says hi! G

"What the hell?" Tiffany grimaced when she realised she'd said that out loud. The six smiley faces Giggles had appended to the end of his message showed he was, as usual, unaware of how much he had infuriated her.

"But, you know," Twitter philosophised, mainly to himself, "you never know whom you're going to meet on the road of life. Anyway, always keep your heart open... no, always keep your arms open... always keep your eyes open on the road of life. Love might be walking towards you and indeed it may pass you by if you're not careful."

Ping. Sigh. Glance.

This latest communication was from Bill.

Have u seen Kyl, Tiffs? She went out to get me headache tablets and didn't come back yet.

For the first time that morning, Tiffany smiled.

Sometimes you want a meal, sometimes you want a snack.
I'll be your hot meal, darlin'. I'll be your tasty snack.
Whenever I give myself to you, you always send the plate back.

Although the atmosphere around Ernie's Sunday dinner table was markedly warmer than the usual atmosphere around Martha's Sunday dinner table, it was still a tad frosty. Ernie, Tiffany, Robin, George, and Martha all felt the icicles in the air. This was because another bitter cold front had swept through Ernie and Claude's warm domestic bliss.

Ernie was a bit sketchy on the details, just hinting darkly about "razor-sharp silences", "death stares", "knicker fits", and "prima donna bullshit".

Apparently, there'd been a profound disagreement about where to go on holiday this summer. A disagreement about flights soon developed into a disagreement about expectations, infidelities, broken promises, broken bottles, and broken door handles.

The net result was that Claude was no longer speaking to Ernie. However, Claude was diplomatic enough to vacate the dining room while Ernie had guests. Instead, he let his absence make his point for him.

The diplomatic thing to do, of course, would have been to ignore his absence.

"So where's Claude today?" Tiffany asked Ernie.

"Oh, he's sulking in the kitchen," Ernie replied with a shrug, "busy tearing up photos of me."

"Goodness." Tiffany didn't bother hiding her smile. "Seems like every couple gets its time in the trenches!"

"Don't judge all couples by your tragic standard!" Martha snapped. "George and I are very happy, aren't we, George?"

"Hmmm?"

"Well, if you call Sudoku puzzles and burnt pancakes the secret to happiness," Tiffany replied, "I suppose you must be happy. That's what you tell yourself."

"Tiffany's got a point, Mar," Ernie piped up, glad to ensure the focus stayed away from his own domestic carnage. "Whatever happened to your sense of adventure?"

"We used it as collateral on our mortgage," said Martha. "Anyway, what happens in our house is nobody's business!"

"If we knew what most couples get up to at night when no one's looking," Ernie said, "we'd be afraid to close our eyes."

"I can barely believe what you pair get up to during the day," Tiffany replied. "You'd make the devil blush with your carry-on."

"George, do you think there's not enough excitement in our life?" Martha turned her death-sentence stare on her Sudoku-distracted husband. "I've never heard you complain."

"Hmmm? Oh... Of course, pumpkin patch. I think the excitement levels are perfectly adequate for the scope and scale of our interdependent variables in real-time analysis..."

"Why can you never give a simple answer?" Martha turned to Ernie. "If you asked him the time, he'd draw you a blueprint for a watch factory."

The tension between Claude and Ernie mingled effortlessly with the tension between Tiffany and Martha, the tension between Ernie and Tiffany, and the tension between Martha and George.

The food, however, was the saving grace, as usual. There were two places in life where Claude excelled: the kickboxing ring and the kitchen. The minestrone soup he'd made was fit for fussy royalty, and George almost wept with gratitude as he savoured each swallow.

"Must you really lick the spoon like that, George?" Martha glowered at her husband. "People will think you're part Labrador."

"You must give Martha the recipe for this soup," Tiffany said to Ernie. "I'd love to see her ruin another masterpiece."

"If you don't like the food in my house," Martha pointed out, for the seventieth time, "you know where you can go. Tell her, George!"

George was still rapt in the glory of Claude's soup. The smell. The texture. The colour. The funny way it seemed to wink at you when the sunbeams caressed it. He almost felt ashamed to eat it. He was unworthy of it.

"I hear you've been seen around town hanging off Robin's gym teacher," Ernie remarked to Tiffany. "How's that going?"

"Well, he hasn't asked me to move in with him yet, if that's what you mean!"

"Don't wait to be asked." Martha took full advantage of the opening. "Just move in with him. Pack your bags tonight and go. I'll even get George to drive you there."

"There's certainly a lot to like about him." Tiffany allowed herself some seconds to bask in the memory of Karl's brilliant smile. "But I'm beginning to wonder if it's all just some meaningless passing phase. Like one of Ernie's pathetic obsessions."

"You even insult me at my own table," Ernie grumbled. "All that venom inside you is going to poison you some day. If Claude doesn't poison us all first."

"Here's another suggestion," Martha persisted, unwilling to give up the advantage. "Just turn up at his door and pretend that he asked you to move in. If he denies it, you'll just have to lie."

"I can't lie," Tiffany protested.

"Why the hell not? Every relationship needs a few white lies to survive. Do you think Claude would stay with him if Ernie always told him the truth about what he gets up to? And don't pretend that you've never lied to Bill!"

"In my defence," Ernie began, fearful that Claude might overhear the conversation, "I must clarify that any lies I've ever—"

"Have you ever lied to George?" Tiffany asked.

"Of course not," Martha lied. "He never listens to me, so I never have to lie. He's not even listening to us now. He's too busy caressing the soup!"

"Do you ever lie to me, Ma?"

"Shut up, Robin." Martha brushed away Robin's question as if it were a fly in a firestorm. "The grown-ups are getting ready to tear strips off each other."

Robin returned his attention to the glories of the soup.

"You'll have to forgive your mother," Ernie said. "She's spent the last fifteen years punishing you for a difficult pregnancy and birth. You were an indecisive little git back then too. You couldn't decide whether to come out or stay in! You obviously took after your father."

"The boy doesn't need to know about his family history, Ernie," Martha argued. "I feed and clothe him. What else does he need?"

"Your poor mother is rebelling against impending old age," Ernie continued, steering the conversation towards Martha's discomfort. "She lost her youth back when you were born. And your father never really was a youth. Isn't that right, George?"

"Hmmm?"

"But remember this, Robin." Ernie put a fatherly hand on Robin's shoulder. "Just because your father is barely aware of your existence, it doesn't mean that he doesn't care about you. He does! He'd probably care about you a bit more if you were a Sudoku puzzle, but don't dwell too much on that."

"What do you mean by impending old age?" Martha asked. "I'm still in my prime of—"

"Stop fooling yourself." Ernie laughed. "You can't stay young forever. That train's going to keep moving, no matter how much you cling to the platform. That's why you're so jealous of Tiffany."

"Why the hell would I be jealous of *her*?"

Having thrown the shark into the water, Ernie knew it was time to vacate the swimming pool. He got up and went into the kitchen to see how Claude's fury was progressing.

"I don't know why you're all so infatuated with this soup." Martha pushed her bowl away from her, with a concerned glance at her departing brother. "I could rustle up a better broth in my sleep."

A diplomatic silence followed this pronouncement.

"George," Martha suddenly ordered, "tell your son to stop slurping into the bowl. We're not at home now."

"What, sweet sherry?" George was still lost in a minestrone dreamland.

"Do as your father says," Martha told Robin. "And stop licking the spoon. Has he taught you nothing but bad habits?"

Robin put the spoon back into the bowl. He had to accept that all the soup was gone now.

"I don't think George could teach anybody bad habits," Tiffany remarked. "How you two have managed to keep your marriage ticking over is beyond me!"

"We're hardly going to take marriage guidance advice from *you* now, are we?" Martha settled into the high moral ground. "You go through men like the cat goes through blankets."

"Are you going to take advice from him instead?" Tiffany nodded towards ashen-faced Ernie, who'd re-emerged from an obviously fraught little encounter with Claude in the kitchen.

He began to clear away the soup bowls. He didn't even notice George's fingers lingering longingly on the bowl.

"I'll get the main course now," Ernie said, getting up with a rattling sigh. "Let's get that over with."

Robin watched Ernie go into the kitchen.

"What's taking him so long to get the food, Ma?"

"Stop moaning like a broken goat, Robin!" Martha reached across the table to slap him with her napkin. "George, why can't you talk some sense into your son? Pretend he's a Sudoku puzzle, if that helps you."

"Your mother's right, Robbie." George had no idea what Martha had been talking about, but he always found it useful to begin any expression of opinion with these words. "You should listen carefully to what she's saying and remember to…. Oh my goodness!"

The dining room was engulfed with the aroma of Sunday roast as Ernie returned with the main course. Roast beef, tender as trifle, succulent as a sponge soaked in the juices of a cow that had died a happy death. Roast potatoes, smooth on the inside, crispy on the outside. Carrots and peas, parboiled to perfection. And the most delicate drizzle of herbs and spices, complementing the flavours into a dizzying carnival of taste.

"Here's the main course," Ernie announced, putting the plates on the table. "As you can see, Claude has once again excelled himself in the kitchen. He won't be joining us, though. He's having… an episode. It'd be safer inviting a bucket of wet wasps to join us for dinner… Are you weeping, George?"

"No, no, no," George whimpered, hastily flicking away a tear of gratitude as he stared entranced at the feast before him. "This food looks… I'm lost for words."

"So is Claude, apparently," Ernie answered, with a sour glance towards the kitchen. "His tongue must have been paralysed by a bout of self-righteous bile. Anyway, I'd like some peace and quiet. I feel like someone's demolishing a cathedral inside my head."

"Have you got nothing to add to the conversation, George?" Tiffany asked. "Or are you too busy trying to seduce that slice of roast beef?"

"Don't expect him to express an opinion," Martha answered with a husband-ward glare. "He's been sitting on the fence so long, he's worn an arse groove into it."

"You really need to develop a kinder, gentler iron fist, Mar," Ernie said, before launching an attack into his meal. "I see you like the beef, Robin."

"Mmmph," Robin answered, as the greater part of a cow got comfortable in his mouth. "Mmmmlllllyyy."

"Another profound contribution from our boy." Martha sighed.

"Poor boy hardly ever gets to eat real food," Tiffany said, with a sad shake of her head. "Of course, just because his mother can't feed him doesn't mean that he has to starve to death. You'd see more meat on a fossil than on that boy."

"I hope you choke on your beef," Martha snapped, slamming her cutlery on the table. "I'm getting really sick of your constant—"

"Please, everybody," Ernie pleaded. "Bring it down a notch. Or better still, put it on mute. There's enough crackling tension in this house already without you adding to it."

Everyone had to agree that the food was too delicious to be ignored any longer. Soon the only sound was happily chewing teeth as a contented silence descended on the table. And the occasional ecstatic moan from George. And a happy sigh from Robin.

At last! Peace and quiet. Blessed silence!

The doorbell rang.

"What fresh hell is this going to be?" Ernie threw his knife on the table and got up to answer the door. "If it's those Jehovah's Witnesses again, this time I really will lock them in the closet."

Everyone was enjoying their food too much to pay any attention to who was at the door. So everyone was surprised to see Ernie return to the dining room. Followed by Bill and Kylie.

Time stood still as everyone took in the scene.

Bill looked like he hadn't shaved, washed, or consulted a mirror in weeks. Bloodshot eyes swam uneasily under shaggy eyebrows. Unkempt hair peeked out from beneath his Eminem hoodie. Myriad stains of mysterious origin laid claim to his jeans.

Kylie, on the other hand, looked like she'd just walked off

a photo shoot. A body-hugging red dress highlighted her ample assets. Golden ringlets cascaded down either side of her tanned face. Her dark brown eyes drank in the room.

As usual, Martha was the first one to release a missile.

"Be careful there, Kylie. Bill might smother you with his cobwebs."

Kylie's laugh was loud, uninhibited, and utterly infectious. The only one who resisted its charms was Bill, who stared at Martha as if she were the Black Death.

"Always a pleasure to see you, Martha." Bill turned his attention to his seething ex. "How are you, Tiffs?"

Tiffany continued to fume in flabbergasted silence.

"I like your dress, Kylie," said Martha, taking advantage of every opportunity to annoy her sister, "even though there's so little of it."

"It certainly doesn't leave much to the imagination," George agreed, wide-eyed and sweating. He was torn between the pleasures of the beef and the pleasures of Kylie. "A very revealing–"

"Since when have you had an imagination, George?" Martha no longer regarded Kylie as a useful ally in her war against Tiffany. "Go back to your Sudoku!"

"What the hell are those two doing here?" Tiffany's boiler

finally exploded. "Get rid of them, Ernie!"

"He can't," Bill pointed out. "After all, he invited us."

"You what?" Tiffany scanned the table for something to fling at her brother. "Are you even stupider than I think? No wonder Claude has stopped talking to you. You're a disaster."

"Let me explain," Ernie interrupted, as another corner of the cathedral collapsed inside his head. "Bill asked me if he could come along today. What could I say? I don't like saying 'no'."

"We know all about that," Tiffany said. "But what kind of brainless hamster would bring that pair into the same room as me?"

"Of course," Ernie said, turning around to Bill, "I thought he was coming here *on his own* to reconcile with you. I didn't realise he was going to bring his latest squeeze with him!"

"I'm glad he brought his squeeze," George enthused. "A most refreshing sight on a Sunday afternoon… Ouch!"

Martha breathed a sigh of relief as her kick struck George's shin with full velocity. She wasn't sure she'd hit the right leg. These under-table assaults were always tricky.

"I didn't know what to do with her," Bill explained. "She gets easily bored when I'm not around. Can't blame her, though. Once someone gets a hit of Bill, they find it hard to be without it, ha ha ha ha."

"Bill, we all know your brain stopped working back in playschool," Martha said, simultaneously preparing to launch another assault on her besotted husband, "but even by your standards, this is a ridiculous stunt. What the hell were you thinking, coming here today?"

"I actually was hoping for some lunch…"

"Why are those two still here, Ernie?" Tiffany grabbed Ernie's arm. "If you don't throw them out, I'll throw the two of them into the oven."

"I miss your spirit, babes," Bill said. "Without you, I find it very hard to get out of bed in the morning."

"Well, have a lie-on then." Tiffany had forgotten how great it felt to spar with Bill. "You'd do less harm that way."

"Can I make a suggestion?" Kylie asked.

"Of course," George enthused, leaning forward in anticipation. "I'm sure it'll be a good one."

"Actually, babes," Bill interrupted, turning to Kylie, "it might be best if you give us a bit of privacy to–"

"Why did you bring her here if you wanted privacy?" Ernie asked.

"Oh, leave it to Bill not to think things through," Tiffany said, with a disgusted snort. "Always the bull in the china

280

shop."

"Actually, I don't mind," Kylie answered with a dazzling smile. "I always love exploring other people's houses. My father used to take me when he was sneaking into–"

"Go explore the kitchen," Bill hastily replied. "No need to give everyone your entire family history."

Kylie began walking towards the kitchen.

"Perhaps you'd like me to show you the way?" George said, temporarily forgetting about the feast in front of him and getting up to follow Kylie. "Allow me to–"

"George!" Martha roared. "Kylie is perfectly capable of finding the kitchen on her own. And I'm perfectly capable of kneecapping you if you don't sit down immediately."

George reluctantly took his eyes from the feast in the red dress and returned to the feast on his plate.

"About the lunch?" Bill asked.

Ernie sat down with an exhausted slump and began darkly chewing his beef.

From the kitchen came the sound of indistinct French mumbling, followed by an explosion of flirtatious laughter from Kylie.

"Oh my goodness," she giggled, "you're just *adorable!*"

"So, how are you, Tiffs?" Bill asked, casting a brief puzzled glance towards the kitchen. "Do you still miss me?"

"Bill, please listen to me." Tiffany was making a supreme effort to be polite and reasonable. The only thing preventing her from throwing her plate at her returned ex was the mind-blowing aroma wafting up from the roast beef. "I never want to see you again. So, you can take that washed-up Barbie doll and drag yourself back home."

French laughter rumbled from under the kitchen door.

"Be careful in there, Kylie," Ernie called. "He's not all sugar and pop. He hides a nasty sting beneath his feathers!"

"I really think I should go in there," George said, about to stand up again, "and make sure Kylie is all right."

"If you don't sit down, George," Martha said, "I'll nail you to that chair. Go play with your Sudoku."

More rumbling and laughter from the kitchen.

"Bill, you had your chance," Tiffany said, returning her attention to the food. "It's time for us both to move on. You've made your mistakes – countless stupid mistakes – and have to live with the consequences."

"That's you all over," Bill replied. "You can't admit you love me, so you just give out to me instead. You seem to think I'm just something to be roared at."

"Perhaps," Tiffany conceded. "Now please stop talking

nonsense and leave us in peace."

"You call that peace?" Ernie asked, pointing an exasperated finger to the kitchen. "You'd get more peace on a rifle range."

"I've often wondered," Martha said, thoughtfully chewing her food, "if Bill says something in an empty forest, and no one hears him, is he still talking shite?"

"I'm *not* talking shite," Bill protested. More rumbling and giggling from the kitchen. "And Ernie, will you kindly explain why your boyfriend is hitting on Kylie?"

"It's his idea of revenge," Ernie answered with a sigh. "The more horrible he is to me, the nicer he has to be to everyone else."

"Remember, Tiffany," Bill continued, throwing a cautious glance towards the kitchen, "when I used to hit on you. Remember how I used to cuddle up beside you in the cinema and lick…"

"I've repressed the memory!" Tiffany shuddered. "For God's sake, Bill, we're trying to eat."

"I never forget our good times," Bill said, kneeling down so he could more easily maintain eye contact with Tiffany. He was rewarded with an icy stare of death. "I think about them every night when I go to bed… I realise my memories are very touching. I can see you're about to start crying."

"I'm about to start vomiting!" Tiffany pushed her plate away from her. "Only you could make this feast taste like raw sewage in my mouth. You're a bigger risk to food than Martha is!"

The briefest of smiles flickered across Tiffany's face. For a second, the ice in her eyes seemed to thaw.

"I look at you," Tiffany continued, the ice settling in her eyes again, "and I simply don't recognise you anymore."

"I understand." Bill nodded. "It's probably because I've started parting my hair from the other side."

"Your hair is the least of your problems. You need to change more than that."

"I have changed," Bill insisted. "I swear!"

"A leopard can't change its spots, Bill."

"No, but it can change its personality." Bill leaned in closer to Tiffany. "You really know how to wound me with your words."

"Right now," Tiffany said, recoiling, "I really want to wound you with my fists."

The laughter and mumbling in the kitchen were beginning to reach fever pitch.

"Ernie, please find out what your… companion is doing

to that poor woman," Martha said. "She's been damaged enough by hanging out with Bill these last few weeks. All she needs is a dose of Claude to finish her off... George, sit down!"

"Don't you think," Ernie said, shuddering as he glanced at the kitchen door, "Bill should be the one to rescue Kylie?"

"I've found my damsel in distress here beside me," Bill said, staring straight up into Tiffany's eyes. "You can go in there, Ernie, and rescue your damsel. You know what I mean. We're both men of the world."

"Perhaps," Ernie agreed, standing up with resigned determination, "but I'm not sure we're of the same world!"

Ernie nervously tapped on the kitchen door before entering.

Tiffany looked over at George. Unable to pursue the pleasures of Kylie, he'd returned to the pleasures of tender beef soaked in warm gravy. Meanwhile, his hand tenderly fingered the beloved Sudoku puzzle book in his pocket. For once, George looked totally at peace with the world. At least, that part of the world he was aware of.

Tiffany would have given anything for that level of simple peace.

When you came back from the farm, there were feathers in your hair.
You came back from that farm, and I saw feathers in your hair.
I know where you were, honey, and I know who put them there.

Tiffany knew that Bill was a creature of habit. She could almost pinpoint the times when he would infuriate her the most.

So, of course, he'd bring Kylie to the Spinning Pig on a Sunday evening. As grimly predictable as a migraine, poor old Bill. Therefore, Tiffany made sure she'd be there with a guy certain to stir Bill's futile jealousy.

The Seagull fit the bill.

She tried to make it seem like it was just another work-related meeting. She said she wanted a *casual* follow-up chat about the recent performance review. Best to discuss it in an informal atmosphere.

The Seagull, needless to say, readily agreed.

He had made a huge effort to appear casual. Well-cut jeans cascaded gracefully down to spotless new burgundy sneakers. The aggressively floral shirt had been meticulously ironed and sat snugly beneath a dry-cleaned blue blazer. His usually groomed hair had a sculpted scruffiness about it.

The poor sod is trying too hard!

Eager to keep her focus, Tiffany ordered an orange juice, despite the Seagull's repeated remarks that it wasn't Monday morning yet. His eyebrows predictably arched each time he said "morning".

The Spinning Pig always had a somewhat tense vibe on a Sunday evening. Saturday night's carefree abandon had been replaced by a sulky determination to eke out a few more hours' diversion from the weekend before the Monday morning alarm clock bellowed people back to their grim commutes and deadlines. Some people were still recovering from the previous evening, casting stricken glances at the bottles behind the bar. Others, having failed to set the town on fire the night before, were desperately poking at the embers of the weekend. The pulsating techno disco riffs of Saturday had faded into a more circumspect soft-rock headache throb.

The Seagull was in flying form, trying to regale Tiffany with risqué tales of his weekend exploits with his neanderthal friends from the rugby club, even though the Seagull's rugby days had long since flown away. He and his friends had been thrown out of some nightclub – Scorpio or Scorchio – for some inane reason – being too drunk or being too sober. Tiffany wasn't really listening.

"Boys will be boys," the Seagull remarked sagely, though

Tiffany suspected that these particular boys probably just bored the other customers to death with their juvenile, unoriginal antics. "Oh, Jesus wept, they will be!"

As the music continued to rumble grimly in the background, the Seagull seemed unsure about whether to portray himself as some incorrigible young buck who could still thrust his way into the heart of the action, or as a wise old wizard smiling indulgently at the escapades of his less-mature friends while he looked for something more stable and sophisticated to satisfy his complex, mysterious needs.

"And how was your weekend, Tiffany?" he asked, finally veering the conversation in Tiffany's direction. "Were you thrown out of any nightclubs?"

Tiffany didn't bother answering because, right on cue, Bill and Kylie slouched into the bar.

No surprises there!

Giggles came bounding in after them.

Okay, that's a bit of a surprise!

When she'd phoned Giggles earlier to tell him about the traumatic lunch, he hadn't mentioned that he was planning to head out this evening. Of course, she hadn't mentioned to him that she was planning to head out either. But still…

Not wanting to indulge in too many negative speculations,

Tiffany decided it was time to focus at least some attention on what the Seagull was saying.

And instantly regretted it.

"...often don't realise how deep I am. Sure, I'm as fond of superficial fun as the next guy, but what women need to understand is that I've moved beyond the wild oats stage and now want to start planting roots. But that requires deep, fertile soils. Do you understand me, Tiffany?"

"I had no idea that you were born on a farm, Gordon" was the only reply that Tiffany could muster.

"It is so hard to find a woman who is tuned into my wavelength. Maybe I'm just a bit too *complicated* for some girls."

"Or perhaps your signal is scrambled," Tiffany suggested, glancing over at the threesome further down the bar.

Giggles was gazing intently at Kylie as she berated Bill over something. Concern and hope battled for possession of his face.

"You seem distracted," the Seagull noted. "I thought you said that this meeting was urgent."

"Oh yes, of course!" Tiffany shook off the unfolding Kylie drama. "I wanted to... to talk to you about... what? Oh, that's it, my career path. I feel like I've been stuck in a pointless rut for too long."

"I see." The Seagull failed to hide his disappointment. "Well, of course, I'd be delighted to help your future in any–"

"My *career*, not my future," Tiffany clarified, wondering why Giggles was paying so much attention to what Kylie was saying. "A transition into management, for example."

"Management? Jesus wept!" The Seagull laughed heartily until he realised that Tiffany wasn't joking. "Oh, you mean you're seriously considering becoming a manager?"

"Don't you think I'm management material?" *It can't be too difficult. You do it!* "I thought you had a great interest in my career."

"Oh, I'm *very* interested in you!" The Seagull tried to unruffle his feathers as the conversation constantly slipped from his grasp. "I think I've made that clear on many–"

"Very interested in my *career*, you mean," Tiffany pointed out, nudging the conversation back into her lane. "You've always been very supportive of my career ambitions."

"Career ambitions?" The Seagull chewed his lips, trying to prevent a guffaw from escaping. "I never realised that you cared so much about your work."

"You're starting to hurt my feelings!" Tiffany was enjoying the Seagull's discomfort. "I didn't realise that you thought so little of my work ethic."

The Seagull spluttered into his drink.

"Your work ethic?" He wiped the foam from his face. "Exactly what work ethic are you talking about?"

"I thought you always admired my work!"

"Of course, I admire you." The Seagull placed a sympathetic hand on Tiffany's arm, which she instinctively swatted away. "We have a really good connection."

"I'm not talking about connections." *I know exactly what kind of connection you want to make!* "I'm talking about promotion."

Another explosion of spluttered beer.

As Tiffany waited for the Seagull to regain some semblance of dignity, she noticed Bill and Kylie walking towards her, with a sheepish Giggles in tow.

Even the background music took an ominous turn – more discordant and scratchier – as Bill approached.

"Hello, Tiffs! I see you haven't forgotten our favourite haunt. We spent many happy evenings here."

"Yes, we did spend many evenings here," Tiffany partly agreed. "Why have you dragged Kylie here?"

"Cavemen like to drag their women around," Kylie replied sourly.

"We're here to have a good time," Bill said, with a puzzled

glance at Kylie. "No matter what mood we were in earlier."

Bill and Kylie looked like they were half-heartedly trying to paper over an earlier row, being reasonably civil with each other while just about restraining themselves from scratching each other's eyes out. Things had clearly not improved too much between them since lunch.

The only happy person in the group was, as usual, Giggles. Tiffany tried to ignore her doubts about the reasons for his present happiness.

"You look rather tense, Tiffs," Bill remarked, calling the kettle black. "I hope you're not still pining for our times together. I'm sure this place brings back many sweet memories for you, but we must resist the seductive charms of poignant nostalgia and move on with determination and renewed purpose in life. Instead of longing for happiness that's past, embrace the happiness that's present. If you can find happiness, of course."

"I've already found—"

"Just look at me and Kylie." Bill wasn't going to get dislodged from his high horse that easily. "I'm very happy with Kylie. And, of course, she's very happy with me."

Kylie rolled her eyes at this analysis of the current state of their relationship.

"When you find your soul mate," Bill ploughed on, utterly oblivious, "you stick with them, through the good times and the bad times."

"Bad times?" Tiffany immediately pounced on this. "I'm so sorry, Bill, to hear that your new fling is already in terminal decline. However, Kylie, I do admire your stoicism in sticking with him for so long. It must be a great way to strengthen your character."

"I think I deserve a medal," Kylie conceded, glowering at Bill. "This man is as self-absorbed as a blow-dried cat!"

"It can indeed be difficult to find true happiness." Tiffany tilted her head sympathetically at the pair. "Thankfully, Gordon and I are very happy together. Perfect synergy, dare I say. In fact, we were just discussing our future together when you all – oh, hi, Giggles. I didn't see you there – strolled in. Isn't that right, darling?"

The Seagull gaped at Tiffany, utterly lost for words.

"Oh dear, you're still in denial." Bill shook his head sagely. "In order to cope with your loss, you just grab the nearest scarecrow and pretend that he can make you happy. Hello again, Gordon, by the way!"

"At least a scarecrow has some use," Kylie remarked. "You're about as useful as an underwater candle."

In the background, as the tensions rose in the group, the music shook itself out of its creepy groove and ambled into a light, silky chord sequence, complete with kitsch saxophone bleating. Some couples smiled and leaned in closer to each other. Others shuddered and recoiled from each other. The music dawdled on regardless.

The couples at the bar had no interest in the music.

"You know, Kylie," Giggles suddenly said, as if to remind everyone that he was still there, "it's not good for you to nurture negative thoughts. We all love your bubbly, carefree spirit. It'd really be a shame to see that sparkle squashed by simple everyday personal conflicts with friends."

"Love?" Tiffany asked.

"Friends?" Bill asked.

"Bubbly?" Kylie asked.

"I just mean," Giggles continued, ignoring the various levels of anger that were enveloping him, "that I can see – we all can see, even Bill can see – how sad Kylie is. My undertaker boss on a wet Monday morning has more sparkle. Something seems to have died inside you, Kylie, and I've no idea why. Ahem."

Giggles cast a quick glance at Bill before devoting all his attention again to Kylie.

"Bill does have that effect on people, Kylie," Tiffany agreed. "Bill's arms are where dreams go to die."

She looked carefully at Kylie. Although she had been going out with Bill for only a short while, Kylie already looked a bit world-wearier than before. Even the cheerful frizz in her hair had dampened into a sullen thatch. Maybe Giggles was on to something after all.

But why the hell is Giggles so interested in how Kylie looks anyway?

"So, Gordon," said Bill suddenly, apparently keen to divert the conversation away from himself and Kylie, "what brings you here this evening? Discussing mission-critical deliverables with Tiffs? I'd say you really know how to show a girl a good time!"

"What Gordon is delivering," Tiffany declared before an increasingly disconcerted Seagull could respond, "is none of your business, Bill! How we meet our targets is our little secret. Isn't that right, Snuggles?"

"Snuggles?" The Seagull gasped at Tiffany. "Really, Tiffany, I think that, given we have other people here, we shouldn't allow things to get out of—"

"Snuggles sees great potential in me," Tiffany explained to the others, ignoring the ever-widening of their eye sockets. "He has one eye on the here and now and the other eye on the future. He certainly doesn't live in the past."

"It's important to live in the future," Giggles agreed, "unless you work in my job, of course. Not much of a future for my clients, unfortunately, except lying flat and decomposing away."

"Oh, is Bill one of your clients?" Kylie asked, grabbing an opportunity to insult Bill before Tiffany could formulate her own snipe. "That sums him up perfectly."

In spite of her best efforts to hate Kylie, Tiffany found herself warming to the woman. Tiffany always gravitated towards women with sharp tongues and strong opinions. Kylie was evolving surprisingly fast. Another result of being with Bill, presumably.

As the cryptic romantic music shook itself into a more desperately upbeat disco–jazz confection, Tiffany noticed that Bill was still glaring at the Seagull. Her strategy was working nicely. Bill was jealous.

A bit more worrying, though, was the fact that Giggles wasn't jealous. He was still laughing wantonly at Kylie's jab at Bill. Anyway, she could deal with that later.

Now that Bill was sufficiently uncomfortable, she could turn her attention back to the Seagull's discomfort.

"So, Snuggles, what are your plans for the rest of the

evening?" she asked in as vampish a voice as she could rustle up while chirpy music jingled incessantly in her ears. "You mentioned something about exploring our data between the spreadsheets earlier."

"Jesus wept! I never did!" Aghast, the Seagull glanced around the bar to make sure no other work colleagues had wandered in. "You told me that you wanted to discuss your performance review. That's *all* I came here to discuss. We need to focus on your career path and your ongoing progression. I don't know why you're—"

"Well, I'm very happy with your performance so far, Snuggles," Tiffany replied, with a wink to Bill. "Five stars, baby!"

"Tiffany!"

"Tiffs!"

The more jealous Bill became, and the more stricken the Seagull looked, the more Tiffany enjoyed the evening.

"For God's sake, Tiffs, try to control yourself." Bill seemed to have forgotten all about Kylie, who anyway was engrossed in a whispered conversation with Giggles. "Remember that you're out in public and people can hear you. I know that our break-up was very tough on you, but you must—"

"Our break-up was as easy and satisfying as an epic bowel movement. A wonderful sense of relief!"

"Bill does tend to have a laxative effect on people," Kylie agreed, briefly tearing herself away from Giggles's anecdote.

Damn, we could be great besties under different circumstances!

The Seagull clearly felt out of his depth in the midst of all this domestic carnage. He was downing the last of his pint, with one longing eye on the door.

"What's your hurry, Snuggles?"

"Actually, I think it's best that we continue our discussions about your *performance review* in a more formal, professional setting, Tiffany. Let's meet tomorrow to put something in the diary."

Before Tiffany could reply, the Seagull was fluttering away through the crowd towards the door, his body swaying with surprising grace in synch with the jazz-fusion froth pouring from the speakers. Tiffany wasn't sure if he was trying to escape or invent a new dance craze.

"Looks like Gordon has forgotten about you, Tiffs."

"Looks like Kylie has forgotten about you, Bill."

And it looks like Giggles has forgotten about me!

As the couples around the bar eased themselves into the frivolous grooves of the bouncy music, Tiffany stood as stiff as one of Giggles's clients. She was now the one who was jealous.

It ain't easy to rise to the occasion, darlin', when you're already over the hill.
You know, it ain't easy to rise to the occasion when you find yourself over the hill.
Bring me over the bottle of whiskey, bring me over that magic little pill.

Tiffany had to get away from the lot of them!

Bill. Kylie. Giggles.

The smug, smiling couples. The silent, scowling couples. The grumpy floor staff. The infuriatingly chirpy music that chipped away at her brain.

It was time for an evening hill walk, away from everyone. Blessed solitude. Total peace. Not a single soul in sight in the smoky twilight.

Except for the sweating, gasping saint beside her.

"Were three men in the one evening just a little *too much* for you to handle?" Bruno had gone to the cinema while Tiffany was at the Spinning Pig, and he was now working his way, with grim determination, through a jumbo box of toffee popcorn. "I suppose even the whore of Babylon needed to run away to find some quality time on her own every now and then."

"I'm not running away from anything," Tiffany lied. "It's been a pointlessly stressful day and I wanted to simply slip away into the graceful beauty of nature. The hills don't judge anybody."

"Lucky for you, then!"

"Can you not feel the peace soak into you, you grouchy old carpet! See how the evening light delicately dances around the leaves, creating beautiful patterns that disappear as soon as you notice them." Tiffany took a deep breath to take in the calming waves around her and then tried to exhale the debacle of an evening from her soul. "Listen to the fragile rustle of the leaves. Listen to the sleepy twitter of the birds as they start to smooth their feathers and slumber into the night. Listen to the… God almighty! Do you have to make such a racket with that popcorn? You sound like a rottweiler in a tumble dryer!"

"I need to recharge my energy after that disaster in the cinema!" Bruno scarfed down another fistful of popcorn before proceeding. "The movie was billed as some jerk's spiritual quest to find meaning among the trees in the redwood forests or something ridiculous like that. I assumed it was a comedy. I mean, who the hell tries to find enlightenment in a forest? Apart from you, of course!"

Tiffany ignored the insult and concentrated on the less

annoying twittering of the birds instead.

"Anyway, comedy, my skinny arse! It was the most boring pile of dust since the Book of Leviticus. I was fast asleep within twenty minutes. And snoring and farting contentedly within twenty-five minutes. By the time I woke up, I had nothing to show for my evening but this box of gooey plastic. Would you like some, by the way?"

"Of course not!" Another lie. The sublime ecstasy of Claude's lunch was starting to fade and Tiffany was feeling peckish again. A mouthful of toffee popcorn would hit the spot just nicely right about now. But she wouldn't give Bruno the satisfaction. "I'm watching my figure."

"I think the problem is that you're worried that no one is watching your figure. That's why you ran away from the three loco amigos this evening!"

"Once again, I didn't run away!" Tiffany didn't want to have that argument again. "I just think it's important to be careful about what you eat. I think I've come to realise this ever since Martha has inflicted her cooking on me."

"It's not Martha's fault. It's Karl's!" Bruno licked some dripping toffee off his fingers as he allowed this insight to sink in. "But just how far are you willing to go to impress him? Anyway, if you ever do make it to the pearly gates, Grouchy

Peter isn't going to be asking you how many salads you ate. Believe me, life is too short to be tossing salads!"

"Your waistline certainly isn't too short!"

"I'm not a fan of diets, as you know. Not since that bastard of a duke tried to starve me to death by locking me in an underwater cage."

Tiffany didn't want to explore the contradictions inherent in another duke anecdote. She tried to block out all the external noise and listen to her inner silence, that core of her being where she could always ground herself in serene bliss.

All she heard was the rumbling of her stomach.

Instead, she focused on the breeze, letting its fingertips massage her ears and smooth away the cares of the evening. All she could hear was nature's comforting whispers caressing her mind.

Her phone pinged a new message.

Ignore it! Ignore it! Ignore… Oh, maybe it's Giggles texting to apologise.

She snatched the phone from her bag while Bruno searched for the last specks of popcorn at the sticky bottom of the carton.

Sure enough! The message was indeed from Giggles.

Im worried abut Kylie. G

Tiffany thrust the phone back into the bag.

She was absolutely sick of men by now. The Seagull with his half-hearted insinuations. Giggles with his inability to focus on what was important. Jehovah with his self-righteous insults. Bruno with his sweaty sermons. And Bill with his... everything.

Part of her would be happy if she never saw another man again.

She then noticed two people jogging towards her.

One was a slim young women in a sleek designer tracksuit, wearing expensive glasses and sporting a confrontational haircut. Tiffany recognised her from the yoga class. Crystal-Orion. Or Jade-Neptune. Something-Something, anyway. Even the sheen of sweat on her glowing face had an elegant touch to it.

The other was Karl, in his evening shorts and deliciously tight T-shirt. No sweat on Karl, needless to say.

Tiffany didn't know whether to ravage or kill him.

"Oh, hi, Tiffany," Karl enthused, slowing down to a stationary jog. "How are you? You remember Sapphire-Starlight from the class, I'm sure."

"Oh, my friends just call me Sapphie," Sapphire-Starlight clarified, with a hyphenated giggle. "Nice to see you out walking, Tiffany. It's good to start easy before moving on to the difficult stuff."

"Wonderful to see you again, Sapphire," Tiffany lied. "Karl, I didn't realise you also gave jogging classes. I would have signed up if I knew."

"This is more of a *private* class," Karl explained, oblivious to the sudden shadows gathering around Tiffany's face. "My platinum clients get some one-to-one tuition."

"Those are certainly platinum ears," Bruno pointed out to Tiffany. "I've never seen ears droop so spectacularly."

"Ah, I see." *Jesus, his ears are a bit odd, now that I look at them.* "Hopefully, I'll be able to be reach platinum status some day soon."

"Well, as Sapphie just said," Karl replied, "you need to take things slowly. You're not at platinum level yet. But it *is* really encouraging to see you rambling the hills. A nice easy way to sneak in some light exercise."

"Yes, I do enjoy the hills." *Rambling? The sanctimonious bastard! I'll rip those jumbo ears right off his head.* "And of course it's a great opportunity to get some mindful breathing in to calm the soul. Right, Sapphire?"

"Oh, indeed," Sapphire agreed. "But you have to do it *properly*, don't you? Otherwise, it's just… well, breathing, and we're already able to do that without much effort, aren't we?"

"I know who he reminds me of!" Bruno scratched the dark depths of his beard. "There was this saint back in the village that got martyred. Gustav always wanted to be martyred, in fact, and to be honest the rest of us were hoping for it too. He was hard work to listen to. He kept saying that we just have to open our ears to hear the voice of the Holy Spirit. Well, the bastard of a duke helped him out with that. He dangled Gustav from the bridge by the ears until he finally dropped into the serpent pit below. He ended up with weeping willow ears, just like Karl."

Tiffany felt she should offer some defence of Karl's ears, but then her phone pinged again. She took it out of her bag.

K seemed a bit off this evening. Hope she's okay.

After thrusting the phone into her pocket, Tiffany turned her attention back to Karl, trying not to stare at his ears and focus on all the other perfect parts of his body.

They're not really drooping, I suppose. More just out of alignment. A bit askew, perhaps…

"So, how many of your clients are platinum, then?"

"Oh, at the moment, just Sapphie and, of course, Kylie."

"Of course!" *Those ears are in serious danger now.* "And what exactly did she do to earn that… status?"

"Oh, Kylie's amazing!"

"The weeping willow speaks the truth," Bruno chimed in. "That woman could convince a saint to climb down from a burning stake."

"What's so amazing about her?" Tiffany was trying to ignore the incessant pinging of her phone. "All I see is a young– a youngish woman somewhat lost in the world, incapable of finding her way anywhere."

"Oh, there's much more to her than that," Karl replied, with unexpected passion. "Her intelligence is remarkable. She's an expert on nutrition and is surprisingly alert to the latest science."

"Intelligence?" Tiffany failed to keep the sarcasm out of her voice, mainly because she didn't really try to. "Kylie?"

"He's right," Sapphire added. "I was talking to her about yoga the other evening and she knew all the history and philosophy behind it and how it ties into mindfulness and spirituality. She's certainly not just another featherhead who simply turns up to class out of boredom."

"Well, obviously I'm glad to hear that she knows how to read books." *Was that glittery bitch having a dig at me there?* "I suppose we're all intelligent in our own way."

"She goes way beyond the norm, though," Karl continued.

"She doesn't just accept what she reads. She challenges it and makes up her own mind. She doesn't let me off the hook on anything, I can tell you!"

"Have you noticed," Bruno asked, "how his ears twitch when he gets excited?"

Tiffany ignored Bruno. She was wrong about Kylie, just like she'd been wrong about Karl, about Giggles, about… She stopped this line of thought.

"Of all my clients," Karl was saying, "I have to say Kylie is the most impressive, with all due respect to both of you here, of course."

"You certainly seem to be impressed with her." *Clients?* "Maybe there's more too her than meets the eye. I suppose I find it hard to see beyond the blinding glare of the surface."

"I'm also impressed by her resilience," Karl continued, with a solemn sigh. "As you may know, she's going out with this absolute train wreck of man."

"Oh yes," Tiffany eagerly agreed, "I'm aware that he's a total train wreck."

"I think she thought she could fix him." Karl shook his head sadly. "But you can't build a new person when they cling to old habits. Apparently, he's still pining for his ex, even though she was totally high maintenance and–"

"High maintenance?"

"Oh yeah," Sapphire agreed, "Kylie did mention that. I don't know how Bill put up with her. But Kylie was very gracious about the situation, stressing that we can't rush to judgement because we don't know the whole story."

"That's so Kylie," Karl remarked, with a smile.

That's so bullshit!

"Anyway," Tiffany said, eager to extricate herself out of what was in danger of becoming a therapy session, "I suppose we all should keep moving."

"True," Karl replied. "We all move at our own speeds, but we are all moving to some extent."

Tiffany allowed herself one last lingering gaze at Karl as he jogged off with Sapphire and her hyphen.

"I've met dismembered saints who were less sanctimonious than that droopy-eared bowl of lettuce," Bruno grumbled, allowing himself one last lingering gaze at Sapphire-Starlight. "Just like every toasted martyr, he's convinced that he's the only one who's got the secret knowledge. Thinks he's closer to God than the rest of us."

"I think the only god he worships," Tiffany replied, starting to walk again, despite the anguished sigh from Bruno, "is himself."

"What's the point of healthy living anyway?"

"We're going to keep walking. You're not getting out of it on some philosophical technicality."

"Everyone has to die eventually," Bruno declared. "Even that bastard of a duke went into the ground finally. Even though he wasn't technically dead when we buried him."

Tiffany checked the messages on her phone.

She hoped Giggles had seen sense and realised whom he should be focusing on.

U havn't seen K, have u? Hope she's okay.

She hoped he would at least remember her.

How r u?

That was promising.

We should meet up.

Even better. Things were looking up.

Have a chat about K.

"Am I high maintenance?" Tiffany turned off the phone. "I mean, I was good for Bill. Without me, he would have eaten himself alive years ago. I saved him."

"Not everybody wants saving," Bruno pointed out, "despite what the Bible says."

"Why would anyone think I'm high maintenance?"

"Sometimes we just don't see ourselves as others see us.

For example, I'm not as confident or gracious as I come across. I have my own little doubts and foibles too. It's not always easy to look at yourself. That's why most people don't like polishing mirrors, except those who adore their own droopy-eared reflections."

Bruno idly massaged his shaggy hair into a more presentable bird's nest, and smoothed his beard slightly.

Tiffany walked in silence, hoping Bruno would keep any further analysing to himself.

"Your problem," Bruno explained, without being asked, "is that you focus on people's faults. You can't see their good points. Now, Karl is an admittedly fine slab of beef. Anyone who spends that much time grooming and polishing and sculpting himself is bound to look reasonably acceptable. But when you were looking at him, all you could see were his faulty ears."

"They weren't really that *faulty*. Just a bit... off-kilter."

"I think God did a rush job on them on a Friday afternoon, but never mind. You have to learn to look beyond people's faults. When someone hands you a bowl of soup, all you can see is the dead rodent floating in it. You lose sight of the warm, tasty vegetable broth."

With some annoyance, Tiffany realised that she was still

hungry. She wondered if she could call round to Claude and Ernie for some leftovers.

However, the thought of walking into the middle of some domestic carnage or other persuaded her to go to the nearest takeaway instead for an evening snack.

It wasn't the perfect solution, but it'd do for now.

Maybe Bruno was on to something.

I try my best to be healthy, honey, but it ain't an easy habit.
How can I be healthy, darling, when it's such a hard ol' habit.
You can eat the lettuce, baby, and I can eat the rabbit.

10

The Devil's Holy Church of the Blues

Nearer my God to thee, the smell still lingers in my nose.
You're standin' so near to me, a part of you lives in my nose.
You took my two feet, and just left me with these ten toes.

"I ask you again, Robin," Martha said, waving a porridge-encrusted spoon at him, "what part of recession do you not understand?"

"Have you not found enough money *yet* to buy me a new pair of runners?" Robin looked down at his two bare feet. "Tatty socks. Tatty runners. A new pair of runners would make me look at least a little bit respectable."

"I thought Lettuce was more interested in your socks than your feet," Tiffany pointed out. "And who can blame her?"

Robin had taken after his father in the podiatry department. His feet, while not exactly ugly, always looked somewhat trodden upon. Feet condemned to follow, never lead.

Martha chewed the lumpy porridge as she formulated her response.

"It's not a good morning for you to try my patience,

Robin," she warned, glancing over at George, who was riveted to his morning Sudoku while also sneaking furtive peeks at the mid-morning puzzle. "I've got a lot on my mind and at four o'clock this morning every one of my little demons decided to hold a disco in my head and–"

"Is that why you were growling in your sleep, peach blossom?"

"Shut up, George!" Martha's voice didn't sound as sharp as usual this morning. "You know what I'm talking about."

What the hell is she talking about now?

"Now, back to you, Robin." Martha stopped gazing at her husband with concern, and she recommenced glaring at her son with fury. "We're still on our austerity drive. That's why I've had to switch to this ganky brand of porridge. I tried to use extra sugar to kill the taste, but it's still horrendous. There's only so much a chef can do. Anyway, while there's an austerity drive on, you have to forget about new runners."

"Everybody at school laughs at these runners!" Robin pleaded. "Even barefoot children giggle when I walk by! You want to make my schooldays a complete misery."

"Your schooldays are the happiest days of your life." Martha allowed herself a few seconds' reminiscence. Then she looked over at her husband. "It's later in life that the real misery gets going."

"I have to invent imaginary friends to get me through the day," Robin declared, before settling into a teenage sulk.

"That's not the worst way to get through life," Tiffany pointed out.

"Well, if he can invent imaginary friends," Martha replied, "he can invent an imaginary mother too. Get her to wash your clothes and tidy your room and put raspberries in your porridge and–"

"Are these raspberries?" her husband asked.

"Shut up, George! And stop rubbing your stomach. People will think you didn't enjoy the breakfast."

Tiffany noted that the breakfast was unusually enjoyable this morning. Really not as horrendous as Martha had said. Yes, the porridge was relentlessly lumpy and the fruit was of unclear origin, but it did taste nice, with a careful blend of sugar, cinnamon, and sesame seeds. Tiffany wondered why Martha was making such an extra effort.

"The breakfast is delightful, strawberry muffin," George assured Martha, clearly happy not to have to lie about her cooking this morning. "It's just that my stomach is sore again today. We'll see what Dr Lambchop says later."

Doctor?

"Explain your symptoms carefully to him, because that so-called doctor wasn't blessed with brains or beauty. Try not to bore him to death. And please, please, don't talk about your work to him."

"I seem to be the only person in the world who cares about my work," George said with a sigh. "I know it's not very exciting, but I enjoy it."

"How on earth," Martha asked, more out of concern than her usual venom, "can you enjoy a job that's so hopelessly boring?"

"Yes, it's boring," George agreed, "but I enjoy it because I know each evening I'll be coming home to you and Robbie. Oh yes, six fits perfectly in that square."

Martha quickly blinked her eyes and gripped her spoon with sudden force. She looked like she wanted to cry.

Tiffany wanted to vomit. But, for once, not because of the food.

She really does love him, despite all his failings. Have I wasted all this energy feeling sorry for her?

Tiffany knew that health scares could bring couples closer. And she'd always enjoyed whenever Bill got sick, but that was mainly because she enjoyed seeing him in pain. But the novelty would soon wear off once she got fed up looking after him.

Bill was a high-maintenance patient. He could turn a splinter scratch into a crucifixion. How would Martha cope if George managed to get really sick?

"You're looking very thoughtful there, Tiffany," Martha suddenly remarked. "Like a nun plotting to run off with the orphans' fund!"

"I've never really seen her as a nun," George argued, returning to silence when his contribution was ignored.

"Just thinking about the future," Tiffany lied, "wondering where I'll be going from here."

"Oh, are you leaving us?" George and Martha asked in enthusiastic unison.

"One step at a time!" *I'll stay an extra month just for that response!* "First I need to sort out where I want to go from here."

They ate in silence for some minutes, each carefully manoeuvring the sticky (but tasty!) porridge down their gullets.

A sudden sigh emanated from George.

"And what's wrong with you now?" Martha asked. "Are you worrying about some stupid work project that no one else in the entire universe cares about?"

"I was just wondering," George said, his voice quaking

slightly, "what'll happen to Kylie if she decides to leave Bill."

What? Is Kylie leaving Bill?

"And why on earth would you be worrying about what happens to that empty-headed blow-up doll?" Martha pointed a ballistic spoon at her husband. "Why would you care about *her*?"

"Oh, no reason at all, cherry plum," George blubbered, as panic set in. "I... I... I just thought that she had a certain charm that I can't quite put my finger on."

"If you put your finger anywhere near that sparkly little tart," Martha warned, "I'll saw it off. Concentrate on your Sudoku!"

George seemed to accept that the tangible benefits of staying alive outweighed the intangible benefits of thinking about Kylie, and lapsed back into his usual obedient silence.

Martha was not silent, though. She continued to grumble and growl, making vague threats to all and sundry.

Tiffany couldn't help smiling to herself, though. Martha was actually jealous. The very idea that George would be interested in someone else had apparently never occurred to her before. This new insight into the workings of her husband's brain, couple with his vague health scare, seemed to have shaken her to the core.

"I was thinking, honey bunch—" George began.

"Tread very carefully," Martha cautioned in her prison-warder voice. "You're walking on razor blades at the moment."

"I was thinking, honey bunch, that maybe we could go for a walk this evening. After I get home from Dr Lambchop. You know, just the two of us." He threw a sour glance at Tiffany. "No one else."

"Steady on, George!" Tiffany laughed. "Don't lose the run of yourself. There's only so much excitement a grown woman can take!"

But Martha wasn't laughing.

She was smiling at her husband.

I believe in Jesus, but he always leaves me in the lurch.
I try to be a believer, but my saviour leaves me in the lurch.
The last time I got on my knees to pray, he set fire to the church.

George wasn't the only one who wanted a walk. Tiffany's head was still spinning after the past few days.

She wandered aimlessly for an hour after breakfast.

She'd told the Seagull she'd be late into work. She now just had to remember to show up at some stage before lunch.

Bruno, of course, was more interested in lunch than work. He was enjoying a pre-lunch snack of a hotdog with chips, casting aside the limp lettuce leaves with disdain as he walked alongside Tiffany.

"The philosophers tell us that it is impossible to prove a negative," Bruno mused, after washing down his latest mouthful with a slurp of strawberry smoothie. "I would have also thought that it was impossible to love a non-entity. But Martha has proved me wrong. Even vacuums have somebody to love."

Tiffany was as nonplussed as Bruno, but considerably less sweaty and gaspy in the morning sun. This morning's insight into Martha's love for George had unsettled her. She had always assumed that Martha had simply *put up* with George because, well, it was a bit too much of an effort to start all over again. She regretted her choice, but had resigned herself to it, surviving on a cocktail of bitterness and mockery. But no, Martha was comfortable with her choice after all. Love wasn't mysterious. It was utterly baffling.

"You assume that everyone in the world is as bitter as you," Bruno declared, after gargling another mouthful of smoothie, sending red bubbles into the air. "You can't get your head around the idea that other people might actually be happy, no matter what a brittle front they put up."

"Martha's front is pretty toxic," Tiffany said. "She certainly had me fooled. I thought it was only a matter of time before she exchanged him for a new couch."

"If George were a couch," Bruno said with a laugh, "he'd be the blandest, most uncomfortable couch in the showroom. People wouldn't fall asleep on it. They'd simply die of boredom. And then they'd... Oh, for God's sake, what the hell are we doing *here?*"

Tiffany looked up and realised, to her surprise, that her aimless saunter had led her to St Anne's church. She'd just wanted to get away from Martha and George. Anywhere would do. She certainly wasn't running to church!

"I suppose the day was bound to come," Bruno sneered, "when all your lavender reeds and shiny crystals and manicured breaths just weren't going to be up to the job anymore. No matter how much they renounce religion, everybody eventually ends up back at the Church of the Desperate, trying to remember their prayers and holy moves."

"Church of the Desperately Unfit, more like," Tiffany retorted, looking at the sweat waterfalling down Bruno's beard. "You really are the worst advertisement for your religion."

"Everyone walks tall when they think they've got everything sorted." The sweat started to steam as Bruno's rhetorical engine warmed up. "But they all end up back on their knees. Just like that guy over there!"

In the distance, Tiffany could see someone kneeling on the grass near the chapel walls. The sun beams caressed him as he bowed his head in the wafting mist. All that was missing was a celestial choir.

Bruno's phone starting ringing.

"Oh, what now?" He crammed the last of the hotdog into his mouth while he dug out the phone from his dusty pockets. "What?"

Tiffany noticed, to her surprise, that the kneeling supplicant was Claude. Being Ernie's boyfriend was likely to drive anyone to spiritual despair. She wondered what calamity had laid him so low.

"It's not my bloody fault that she won't listen to reason, is it?" Bruno roared down the phone. "You always set us up for failure. You're never happy until we're being crucified on a burning cross or being fed to toothless piranhas by that bastard of a duke. And I'm now beginning to realise that that bastard of a duke was an angel compared to you, you sadistic, psychotic lunatic! No wonder the nuns all worship you."

Tiffany was glad to see that Bruno's relationship with his boss was as dysfunctional as her own relationship with the Seagull. She made another mental note to remember to go to the office at some stage before lunch. But first, she had to tackle Claude.

"What brings you here, Claude? Are you on Ernie's Bible kick now too?"

Claude looked up, startled. Then smiled when he saw Tiffany.

"The only prayers I'm saying," he replied, "is that these mushrooms aren't poisonous!"

Tiffany then noticed that Claude was actually kneeling in front of a cluster of mushrooms on the grass near the building.

"I don't know what they put in the soil in this church," Claude explained, "but the mushrooms that pop up around here taste amazing!"

"It must be all the bullshit they spew from the pulpit," Tiffany suggested.

Claude laughed as he stood up, wiping the dusty earth from his designer jeans.

"And that's another thing," Bruno was shouting down the phone, "why the hell do you let food grow in your soil that can actually poison us? Do you enjoy torturing us, just like the bastard of a duke does?"

Things were obviously still a bit fraught with Ernie. Claude's hair was expertly sculpted and groomed, a sure sign he'd spent more time attending to his appearance than talking to Ernie. He always retreated to the mirror in times of difficulty.

"No, for your information, it's not some other gigolo she's trying to get her desperate claws into," Bruno explained, absently fondling his own hair. "It's just her brother's boyfriend. I think he's safe for now... Well, what the hell's that got to do with anything? You made him like that, so you can't start complaining about it now."

"I take it things are still somewhat frigid at Chez Ernie," Tiffany ventured. "Are you still both plotting murder?"

"Murder by mushrooms," Claude said, with a grin. "I'll put the poisoned ones in his pot. But, knowing my luck, he'll probably survive."

"Oh yes," Tiffany agreed. "He's as resilient as a nettle. Mother tried to drown him in the bath many times, but he always managed to wriggle away."

"He certainly is slippery!" Claude's grin faded. "Even more so these days. His latest craze is yoga. You can probably hear his bones creaking from here."

Tiffany noticed that Claude's hair was fading to grey in places. Living with Ernie would prematurely age anyone. She and Martha adored Ernie, despite his countless faults, but they could adore him from a safe distance. They knew that Claude's adoration was a much more frustrating journey.

"Maybe the yoga will calm him down and you'll both be okay again," Tiffany reassured Claude. "If Martha and George can survive, anyone can."

"At least Martha loves George. Anyone can see that." Claude shrugged. "Sometimes I think I'm just another trophy for Ernie."

"Well, at least you're more of a trophy than he is!"

Although Claude didn't quite rise to Karl's level of physical magnificence, he was certainly a finer specimen than her brother was. The beauty genes in Tiffany's family tended to flow towards the females.

Meanwhile, the physical catastrophe behind her was still arguing on the phone, curses and spittle flying with abandon.

"I've done my duty. I've protected her from the worst of her mistakes. So far. She danced with fire a few times, but at least she hasn't gone up flames yet. Joan of Arc could have learnt a thing or two— Have you no sense of–? Okay, I won't mention that again."

"I'm sure things will get better again," Tiffany told Claude. "Some people just pretend to hate the ones they love. They blame all their suffering on some bastard of a duke, yet they can't stop talking about them either."

"I know what you mean," Claude agreed. "It's like when you have a pebble in your shoe. It's a constant irritation, but when you take the pebble away, your foot feels a bit lonely. I suppose Ernie is my pebble."

"You should aim to be more than a foot, Claude," Tiffany advised. "Unless you plan to walk all over him. And that wouldn't end well, given how our family react when on the defensive!"

"Maybe a nice lunch will help to calm him down again." Claude glanced at the mushrooms. "The problem is that he enjoys all the fights. I don't know why you all love confrontation so much. It's great fun for you, but it wears out the rest of us. Just because life has treated you all badly, you think it gives you the right to treat everybody else badly too."

"We don't treat *everybody* badly, do we?"

"Someone once told me that the mind is a garden, full of weeds and flowers," Claude continued. "Some people water the flowers. But your family, it just waters the weeds."

"You're only happy when you're creating havoc!" Bruno

had worked himself up into a steaming dervish. "You unleash carnage and then expect people to just put it down to God's mysterious ways. Of course, when we actually need your help, when it would be useful to have a host of angels descend and rescue a person from the maw of a hungover lion belonging to that bastard of a duke, all the angels are too busy droning away on their harps!"

"Anyway," Claude said, "I suppose I should go back to the House of Eternal Tantrums. You and whoever should come join us for lunch some day soon. You manage to calm down Ernie a bit. He'd never admit that, of course. He looks down his pointy old nose at you, but in reality he does look up to you. Maybe he's just the tiniest bit jealous of you and Martha."

Claude walked away, the bag of mushrooms dangling from his hands.

"Okay! Fine!" Bruno ended the call by thumping the screen and throwing the phone on the ground. "Seems like I've been summoned by my boss!"

"Oh yeah!" Tiffany had completely forgotten about her work. "My boss."

"We all have some sanctimonious, self-important, incompetent hypocrite to report to, I suppose. But at least my boss isn't trying to flirt with me. Too in love with Himself for any of that nonsense."

Tiffany looked at the retreating figure in the distance, admiring his poise and patience.

"Poor Claude deserves a medal for putting up with Ernie," she remarked.

"And poor Bill deserved a medal for putting up with you! Anyway, I suppose I'd better go and prepare for my meeting."

"I need to prepare for my meeting too. The Seagull wants to finally wrap up the performance review. More carnage in the café, no doubt. I need to make sure he doesn't flirt with me the way you flirted with that bastard of a duke back in the day!"

But Bruno didn't hear her. He was already stomping into the chapel.

Pour me a coffee, baby, I like my sugar nice and sweet.
Pour me a coffee, honey, give me sugar sweet.
She held my lonely hand, before she walked away with my feet.

The café was busy with the usual jaded lunch crowd. Thankfully, this meant that the Seagull was less inclined to declare his undying infatuation for Tiffany. Especially after the debacle at the club.

He was looking well rested today, Tiffany noticed. Face smooth and relaxed, hair neatly parted, and ears in perfect alignment.

Looking rather good, in fact… Jesus, I need coffee quick!

The Seagull was in full flight, talking about mission-critical interfaces and cutting-edge paradigms, getting lost in his own jargon jungle while Jesus wept.

Tiffany nodded randomly, barely pretending to listen. Her attention was taken up by another meeting in the café.

Karl and Kylie were deep in thoughtful conversation, tapping and scrolling through tablet screens, muttering and murmuring respectfully. As usual, Karl looked like he could raise the morale of a nation, and Kylie, of course, had those legs that could start a war. However, Tiffany couldn't detect any chemistry between them, apart from some weird intellectual chemistry based on shared ideas rather than shared passions. Kylie was proving a fit match for Karl's questions about nutritional best practices and emerging trends. Unawed by his beauty, she challenged his assumptions and corrected his errors without mercy.

Tiffany felt slightly jealous of her again, but for different reasons this time.

The Seagull was rubbing his hands as he reached the

crescendo of his monologue. Tiffany noticed, with some surprise, how well manicured his fingernails were. Not fastidiously scraped and buffed like Karl's, but neat and appealing in their own inoffensive way. A man who knew how to make himself presentable. A lot to be said for that, she had to admit.

Oh shit! I've no idea what he was saying!

"Maybe, Gordon, you could elaborate a bit more on your main point."

"Well, I was making only one point, but anyway." He smiled and shrugged. Nice white even teeth, Tiffany noticed. Nothing to complain about with the shoulders either. "What do you think your greatest challenge will be this year and how will you overcome it?"

"Where to start?" Tiffany laughed bitterly. "Oh, you mean about my job! Well, I suppose that I'd like to have more autonomy in my–"

"More?" The Seagull's well-tended eyebrows shot up. "Jesus wept! There are countries that have less autonomy than you do. I barely know what you're doing half the time."

"Oh, that's just because I don't like to burden you with the details." *Your ignorance is my bliss.* "Best I get on with my job and you get on with yours. That way, both of us can–"

"Do you two ever hold a meeting in the office?"

A shadow fell across Tiffany's face as an all-too-familiar voice suddenly interrupted her. She looked up with an exasperated sigh.

Jehovah had popped into the café to grab lunch on the hoof. A peppermint tea and an oatcake. He was as spartan in his appetites as he was in his emotions.

"We're in the middle of a performance review," Tiffany explained. "So please bugger off back to the office or some blues club or some soapbox on the corner. We're busy."

"This has to be the longest performance review in history. You two are spending an *awful* lot of time with each other lately."

"We like spending time together," Tiffany lied. "It can be good to get away from the toxic bullshit in the office. And away from nasty interfering gobshites."

"It'd be terrible if, ahem, rumours started to, ahem, develop." Jehovah looked pointedly at the Seagull. "HR takes a dim view of all that, especially these days."

"It's just a performance review," the Seagull explained, through clenched, even, sparkling teeth. "Absolutely nothing inappropriate going on here."

"Well, that depends on how you define 'inappropriate',

Gordon!" Tiffany laughed and slapped Gordon's hand. He withdrew the hand as if he'd been scalded. "There are meetings and then there are, ahem, meetings."

"This is a completely *appropriate* meeting!" His feathers now truly ruffled, the Seagull began to blush and sweat. Tiffany found it endearing. And hilarious. "We are two professionals engaged in a professional discussion about professional things."

"If that's what you say." Jehovah smirked at them both. "It's not me you have to convince."

"There's nothing to convince anyone of!" The Seagull was spluttering now. Tiffany was delighted. This review was going much better than she'd expected! "I have absolutely no interest at all in Tiffany, apart from her career path and performance metrics."

Tiffany jerked back a little.

That sounded a bit too genuine. Did the Seagull really have *no* interest in her? Had she misread him too? Or had he simply changed his mind? As she watched Jehovah skulk back to the office, Tiffany found her brain doing multiple recalculations.

"I'm sorry about that, Tiffany," the Seagull said. "Sometimes, people forget how poisonous office gossip can be."

"Oh, I'm not worried about anything that malignant little sanctimonious runt has to say about anyone." *I must remember to put some salt in Jehovah's coffee this afternoon.* "Boring people are easily bored, and they have to make up stories to amuse themselves."

"Yes, that's it exactly!" The Seagull eagerly grasped at the chance to explain himself. "It's just a made-up story. A fiction. A crazy fairy tale. No truth in it at all."

"Yes, of course." *Steady on there, Gordon! The idea isn't that crazy.* "Let's just let things take their natural course."

"No, that's not what I meant." The Seagull was losing his grip on the conversation again. "There's nothing to take its natural course. There is no course. Nothing is flowing. Everything is... Look, let's just focus on your ongoing performance."

"Of course, Gordon. You have my full attention!"

"Hey, Kylie!" Another familiar voice chirped across the café. "How are you today?"

Tiffany looked over at Giggles. He didn't see her because his attention was focused solely on Kylie.

Has the entire town decided to come into this café for lunch today?

"Oh, hello," Kylie replied, without warmth, glancing up fleetingly from the tablet. "How are you?"

"The more important question is: how are *you?*" Uninvited, Giggles walked over to their table. "Are you keeping well?"

"Hi, Giggles!" Tiffany shouted across the room. "I'm keeping well, thanks for asking."

"Oh, hello, Tiffany," Giggles replied, looking over at her. "I didn't see you there."

You haven't seen me for a while!

"Tiffany," the Seagull pleaded, "is there any chance that we can wrap up this performance review *today?* I have HR breathing down my neck about it."

"Well, we don't want to give HR any ammunition to use against us, do we?" Tiffany grinned at the Seagull. "After all, they're already talking plenty about us! Let's give them something to really sink their poisoned teeth into while we're at it."

"Now look, Tiffany, I thought we'd already–"

"Say, Tiffany," Giggles interrupted as he walked up to the café counter, "do you think Kylie's okay? Oh, hello again, Jeffrey!"

"My name is–"

"If you're so worried about Kylie," Tiffany replied, glowering at Giggles, "why don't you set up home with her and look after her?"

"Well, that's exactly what I want to do, but I have to tread carefully because–"

"You have no idea how carefully you have to tread, Giggles!"

"Anyway, thanks for the advice. You've given me something to chew on. Oh yeah, that reminds me why I came in here. I need lunch. Talk to you later. Great to see you again, Jeffrey. You make a nice couple."

"We are not... How many times do I have...? And anyway, I'm not bloody Jeffrey. My name is–"

"Didn't you want to focus on the performance review?" Tiffany reminded the Seagull, eager to take her thoughts away from Giggles. "Or do you want to wait until we're ready for retirement?"

Relief swept across the Seagull's face.

"Yes, that's exactly what I–"

"Retired and happy. Sitting together in our cottage near the sea. Knitting sweaters by the fireside."

"Tiffany! Please!"

The Seagull's discomfort helped take her mind off her annoyance with Giggles. She knew, deep down, that Giggles was only good for a laugh, but still... She expected more of a spark between them. And she expected him to remember the spark for a little longer.

But whatever! She listened to the Seagull prattle on and tried to concentrate on her career for once.

I wonder what aftershave he uses. He smells really nice today.

Giggles gave her a quick nod as he walked back with his lunch. A mocha, a sausage roll, some biscuits, and a cream doughnut. He went straight over to Karl and Kylie's table again. They looked in horror at his lunch.

"Are you seriously going to eat *that?*" Karl asked.

"Well, I don't plan to put it in a museum." A hearty laugh from Giggles. Silence from the table. "Actually, would you like some, Kylie? A little sugar to sweeten the day?"

"That food would corrode my day," Kylie replied. "Have you any idea how much damage you're doing to yourself?"

"Have you any idea what I'm talking about, Tiffany?"

Oh shit! What he's on about now?

"Sorry, Gordon. I was distracted by those jokers over there. Say again."

Karl and Kylie were patiently explaining to Giggles the damage he was doing to himself. The sugar. The cream. The full-fat milk. The salt. The processed chemicals. The complete lack of any natural food on his plate

"The jam has strawberries in it," Giggles protested, with a

laugh. "And anyway, I get a lot of exercise. I can burn off anything that lingers around."

"You can't exercise your way out of a bad diet, Giggles," Kylie explained. "That's like trying to smoke yourself fit. You should sign up for some of Karl's classes to get your body back into shape."

"Do you go to the classes?" Giggles asked, too quickly.

Before Kylie could answer, Karl launched into a convincing pitch for his personalised training programme. Kylie helped explain and clarify the many points that Giggles was confused about.

"...in the third quarter, before progressing to asynchronous messaging in the fourth... Tiffany!"

"Yes, I understand," Tiffany agreed, not sure what she was agreeing to. "Four quarters. Yes, we'll stay on top of all four."

Trying her best to ignore the health conference in the other corner of the café, Tiffany focused on the Seagull. She tried to listen to what he was saying, but the low-level drone of his voice made that difficult.

However, she was able to occupy herself by examining him. Although he wasn't exactly hot, or even handsome, he was not repulsively unattractive. When she separated the person from the boss, she was able to judge him more objectively. The smoothly shaven face. The carefully chosen, complementary clothes. The eyes of that appealing light blue. The proper ears. She doubted there was a six-pack beneath the neatly ironed shirt, but there was no evidence of a beer gut either.

He lacked Karl's physical splendour. He lacked Giggles's charm. But when she stopped thinking about what he lacked, she could see what he offered. It wasn't much, in fairness, but it wasn't nothing either.

"…we could maybe then start looking to position you into more strategic roles in the future."

"Anything's possible in the future, I suppose," Tiffany agreed. "That page hasn't been written yet, after all."

Maybe Bruno was right. Maybe it is time to settle down. Stop looking for perfection or beauty or hilarity. Look for something more stable. And now is the perfect opportunity to open that conversation. All this talk about future goals. No harm in asking him out for a little date, just to see how things go. A proper date this time, not like that charade at the Spinning Pig. I just need to take a deep breath and ask the question. Here goes…

"Hiya, Tiffs! Do you ever go to work these days?"

Tiffany was jerked out of her thoughts by an unwelcome voice. She looked up to see Bill standing at their table.

"What the hell are you doing here?" she asked. "Can Gordon and I not have one second of peace together."

"Well now, William," Gordon jumped in to explain, "this is just a—"

"I heard they do a nice lunch here," Bill explained, "and I decided to expand my horizons."

"You look like you've expanded your waistline!"

Bill did look a little rough today. Unshaven, uncombed, probably unwashed. He threw mournful bloodshot eyes over at Kylie, who looked the other way, concentrating on Giggles.

"Anyway, William," Gordon said firmly, "can you please just... leave us alone? You look like a mess and you smell even worse. Tiffany and I have important corporate strategies to discuss. Some of us *work* for a living!"

Something in the Seagull's tone made Tiffany recoil. She suddenly remembered every time he had infuriated her at work with his curt, dismissive tone, his assumption that he was more important than everyone else. That sense of entitlement that made him take people for granted.

A burst of laughter exploded at the corner table, as Karl, Giggles, and Kylie got up to leave. They looked over at Bill and laughed again. They were still giggling as they walked out the door.

Bill looked sadly at the departing trio, before looking back to Tiffany again.

God almighty, I nearly made the worst mistake of my life.

"Gordon's right," Tiffany said to Bill. "You look like something a dog threw up."

"Exactly," the Seagull agreed. "A total disgrace and an absolute—"

"You'd better come with me and get yourself sorted out," Tiffany said, standing up. "We need to make you fit for human company again."

Before Gordon could respond, Tiffany was frogmarching Bill out of the restaurant, leaving her lunch and her career path unfinished on the table.

She had just narrowly avoided one terrible mistake. As she walked through the door with Bill, Tiffany wondered if she was just about to make another one instead.

My woman helped me find religion, she touched me deep in my soul.
This woman of mine got religion, she touched me right down in my soul.
She tore the heart right out of me, and she threw it right down in the hole.

Her mind still reeling, Tiffany stumbled back to the one place she found herself at peace.

The silence of St Anne's church gave her time to gather her thoughts and plot her next move. However, the silence was short-lived.

"You brought me to a church?" Bill moaned.

Tiffany had to hand it to Bill. He had an unerring ability to turn her sympathy into irritation within a matter of seconds. The whole way to the church, he had got on her nerves. She was eager to quickly put as much distance between herself and the Seagull as possible. And herself and Giggles. Oh yes, and herself and Karl. In fact, the only person she was keen to chat with was Kylie, but never mind. First things, first.

Bill had lurched between charm and complaining the whole walk over. He complimented her on her hair – which actually was rather elegant today, Tiffany thought – and her clothes – which had been flung on without much thought this morning. He complained about Kylie. And Giggles. (Tiffany quickly changed the subject whenever Giggles was mentioned.) And even the Seagull.

"I brought you here so that we could catch our breaths away from everyone," Tiffany explained. "That café was like Grand Central station today! So shut up for a minute and gather your thoughts. Embrace the silence and focus on your breathing."

Tiffany looked at the painting of St Bruno. She could really do with a heart-to-heart with him right now. But she suspected that she wouldn't be talking to him again. His boss had summoned him back to heaven, no doubt to give him a new assignment. The next stage in his evolving celestial career path. Or maybe he'd spend the rest of eternity locking horns with that bastard of a duke.

He looked as ferocious as ever in the painting. Fuming mouth, waving hands, stamping feet, swirling hair. His tunic fluttered loosely around his plump body as he raged against the corruption of humanity. But somewhere deep in his eyes, Tiffany could see the smallest hint of that devilish mischievous twinkle.

"That's one scary-looking bastard," Bill remarked, pointing to Bruno. "He'd make a lion take its teeth out."

"He is very scary," Tiffany agreed. "I wish you'd met. He might have scared some sense into you."

"What?"

Before Tiffany could reply, she heard gentle footsteps approaching from behind. She looked around to see the two nuns approaching her.

"We'd knew you'd be back," the taller nun remarked.

"And this must be the notorious Bill!" The smaller nun

giggled. "He doesn't look nearly as awful as everybody says. At least he has decent ears."

"But he doesn't exactly look like the last of the famous international playboys either," the taller nun said, looking Bill up and down. "I've seen more presentable souls in purgatory."

Bill looked nervously around the chapel, as if he were worried that hostages were routinely sacrificed on the altar.

"Who are these two?" he asked Tiffany.

"Oh, just two interfering busybodies here with their final sermon," Tiffany replied. She stared defiantly at the nuns. "Let's be having you. What's your great happy-ever-after?"

"Oh, life isn't a fairy tale," the smaller nun said, shaking her head sadly.

"Well, maybe it is in a way," the taller nun countered. "Life has a plentiful supply of dragons and poisoned apples." She glanced at Tiffany. "And toxic witches." And then glanced at Bill. "And goblins!"

"Yes, that's true," the smaller nun agreed thoughtfully. "But, on the other hand, not every frog you kiss turns into a prince."

"Some even retain a lot of their frog DNA," the taller nun said, with a quick nod to Bill.

"Tiffs," Bill said nervously, "are these two wagons your

friends?"

"I get it," Tiffany said, ignoring Bill. "Life's imperfect. That certainly was a lesson worth waiting for!"

Tiffany noticed that the merriment in Bruno's eyes seemed to have faded away since the nuns came into the church. He scowled at them with unrepentant fury.

"Yes, imperfection is our lot in life," the smaller nun agreed, with a sigh. "God made the world in six days. It was a rush job, so of course he botched it."

"He cut a few corners here and there," the taller nun clarified, looking at Bill.

"Oh, go easy on him," the smaller nun said, nudging her colleague. "He's not the worst specimen we've ever seen. I'm sure that in a certain light, he might almost be considered handsome."

"He actually looks passable in starlight," Tiffany agreed, surprising herself with the compliment, "when there's no moon."

Bill looked at the saint in the painting, retreating to the one person in the church who wasn't attacking him.

"You ask for too much from men," the smaller nun told Tiffany. "Bill's not an entirely hopeless case. He's upright and he's got a functioning body."

"Well, *most* of it functions," Tiffany clarified, arching her eyebrows and suppressing a snicker.

"Oh, don't let that stop you," the taller nun said. "Many a warrior has survived the battle with a broken spear. No matter how *small* the spear."

Bill looked increasingly uncomfortable as Tiffany and the nuns giggled away.

Tiffany was never happier than when insulting Bill. It was nice to feel happy again, even if she had to share the moment with two stoned, giggling nuns.

"Why do you think that you have a greater right to happiness than anyone else?" the taller nun suddenly asked, as if reading Tiffany thoughts. "Sometimes it's enough to be happy enough most of the time."

"And exactly how happy is happy enough?" Tiffany asked, pointing at Bill. "Is he supposed to be *enough*?"

"Your sister is happy enough," the taller nun continued. "She's madly in love with that faded doormat she's married to."

"How can you say Martha's happy? She's never happy. And now she's got George's mystery illness to worry about."

"Your sister will be okay," the smaller nun assured Tiffany. "She needs to be needed. She'll enjoy looking after George."

"But who will look after you?" the taller nun asked.

"Oh, here we go! Listen, you two. I'm not religious, not after how your colleagues behaved when I was at school. These days, I'm more of a *spiritual* person."

"Oh, that's just because you're too lazy to apply yourself to any religion," the taller nun retorted. "You think you can find the answers to all of life's problems by looking deep inside yourself. Or by looking at the man across the table from you."

"By the way," the smaller nun asked, prodding Tiffany, "were you seriously considering flying off with the supercilious seagull? Have you really learned nothing from all your mistakes?"

"What's with all the criticism and blame?" Tiffany glared at the two nuns. "I thought you pair were all about forgiveness."

"We forgive sins, dear," the smaller nun explained. "We don't forgive idiocy."

"Thankfully, stupidity isn't fatal," the taller nun added. "If it were, all men would have died out years ago."

"Speaking of stupidity," Tiffany added, "can you please give me some time alone with Bill? It's clear that he completely fell apart without me. I now need to start thinking about how I can put him back together again before he destroys any more lives."

"That's true," the taller nun said, radiating that beatific smile that so infuriated Tiffany, while the smaller nun rummaged for something deep inside her robes. "But, of course, you also fell apart without him."

Before Tiffany could unleash her fierce response to this analysis, the smaller nun stepped forward and handed Bill her harmonica.

"Here you go, dear," she said to Bill. "I think you're going to need all the help you can get."

Silence fell on the church as the two nuns swished back down the aisle before disappearing into the inner sanctum.

Silence fell on the church as the merriment crept back into Bruno's eyes.

Silence fell on the church as Tiffany glared at a speechless Bill.

Outside, the clouds parted, and a few tentative rays of afternoon sun fell on the church, delicately caressing the dusty stained-glass windows.

Somewhere inside the church, saints prayed for martyrs and sinners. Somewhere inside the church, the holy spirit drifted in the air among the wisps of smoky incense.

Somewhere inside the church, Tiffany looked up into the

blazing eyes of a reluctant martyr.

Somewhere inside the church, a harmonica began to wail.

The bridges all are broken, and the dirty waters are too deep.
All them bridges is now broken, them dirty dark waters are too deep.
She haunts all my dreams, she walks all over me when I sleep.

THE END

Printed in Great Britain
by Amazon